Ovidia Yu is one of Singapore's best-known and most acclaimed writers. She has had over thirty plays produced and is the author of a number of comic mysteries published in Singapore, India, Japan and America.

She received a Fulbright International Writing Fellowship to the University of Iowa's International Writers Program and has been a writing fellow at the National University of Singapore.

Facebook: www.facebook.com/OvidiaYuDoggedAuthor

The Frangipani Tree Mystery

Mystery

Ovidia Yu

CONSTABLE • LONDON

CONSTABLE

First published in Great Britain in 2017 by Constable

3 5 7 9 10 8 6 4

Copyright © Ovidia Yu, 2017

The moral right of the author has been asserted.

A CIP catalogue record for this book is
available from the British Library.

ISBN: 978-1-47212-520-0

Typeset in Contenu by SX Composing DTP, Rayleigh, Essex
Printed and bound in Great Britain by CPI Group (UK) Ltd, Croydon CR0 4YY

Papers used by Constable are from well-managed forests and
other responsible sources.

MIX
Paper from
responsible sources
FSC® C104740

Constable
is an imprint of
Little, Brown Book Group
Carmelite House
50 Victoria Embankment
London EC4Y 0DZ

An Hachette UK Company
www.hachette.co.uk

www.littlebrown.co.uk

This book is dedicated to the memory of
René Onraet (1887-1952) and Sophia Blackmore (1857-1945)
and to Richard (here and now)

Prologue

———◆———

Charity Byrne had come to Singapore to look after Dee-Dee. She was also to supervise her lessons and manners, and had taught her to play hide-and-seek, which was why Dee-Dee was hiding in the bougainvillaea bushes under the frangipani tree. Dee-Dee giggled, thinking of the clever trick she was playing on Charity. It had rained in the night and Charity's shoes and dress would get muddy, which she hated. Dee-Dee was already covered with mud but since she didn't do her own washing she didn't care . . . But why wasn't Charity coming?

'Mary! Mary! No!' The scream came from the balcony above.

As Dee-Dee stood up to get a better look, a large form fell through the branches of the frangipani tree and crashed heavily onto the stone paving slabs in front of her.

Charity Byrne lay sprawled, her neck twisted at an awkward angle, at Dee-Dee's feet. Charity's eyes and mouth were wide open in what seemed a crazed grin. Dee-Dee opened her mouth, too, and started to scream.

There would be no lessons from Charity that day or ever again.

This Is 1936!
Women Have Rights!

———◆———

'No! No! No! No! No! You ignorant, backward man, you can't just marry off Su Lin! Don't you see what an utter waste that would be? Your niece has her School Certificate! This is 1936! Women have rights! Women have responsibilities!'

Miss Vanessa Palin might not be shouting ('A lady can always make herself heard without shouting') at the large, bald Chinese man (my uncle Chen) facing her, but she was certainly declaiming at the full volume of a voice she was always reminding us should be 'soft, gentle and low, an excellent thing in woman'. It was not surprising that Uncle Chen looked uncomfortable, but he was standing his ground. Although she was not a teacher, Miss Nessa lectured regularly at the Mission School on 'The Proper Pronunciation and Enunciation of the King's English' as well as 'Table Etiquette and Hygiene for Young Ladies'. This indefatigable woman was tall, clever, and resembled Mrs Virginia Woolf, the writer. She was the unmarried sister of Sir Henry Palin, acting governor of Singapore, and some believed he owed his position and much of his success to her. I know I was not the only student at the school who took her as my role model.

I was Miss Nessa's star pupil because I could mimic her accent perfectly. I was one of the girls most often invited to 'tea and conversation' with visitors she brought to view the Ladies' Mission. Miss Nessa and her visitors didn't know my fluency in English came from my grandmother's shortwave radio. Since Ah Ma had sent me to study English at the Mission, it had been my nightly duty to translate into Hokkien and Malay for her the BBC Empire Service programmes 'for men and women so cut off by the snow, the desert, or the sea, that only voices out of the air can reach them'. Chen Tai (as everyone outside the family knew Ah Ma) had no great love for the British but, like Sun Tzu, she believed in knowing her enemies.

Knowing Miss Nessa had a soft spot for me, I had asked her to help me find a job. I could not tell her that I longed to be independent like her, and see the world beyond Singapore, so I might have exaggerated my fear of being married off now my schooldays were over. In truth, Ah Ma might have kept me at home with her to recoup the investment she had made in sending me to learn English reading and writing at the Mission School. I had been considered 'bad luck' since my parents had died from typhoid, and childhood polio had left me with a limp. It had seemed unlikely my family would ever be able to marry me off, but since I was the only child of Ah Ma's favourite son, she had decided to educate rather than sell me. My grandmother's moneylending and black-market businesses had made her rich in the continuing Depression, and she could afford to keep me at home to translate for her, run errands and monitor the household accounts. But, grateful though I was to her, the school run by the Mission Centre had opened my eyes to a whole world of possibilities. I wanted more than a lifetime of toil under my grandmother or a mother-in-law. If I was to escape domestic captivity, I would need my own money, which was why I had to find a paying job. (It would also have been easier if I had been an English woman rather than a Chinese girl, but I didn't worry about what I couldn't change.)

Unfortunately, Uncle Chen heard that the Mission Centre was getting me a job and decided that he, my dead father's eldest surviving brother, should rescue me from the shame of employment. Last night he and his wife Shen-Shen had presented Ah Ma with the names of three men willing to marry me on the condition she released them from their loan obligations to her and provided them with equipment and supplies to set up a laundry or food business in a shop-house, rent-free, for five years as dowry. Two were already married, but they were all family employees and their wives would accept Uncle Chen's crippled niece as a second wife. Uncle Chen and Shen-Shen told Ah Ma that unless she had me married off at once, my Mission School friends would match me up with some relative of Parshanti (bad because Indian) or Grace (worse because Christian). The whole family, ancestors and descendants included, would be disgraced for ever.

'I must think about it,' my grandmother told them. 'Five years' rent is a lot of money.' My grandmother disliked giving away money almost as much as she disliked being told what to do.

I wasn't against marriage. I just didn't want to marry a man as a business deal. I asked Uncle Chen for a job instead of a husband, but Uncle Chen was one of those old-fashioned men who saw all working women as servants or prostitutes, even though he deferred to Ah Ma in important business decisions.

I had taught myself shorthand and typing, and thought I could earn a salary as a secretary. My dream was to train for a profession. Thanks to Miss Nessa, I knew that women in England and America trained to be teachers, nurses and even doctors, and I was sure that, given time, I could talk Ah Ma round to accepting that. First, though, I had to earn my training fees. That was why I had slipped away from home that morning to meet Miss Nessa and my potential employer.

One of the servants must have told tales, which had resulted in Uncle Chen charging into the Mission Centre to save me from myself and Western influences.

'You ignorant fool! You should be proud of Su Lin! She is very intelligent! She came top of the class!' Miss Nessa raised her voice over Uncle Chen's Hokkien tirade, which concerned the unclean state of Nessa Palin's genitals and how he would never allow a skinny sterile white woman to rob the Chen family of a precious granddaughter (he meant me). He jabbed me in the back to translate while glaring at Miss Nessa.

I had stopped translating when they started talking at the same time, but that had not stopped them. Very likely they hadn't even noticed. After all, they understood themselves and neither was listening to the other. Now Miss Nessa was watching and waiting for me to translate her words. The large black handbag she was swinging vigorously looked dangerous.

'My uncle says my grandmother wants only what's best for me,' I told Miss Nessa, then to Uncle Chen, 'My teacher respectfully says she wants to help me not be a burden to my family.'

They both snorted. A noise at the open doorway sounded like a laugh. I turned and saw a tall, dark Englishman hesitating just outside. He had clearly come to keep an appointment – and it was even clearer that he was thinking of leaving without fulfilling it. Even from the street outside, the row going on inside must have been entertaining.

'I think Chief Inspector Le Froy is here,' I said warningly. I recognized him from the newspapers. Once my friend Parshanti and I had been studying at the back of her parents' shop when he had come in to ask Mrs Shankar to help identify a button found at a crime scene. We had watched through the curtains. Unfortunately, she had not been able to help him and he had not stayed long. This was the first time I was seeing him at such close quarters and I couldn't help staring. Thomas Le Froy was the closest thing Singapore Island had to a Rudolph Valentino, a Douglas Fairbanks or a John Barrymore, all combined in the person of one genuine hero . . .

I must digress. Unless you are aware of the awe with which Chief Inspector Le Froy was regarded, you will find it impossible to understand how great a favour Miss Nessa was doing me. Thomas Francis Le Froy, of the Criminal Intelligence Department, was a legend in the Crown Colonies. He spoke fluent Hokkien and Malay; he had pulled rickshaws and infiltrated gambling dens disguised as a Chinese drains inspector. Most of the single ladies in town (and a good number of the married ones) were in love with him, but even top investigative

7

gossips, like my grandmother and Shen-Shen, had no stories of female companions. In fact, I suspected Miss Nessa hoped to use me to insinuate herself into his life, much in the way that a young man gives a puppy or kitten to the object of his affections. 'Give me all the details of his household and I will tell you how to go about your duties,' she had told me. Despite the height, large feet and sharp features that protected her from the sin of vanity, Miss Nessa was not immune to Le Froy.

Years of balancing home and Mission School life had taught me to seize all opportunities as soon as they arose, before they could be snatched away. Thomas Le Froy was the work opportunity Miss Nessa had engineered for me, promising, 'You will be safer with him than with any old woman. He's too engrossed in his work to have time for women, and where can you be safer than working for a policeman? Even your family won't dare to touch you there. And I hear that he is in desperate need of a housekeeper.'

'Chief Inspector Le Froy?' I stepped forward as he turned to me, looking surprised. 'I am Chen Su Lin. I believe Miss Nessa spoke to you about me?'

I had not planned to work as a cleaner or housekeeper but anything that took me away from Uncle Chen's suitors was a step in the right direction. And, if I made myself useful, who could say how swiftly I might move up from housekeeper to assistant and even secretary?

'You're late, Chief Inspector!' Miss Nessa snapped. Then, collecting herself, 'Good morning.'

'It is not yet eleven, Miss Palin. What is the mysterious affair you wish to discuss?' Le Froy's eyes returned to me. I thought I saw discomfort in them, even a touch of distaste.

'No reason to rush. Some tea, I think – Su Lin, if you would–' Miss Nessa tried to return to her carefully planned introduction, but was interrupted again when Uncle Chen grabbed my arm and walked me towards the door. Miss Nessa seized my other arm. Like the baby in the Bible story, I was being pulled apart, but without a true mother in the picture.

'Chief Inspector! You must make this man leave at once!'

'It is best not to interfere in domestic situations.' Le Froy turned to the door, hoping for an excuse to escape. He looked exactly like the Mission kindergarten children trying to avoid questions when they hadn't prepared an answer. The thought made me grin just as he glanced at me. Did that trigger a curiosity that made him stay?

'Perhaps you would permit me to close the front door, Miss Palin.' A small crowd of hawkers, coolies and rickshaw-pullers had clustered outside to watch what was going on within. Among them I recognized a couple of men who worked for Uncle Chen. If Le Froy knew these people as well as I did, he would be aware that they were already placing bets on which of us the chief inspector was going to arrest and take away. A Singaporean never missed the chance to gamble.

'May I?'

'That's a good idea. You are a practical man, Chief Inspector.' Rather than accept his offer, Miss Nessa swung the doors shut and tugged at the flat bolt, which was meant to lock them. Like so many things at the Mission Centre for which volunteers had been responsible, it didn't quite fit and stuck, but the doors stayed closed.

'Please take a seat, Chief Inspector,' Miss Nessa said, with abrupt dignity. 'I must apologize for the circus here this morning.

9

This man . . .' She looked severely at Uncle Chen, but he was suddenly fussing over me, straightening my shirt over my shoulders and patting down my hair. In other words, establishing family authority in the way that a farmer claims ownership of a pig at the market. I respected my uncle, who indulged his mother's fondness for me, had never stinted on my food or clothes after my father's death had left him head of the Chen family, and had not thrown me out when fortune-tellers told him his own childless marriage was due to my bad-luck presence. Uncle Chen had taken only one wife so far and, though married for more than ten years, Shen-Shen was barely in her thirties. And although Uncle Chen was trying to strong-arm me into marriage, he had tried to reassure me: 'Don't be scared. If your husband beats you or doesn't give you children, you tell me and I'll make sure he dies without children!'

'Good morning, Miss Palin,' Le Froy said. 'You did say eleven o'clock? I can return at some other time if this is not convenient.' He glanced at my uncle again. His eyes darted constantly around the room as though he were taking stock and assessing everything in it.

It was said that Le Froy was a fair man, known for his willingness to work with – and against – men of any race, language or religion. Since his arrival on the island, he had promoted good local people based on the standard of their work and pursued Europeans who had broken the law. He was at the Mission Centre that morning thanks to Miss Nessa. After all Miss Vanessa Palin was the sister of Singapore's acting governor, Sir Henry Palin, currently based in Government House on Frangipani Hill. Sir Henry represented British colonial authority in Singapore, and

Nessa Palin represented Sir Henry. Chief Inspector Le Froy might be head of the Singapore Police but, like everyone else on the island, he was subject to the Crown and colonial authority.

'Oh, no, Chief Inspector. Of course this is convenient. You have an appointment, after all. Some local people do not understand how to make and keep appointments.' Miss Nessa threw a triumphant glance at my uncle. She had never doubted her victory but it was still nice to see rivals crumble as reinforcements arrived.

Uncle Chen did not crumble. He locked strong plump fingers around my arm and started to pull me towards the exit again, muttering rude things under his breath. I didn't know whether he had recognized the policeman but Le Froy was an *ang moh* – a white man – and Uncle Chen did not trust *ang moh*s. Again, Miss Nessa seized my other arm, effectively halting progress.

'I don't know what the man is talking about.' Miss Nessa's voice rose to drown Uncle Chen's rant. 'Can't you get one of your men to put him out? You're supposed to be keeping order here. Please make sure we're not bothered by gaga natives.'

'He's threatening to come back and burn down the Mission building if you try to keep his dead brother's orphan daughter prisoner here,' Le Froy translated calmly.

I noticed he had kept the more colourful parts of my uncle's tirade to himself: he had not told Miss Nessa she had been called an immoral white ghost, a tigress, and less useful than what comes out of the hind end of a barren chicken. Nevertheless I was impressed by his fluency. I was even more impressed when he turned to my uncle and said, in flawless Hokkien, 'It's against the law to burn down buildings, sir.'

Uncle Chen paused to assess him, still suspicious but some-what mollified by his respectful use of 'sir'. Most *ang mohs* demanded respect without giving it. Uncle Chen focused his attention on Le Froy, sniffing like a suspicious guard dog trying to decide whether to bite. Many Chinese people said *ang mohs* smelt of dead cow because of all the beef they ate. Perhaps he'd caught a whiff of it.

'Who are you?'

'My name is Thomas Le Froy. I am a police officer. I am here to keep the peace and protect your rights. What may I call you?'

'Chen. If you are a police officer, you'd better tell this unmarried white she-devil to give me back my dead brother's daughter.'

Le Froy returned to Nessa and the English language: 'Miss Palin, have you taken Mr Chen's niece away from her family?'

'Don't be absurd, Chief Inspector. Why would I want to do that? I am only trying to help her! Su Lin, tell the inspector what your family is trying to do to you!'

They all turned to stare at me. I could easily act the part each expected of me, but I had shown these people such very different sides of myself that I couldn't think what to say to them together. I froze.

'She's shy,' Miss Nessa said confidently. 'And she's scared of her uncle. He wants to marry her off to some old man.'

'Miss Chen Su Lin? This man is your uncle?'

'Yes, sir.'

'You can speak English. I assume you were translating for them?'

'I was, sir, but I couldn't keep up.' Since he had heard them shouting there was no need to continue.

'Perhaps you could explain to me how things stand.'

'Su Lin has been a model student at the Mission School for years.' Nessa Palin was not used to hearing anyone else explain anything when she was around to do it better. 'Last year she was one of the first girls in Malaya to sit for the Cambridge School Leaving Certificate Examination and pass. It would be criminal and irresponsible to marry her into virtual slavery!'

Le Froy hushed her with a small hand gesture. 'I want to hear from Su Lin. Start at the beginning.'

I was wearing a plain Western-style cotton frock and spectacles (which I didn't really need, except for reading), but my long hair was plaited and wound around my head in traditional style. I was sure there was nothing to make me stand out in a crowd, yet Le Froy seemed to be studying me with attention.

I was sixteen but most people thought I was younger. Despite the limp, I was sure I looked too clean and well fed to be a runaway *mui tsai* or indentured (slave) girl. The way in which he was inspecting me would have been rude – though routine for an *ang moh* in authority – if he had not given me a small, polite nod of acknowledgement when our eyes met. Now that was unexpected. I was so taken aback I nodded back automatically. He smiled.

Perhaps he was not only interested in my appearance. Most Chinese girls encountered in town would either smile flirtatiously or stare, speechless, at their feet. I should have decided in advance which of these examples to follow. Instead, betrayed by my own curiosity, I had been staring hard at him.

13

'Why did your parents send you to the English school? Why don't you want to marry the man they have chosen for you?'

'My parents are dead. My grandmother sent me to the English school so that I can earn my own living because I would bring bad luck to the family I marry into. That is why Miss Nessa is helping me to find work. My uncle wants me to marry a man without family so that I will have a husband to look after me, but...'

But a man without family would hardly be an honourable match for me.

I did not really expect an *ang moh* to understand. Although Ah Ma ruled the family and the family businesses in everything but name, girls were worth little. Locals worried that the 'Mission Girls', as we were dubbed, would learn Western ways and be difficult to marry off. However, most of the other Mission Girls had been snapped up as soon as they showed their noses outside the schoolroom and, so far, our years of study had not produced the cross-eyed babies predicted by superstitious traditionalists. Only a few of us remained on the shelf: my friend Parshanti, because of her mixed Anglo-Indian origins, and myself, because of my limp and my reputation as bringer of bad luck, or so I liked to think.

'Who do you want her to marry, sir?' Le Froy asked Uncle Chen, in Hokkien.

To my surprise, Uncle Chen answered him: 'Chang is one of my associates. He comes from the north, Negri Sembilan. He is a younger son with many brothers so he can't expect much from his family.' That was probably why he was willing to marry a polio victim. Uncle Chen turned to me. 'Chang is a good man.

He has no debts, and if he marries you, I will give him one of the Tiong Bahru supply shops to run. Tiong Bahru is a good location. You can help him and you will live well.'

'Have you discussed this with Su Lin?'

Uncle Chen seemed to think there was no need for discussion. 'The man was married before but his wife died. He already has three children. It is about time she learned to look after children.'

'So, as we agreed, you will take Su Lin as your assistant and housekeeper?' Miss Nessa interrupted. She did not understand Hokkien but I suspect Le Froy's lack of aggression towards Uncle Chen worried her. 'No man will dare interfere with Su Lin if she is under your protection.' She looked meaningfully at Uncle Chen, then turned back to Le Froy, 'And it would be very good for you to have someone looking after you and managing your servants.'

Le Froy gazed at my uncle, clearly expecting more protests. But Uncle Chen was watching him with a guarded, calculating expression. The chief inspector glanced at me, and as our eyes met, I saw his apprehension. Chief Inspector Thomas Le Froy, whose name struck terror into the hearts of all the toughest gangsters and gamblers in Singapore, was frightened of the teenage housekeeper a woman was trying to manipulate him into hiring! I couldn't help it – I laughed. Le Froy looked startled, but then he shook his head with a wry grin.

Le Froy might have been a hero but that morning he was clearly a weary one. His square shoulders slumped and his eyes avoided Miss Nessa's. I had heard rumours that, although the chief inspector would take on any man in a fair fight, he preferred not to deal with women. In the newspapers he had been quoted as saying that the police force would never employ female officers because it was impossible to work with irrational persons. Miss Nessa was rational as long as she had her own way, but at that moment I felt sorry for Le Froy.

'Well?' Miss Nessa might have been prodding a terrified student for an answer.

Before he could respond, there was a series of quick knocks and the unbolted door was pushed open. 'Chief Inspector Le Froy?' The newcomer's khaki shirt and shorts marked him as a junior police constable. 'I was told you were here. I have a message for you.'

'What is it?'

'News of a death on Frangipani Hill.'

'What?' Miss Nessa's normally strong voice faltered. 'Don't be ridiculous!'

Frangipani Hill was where Government House stood. The governor's Residence, where Miss Nessa lived with her brother's family, stood just behind it. 'What's happened? Is it Sir Henry? Was it an accident? A shooting? Who is dead, man? Tell me!'

The officer ignored her, looking to Le Froy for directions.

'Who is dead?' Le Froy switched into professional mode, somehow looking taller and more authoritative. I doubted he would have been notified if one of the servants or local administrators had died. It must be someone more important, one of the white officials at least. Uncle Chen was silent. I could see he was trying to take in all he could without calling attention to himself.

'It's the girl who was helping to look after the *tan bai kia*.'

Tan bai kia is a local phrase, often used as an insult. Translated

16

literally from the Chinese Teochew dialect, it means 'retarded child' – in other words, the Palin girl.

'The *tan bai kia* is dead?'

I had always suspected my uncle understood a great deal more English than he let on. Now he was even trying to speak it. I whispered back to him, 'No, Uncle. The white girl looking after her is dead.'

'Charity,' Nessa Palin said. She was clearly relieved that her brother was alive but she seemed shocked and, for a moment, swayed on her feet. I moved a chair behind her and took her arm to guide her onto it. She sat without protest, as though, with her attention fixed on the policeman, she was not aware of what her body was doing. 'Charity Byrne. Someone killed Charity? Why?'

Le Froy looked at her curiously but only asked the policeman, 'Who is there now?'

'Sergeant de Souza, with three men. He sent Constable Kwok to fetch Dr Leask and me to get you. He said he will see to things until you come.'

'Sir Henry came to the police station himself?'

'No, sir. He sent a rickshaw runner with a note. He says it was an accident – a girl fell off the balcony on the upper floor of the Residence.'

Charity Byrne had been another of Miss Nessa's projects. She was an orphaned Irish girl, who had come to the colony as nanny to Deborah Palin. I had met Charity when Miss Nessa brought her to the Mission Centre 'to meet some local girls your age'. Miss Nessa had clearly wanted Charity to spend her free evenings volunteering with young women rather than in the company of young men, but Charity would have none of it. And there had always been plenty of young men – junior government officials and non-commissioned officers – vying for her attention.

The Charity Byrne I remembered had been sparking with energy, outspoken, and had openly contradicted Miss Nessa. She had shocked – and impressed – me.

'You must drive me back to Frangipani Hill at once,' Miss Nessa told Le Froy. 'The car won't be here to collect me for another twenty minutes and I must get back immediately.'

'What about Su Lin?' Le Froy asked.

Miss Nessa looked blank. Le Froy nodded in my direction and her blue-grey eyes moved over me. She seemed to be trying to remember who I was. She made a dismissive gesture with her hand. 'Another time. Another day. It's not important now. Su Lin, I will be in touch when I can. Don't let them marry you to anyone until you hear from me. I must get back to Frangipani Hill.'

Le Froy looked at Uncle Chen and probably saw a glowering, dangerous Chinese man. 'Come,' he said to me. 'Be quick.'

Motor-car

————◆————

'Do you have your things with you?' Le Froy asked me.

I showed him the portmanteau I had grabbed from behind the door as he hurried me out. I had packed a week's worth of clothes, assuming I would return home on Sunday, like the maids from rural villages who worked at my grandmother's house during the week. He tossed it onto the back seat, then held open the front passenger door for me.

'Have you ever been in a motor-car before? It's quite safe, I assure you.'

I had indeed. My grandmother had a 12-horsepower Armstrong tourer that she had driven around in to collect rents, and I had often gone with her when it rained. I had only hesitated because I had never had a man open a door for me before, let alone an *ang moh*. The enormity of what I was taking on began to sink in, but the alternative, in the shape of Uncle Chen, had followed us out of the Mission Centre. Two of his men, who had been squatting outside, straightened up and I saw Le Froy keeping an eye on them as he helped me into his car.

Miss Nessa tried to follow.

'Miss Palin, please step aside.' Miss Nessa was not used to having her instructions ignored and Le Froy had to raise his voice as well as his arm. 'You can wait here for your driver and not disrupt your schedule unnecessarily.'

Uncle Chen looked worried. I saw his lips automatically moving in a Chinese farewell blessing: *May good winds speed your journey*. Uncle Chen was loud and strong, but I had started helping him with his business accounts when I was eight and knew he was not the smartest of men. People never let him forget that he did not measure up to my dead father, who had been the smart, fearless son and intended heir. Uncle Chen often told me I took after my father, and that he would always watch out for me because my father had been good to him. If I had been a boy he would have brought me into the family business with the intention of handing it over to me. Instead, the best he could do was to marry me off to a man who would not beat me. No, there was no future for me in doing what my family wanted. I would take a chance on making a more interesting future for myself.

Le Froy kept his eyes fixed on the road as he pulled away from the kerb outside the Mission Centre and edged slowly through the crowds of people, bicycles, rickshaws and occasional bullock carts. I gazed out of the car window, trying not to feel too excited. Le Froy's black-and-green Plymouth went much faster than my grandmother's old tourer – as buildings and people moved past with increasing speed, I experienced the dizziness of swooping downwards on a rope swing. I closed my eyes.

'Look into the distance.'

'What?'

'Otherwise you'll get motion sickness. The brain finds it difficult to process too much too quickly. Is this the first time you've been in a motor-car?'

I realized I was clutching the little strap by the door with both hands and folded them in my lap, according to Miss Nessa's instructions, as he added, 'You must admit they are fast.'

'They can't run for as long as horses or pull as much as oxen.' I quoted my grandmother automatically.

'Mrs Bertha Benz travelled more than fifty miles from Mannheim to Pforzheim in one of the vehicles her husband Karl created,' Le Froy said conversationally. He slowed down to navigate past a couple of buffalo carts being unloaded at the side of the street and I felt better.

'Are there women drivers?' My dizziness was eclipsed by my interest.

'Oh, yes. And since motor-cars are driven with skill rather than with strength, women are at no disadvantage.'

Oh! If only I could persuade Ah Ma to let me drive her around in hers!

There was less traffic once we turned onto Bukit Timah Road and headed northwards alongside the canal. There, the roadside grasses were dried brown as the earth, but the row of thick-trunked trees lining the canal blocked the worst of the sun. I relaxed a little with the wind blowing in my face, and I remember thinking that moving effortlessly fast had to be what pure joy felt like. The short Sumatra squall earlier had left the roads damp but an ashy scent was coming through the car windows from the paper offerings people were burning.

It was the first day of the Chinese Seventh Lunar Month, when the spirits of the unhappy dead are released from Hell to collect their offerings and settle scores. For the first time in my life I would not be at home to watch the traditional evening burning of the bundles of green 'Hell money'. I doubted I would be missed by either humans or spirits: after Uncle Chen had lit the first joss sticks and put the first green bundle into the burning bin, the servants would take over.

We headed northwards to where the largest cemeteries were located. Local people avoided living close to dead bodies but *ang mohs* seemed not to mind. As we passed makeshift stages set up for concerts to entertain the dead later, some no more than planks on bricks in front of stools and mats, Le Froy spoke again: 'Joss paper for Ghost Month,' he said casually. I saw he wanted to impress me with his local knowledge so I looked properly surprised. I always try to please people when I can, especially if it doesn't cost me anything. It makes them easier to deal with. 'Would you prefer to speak Malay or Hokkien, Su Lin? Am I pronouncing your name correctly? "Su" as in "suit" without the *t* and "Lin" as in "linen" without the "en"?'

Le Froy's Chinese pronunciation was good. I knew he was trying to put me at ease and almost replied, 'Correct, as in "carrot" but reversing the vowels phonetically.' However, I reminded myself in time that I was hoping to get a job with him (a real job – house-keeping was just the first step; I could figure out the second later), which meant making him think I'd be easy to work with, so I said, 'Yes, thank you, Chief Inspector. I am quite comfortable with English.' I was happy to show off *my* proficiency in *his* language.

'So, you don't want to marry the man your family chose for you. Is there someone else you do want to marry? And why does your uncle want to marry you off now?' His eyes were still on the road. 'In the Seventh Month? Isn't that bad luck?'

I had to admire his awareness of local superstitions. During the Seventh Lunar Month, or Ghost Month, Chinese people consider it bad luck to start new projects, from jobs and marriages to moving into new houses.

Before I could answer he added, 'Is that man Chen really your uncle?'

Many years later Le Froy told me that Miss Nessa's actual words to him were: 'The girl is being married into slavery and you need someone to do your cleaning and cooking, and take messages when nobody knows where you are!' He had already rejected several of her previous attempts to provide him with English-speaking servants, who would help her organize him, but Miss Nessa was not a woman to notice rebuffs.

Le Froy had made sure he and I were alone in his car so that he could question me with neither Miss Nessa nor Uncle Chen present. I had assumed he had been too distracted to register Miss Nessa's demand for transport, but as I realized later, there was little he didn't hear. He simply applied a powerful filter to the world around him and ignored whatever he considered irrelevant.

'Yes, Uncle Chen is my uncle. He is my late father's younger brother – the only living brother.' Perhaps I should have been offended on Uncle Chen's behalf, but I could understand Le Froy's suspicion.

Rumour had it that at least seventy thousand prostitutes operated in Shanghai alone, not counting bar girls, masseuses and tour guides. As Chinese workers moved south to Singapore, so did the vice-dealers who served them. Singapore had more than three thousand licensed prostitutes registered at the Chinese Protectorate, as well as maids, singers and actresses, who were really unlicensed whores. Unfortunately for my dream of independence, prostitution was the only profession that seemed open to Chinese girls on the island. Le Froy was making sure I had been not been bought or kidnapped to become a concubine or to be sold to a brothel.

'Don't worry,' I said. 'I wasn't kidnapped from or sold by my family and I'm not a runaway. I can read, write and speak English, Mandarin, Malay and Hokkien, and I can do cleaning, housekeeping and accounts. My uncle came up with his marriage arrangement after he heard Miss Nessa had found a job for me. Uncle Chen means well.' Despite his blind faith in temple fortune-tellers, I was fond of him and didn't want to get him into trouble with the authorities.

'Your uncle can't find you other work?'

'He's afraid I'll bring bad luck to whoever I work for.'

Le Froy glanced at me. 'Bad luck?'

'Because my parents died and I had polio.' It was good luck as well as bad: if my parents had lived, I would not have gone to school.

'So you asked Nessa Palin to find you a job. Times are not easy here, and it's worse in Europe. Even men are finding it difficult to get jobs. If, by any chance, you have some idea of finding work and travelling, I doubt you will.'

'I want to see a bit more of the world before I get married.'

Ever since Miss Nessa had lent me her copy of Henry James's *Portrait of a Lady* I had wanted to be a lady reporter, like Henrietta

Stackpole, whom I had found far more interesting than the book's heroine. I knew it was no use saying that. I longed for a life like Miss Nessa's (she reminded me of Henrietta Stackpole in brains and bluntness), and the last thing I wanted was to be locked into a marriage before I was twenty.

'About your parents, my condolences. You don't look like a victim of kidnap, but it's always safer to ask. Miss Nessa mentioned you have your School Certificate. That's unusual in this part of the world, isn't it? Especially for a girl with no parents?'

'My grandmother takes care of me. She says my father always regretted not having gone to school and he would have wanted me to.'

'What was your father's name?'

'Chen Tou Liang.'

'Ah . . .' The car was still moving but Le Froy gave me a long look. 'So you're one of those Chens. Your uncle Chen must be Chen Tou Seng and your grandmother is the famous Chen Tai. I see.'

I wasn't sure what he saw. People did not gossip to me about my own family but I knew my grandmother was reputed to be a shrewd businesswoman. People whispered that she, rather than my late grandfather, had built up the Chen family fortune, and that it was Chen Tai, rather than Uncle Chen, who ran the Chen family businesses. Some claimed my grandfather's family in China had cut him off after he had angered them by marrying a Straits-born woman without bound feet. It was their loss. Despite Ah Ma's flourishing business, it was said that her pride had brought its share of bad luck. Her husband had died in a cholera epidemic, followed by four of her children, including my father, my mother and my infant brother.

OVIDIA YU

Then there was me, the bad-luck girl. This curse would frighten off parents of respectable suitors, despite my family's standing in the community. And my education wouldn't help: many wealthy Eurasian and Indian families sent their daughters, as well as their sons, to school, but few Chinese did.

'What do you know of the Palins?' Abruptly, Le Froy had changed the subject. His tone was so light he might have been making social chit-chat, which made me suspect he was really asking what the local people knew of the acting governor and his family. Well, if I could help him there, he might find it worth his while to keep me on.

I replied cautiously, with my best enunciation, 'They are rich, respectable people.'

He nodded, keeping his eyes on the road. I sensed I had disappointed him so I continued, 'Sir Henry Palin is a former planter who still owns estates in northern Malaya. He is a committee member of the Singapore Polo Club, although he does not play or own ponies. He lives with his second wife, Lady Mary Palin, his unmarried sister, Miss Vanessa Palin, and the two children from his first marriage. Harry Palin is in his early twenties and Deborah is said to be funny in the head.'

'Very good,' he said, and I could tell he was pleased – as though I had proved a point for him. 'Lady Laura Palin, Sir Henry's first wife, died of a tropical fever in India when Deborah was seven. Deborah was also very ill for a long time, and although she recovered physically, mentally she has remained a seven-year-old. I've often thought that if only Deborah Palin had been born into a poor Asian family, with a web of relatives and social connections, she would have had her own place within the community by now. I've seen children younger than seven tending goats, selling vegetables, catching and drying fish and caring for younger siblings or ageing grandparents. I'm sure you were looking after yourself when you were seven, weren't you, Su Lin? But since everyone treats Deborah Palin like a helpless child, she has remained so, needing to have everything done for her. That's why they brought the Irish girl, Charity Byrne, in to help with her.' He paused. 'Did you know Charity Byrne?'

Of course I'd known who Charity Byrne was. The local gossip system monitored the doings of the *ang moh*s with as much attention as the *ang moh*s followed the doings of their – our – king, Edward VIII, and his lady-friends.

'I met her. She came to the Mission Centre with Miss Nessa a couple of times.'

'Indeed. What did she do?'

I had to think about this. Charity had never stayed long or said much. 'She would just say hello. She had to look after Deborah Palin.'

———◆———

It was just past eleven thirty when we reached the bottom of Frangipani Drive.

We were in the Bukit Timah, 'Mount Timah', district. This was the geographic centre and the highest point on the main island of Singapore. From there the rest of the diamond-shaped island slopes down to the coast in all directions and Frangipani Hill is part of the foothills. The gates at the base of the upward-curving drive stood open and unguarded. Le Froy tightened his lips in disapproval. He slid the car off the driveway between two trees and turned off the engine.

'You had better come with me,' he said. 'You can leave your bag in the car.'

I saw his eyes darting over the surface and sides of the road as we continued on foot up the driveway. I couldn't tell what he was looking out for. On both sides of the road there were rows of the trees that had given Frangipani Hill its name. Beyond them rose a tangle of semi-wild rainforest. I saw clumps of sugar cane, tapioca, and a great many banana trees flourishing untended. I could hear insects and caught the not-so-distant call of a wild cockerel. The earth smelt good and I took a deep breath.

'What are you looking at?' he asked, pausing. The driveway was fairly steep, and I was glad to stop for a rest.

'It's good rich earth. There are probably wild pigs and wild chickens around here. It would be good land to farm.'

'You think it's wasted?' He started to walk uphill again and I followed a respectful step behind him.

'Europeans only grow flowers and grass.' I didn't understand why Europeans who owned land preferred to buy, rather than grow, fruit and vegetables.

'The European community here is not homogeneous,' Le Froy said. 'In fact, most of the "Europeans" in Singapore now are not even European – they don't come from Europe. When in England these people would very likely call all the Dutch, Swiss and French people who come from beyond the English Channel "foreigners". The main reason they call themselves "European" rather than "British" here is to distinguish themselves from local residents in this British Crown Colony. But if you've met any Eurasians you'll know that they're more patriotically British than more recent arrivals from Britain!'

Of course I knew Eurasians: several of my teachers at the Mission Girls' School had been Eurasian women, who were more likely to work outside the home than other women. Most Eurasians were Christians, which gave them access to Mission schools and, subsequently, lower-ranked civil-service positions, the higher ranks reserved exclusively for white people. Although almost aggressively British now, most in this exclusive ethnic enclave traced the European part of their ancestry to Portuguese, Dutch, Danish or Spanish settlers as far back as the sixteenth century. There were around seven thousand 'official' Eurasians in Singapore. My school friend Parshanti Shankar was Euro-Asian. She had a Scottish mother and an Indian father and was not accepted as 'Eurasian': the Eurasian Association acknowledged only those whose fathers were of European origin and had European surnames.

I sensed Le Froy was talking to distract me while he watched me walk beside him and his next words proved me right.

'Is something wrong with one of your shoes?'

'No, sir. I had polio when I was young.'

'But I see you can walk.'

'I can walk and do housework, also office work, sir.'

'Ah.' I heard satisfaction in his voice, as though a piece in a puzzle had clicked into place for him, but it must have been an unimportant puzzle because he immediately returned his attention to the surface and sides of the road. 'Come. I believe there's a body under that frangipani tree.'

The Body Under the Frangipani

————◆————

There were two large buildings on Frangipani Hill. Le Froy had stopped where the road forked: on the left, a circular drive led to Government House, and on the right, the steeper track went to the Residence. Looking up, I saw the two buildings were connected by a shaded walkway, lined with frangipanis, which ran between the back of Government House and the side porch of the Residence.

The Residence was a large, raised, two-storey black and white bungalow, longer than it was wide. The lower storey was at least twenty feet high and, like many other houses built for the colonial masters, it was made of brick below and wood above, with verandas that ran the length of the house on both sides on the ground and upper floors. The house was on a slope, so there were more stairs up to the front porch than to the veranda.

I was to come to know the bungalow on Frangipani Hill very well, but on that long-ago first day I was young and awestruck, and what I remember best is how dusty, dark and stuffy I found it. A great many heavy curtains and blinds kept light and air out of the house and there were dead animals and animal heads along the dim corridor we walked through to the covered porch on the far side of the house.

Once there, the dead white girl under the frangipani tree made it difficult for me to notice much else.

The only people visible were policemen standing in the porch, their photographer and his assistant, who was holding up a sheet, but I sensed many watching eyes. As we approached, there was a flash of light and a belch of evil-smelling magnesium flash – the photographer was finishing his work. His assistant had already started to pack away the equipment. The barrier was lowered for Le Froy, revealing a blanket thrown over what looked like a rag doll. Dark stains showed where blood had seeped into the gravel between the paving stones on which it lay. Sunlight filtered through the leaves and branches of the large frangipanis.

'Very *pantang*,' my grandmother would have said, meaning bad luck.

As the old childhood rhyme went,

> Pokok kubur
> Tumbuh dari
> Darah daging orang mati

The frangipani tree, so the verse says, is the essence of grave-yards, growing on the blood and bones of dead bodies. It is considered bad luck and some people, especially the older ones, avoid its flowers because it is said their lovely fragrance comes from unhappy female spirits. I didn't quite believe that, although I preferred to stay away from graveyards at night – more to avoid mosquitoes than ghosts. I wondered whether Chief Inspector Le Froy had been on the island long enough to know the superstition. He certainly eyed the frangipani tree with some attention, but he also seemed suspicious of the flat paving stones, the granite-chip driveway and the local servants, who were standing at a distance, staring at us. The other police officers stood back as Le Froy took his time pacing around, his lips moving rapidly but silently.

I knew Miss Nessa pooh-poohed such superstitions as heathen ignorance. Europeans had their own superstitions, like wearing shoes all the time, even indoors, and not eating the heads of fish or the feet of chickens. But they obviously didn't mind tree spirits. Why else would they have planted so many frangipani trees around Government House?

Charity Byrne must have fallen from the balcony on the second floor. Looking up, I saw a waist-high wooden railing with upright supports. How could anyone have fallen over a waist-high railing by accident? Had someone pushed her over in a joke gone terribly wrong? Drunken European sailors were always pushing each other into the harbour waters at night and drowning. I shivered. Charity had not been much older than I was. Death was no respecter of average life expectancy. I would remember that the next time someone told me to be patient because I was still young . . .

Le Froy finally turned to the nearest policeman. 'Where is everyone? The family?'

'We asked the governor and his family to wait inside until you got here, sir. The nanny, Miss Charity Byrne, fell from the second floor,' he gestured upwards to where the balcony extended beyond the veranda around the house, 'and broke her neck. But Sir Henry insisted she be left where she was till you got here.'

The local police looked hugely relieved to have Le Froy take charge. It was probably their first experience with a death in an acting governor's household and there was no protocol to follow. The arrival of a senior European officer meant the situation was no longer their responsibility. 'We didn't move anything. We took photographs but that was all.'

As the police photographer and his assistant finished packing his equipment and left, the officers ushered Le Froy towards the body. I followed. My earlier excitement was fading and I was beginning to feel out of place, in the way and slightly nauseous, but I was not going to back away from the only excitement that had ever come into my life. (Though admittedly I had dreamed of an exciting job rather than a dead body.) I could have gone back to Le Froy's car and waited there but I reminded myself that Henrietta Stackpole would have seized the opportunity to watch a police investigation. If I were ever to become a reporter I must learn to observe and record facts, without feeling ill or fainting.

Le Froy stooped carefully beside the covered figure and, at a nod from him, one of the policemen bent to pull back the blanket. Charity Byrne lay on her back, her hands together on her chest. Her eyes were closed. At first glance she might have been in peaceful repose, her dark brown hair damp and matted against the side of her head.

Le Froy frowned. 'She's been moved. Who moved her?'

'No, sir. We never.'

'Nobody moved her. She's still here. This is where she landed.'

'After falling off the second-floor balcony and breaking her neck, she landed here flat on her back with her legs straight, skirt smoothed down and hands together?'

'She has not been moved since we got here, sir.'

'Ah.' Le Froy looked in the direction of the house. 'You have a list of the people here? I want to know who found her and who laid her out.'

I looked at the small shape on the ground. At least someone had cared enough to lay her out decently.

'Oh!' I was startled into crying out at a sudden flicker of the fabric. For a moment I fancied Charity was alive, that all this was just one of her jokes, but then a common tree lizard, which had sought refuge beneath the blanket and been startled by its sudden exposure, flashed across the paving stones and up the tree. Terrified, it left behind its twitching tail as a gruesome distraction. Le Froy looked at me. I tried to sound calm as I said, 'Sorry,' and he turned back to the men.

'She fell? From upstairs?' He looked up through the branches of the tree. 'At this point? She would have caught in the tree. Where is her room? At the side of the house? Was anyone with her? Was she sneaking out to meet someone? Have you found any other injuries on the girl?' His eyes went back to Charity as he spoke, darting from her face to her fingers and feet, then back to the lines of her dress.

The policemen were silent under his rapid barrage of questions. It was not clear whether he was expecting answers from them or thinking aloud. An officer cleared his throat. 'From the balcony, sir. She landed here. Must have fallen down through the tree. But there is something you should see, sir.'

The policeman who had lifted the blanket from the body moved forward and pointed to the dead girl's side. Charity's light blue blouse had four layers of frills starting at the collar. The largest and lowest frill reached beyond the high waist on the dress. The policeman lifted the frill and indicated the girl's side: there was a jagged rip in the material.

Le Froy, now on one knee beside the body, lifted the fabric and peered. I saw a slash in Charity's underwear – and smears of blood, as though a blade had been wiped on it before the blouse had been rearranged to cover the damage.

'The wound in the girl's side suggests she was stabbed before she fell,' the police officer said, as though presenting a report.

'So, this was no accident.' Le Froy said, getting slowly to his feet. 'Miss Charity Byrne was killed – murdered. Did you find the weapon?' Though he spoke softly there was force and authority in his voice. It made me feel I ought to salute and do something useful, if only I knew how to. That was very different from my response to authority at home and in school, which was to keep quiet and stay unnoticed.

'No, sir. We already asked the family. They say they saw nothing of the sort.'

'The weapon seems to have been some kind of knife blade.' I had drawn forward as Le Froy lowered his voice and, squatting just behind him, I was close enough to hear his low voice say rapidly, 'I would say no more than six inches. Not serrated. Make sure it's not in the area. And check upstairs.'

'It sounds like it could have been a local hunting knife,' I said, 'A *keris.*'

Le Froy started, and I realized he had forgotten I was there. 'Yes. Possibly a *keris,*' he said. 'Have you found anything of the sort?'

'Not yet, sir.'

'Tell the men to keep looking. Inside and outside the house.'

'You want us to question the locals around here? Find out who carried a knife like that?'

'Won't do any good. Westerners often collect such objects as novelties or souvenirs.'

I suspected he had said this for my benefit, but I was not surprised by it: Westerners collected everything from dead animals to religious objects, which they displayed as decorations.

One of the police officers moved away and I heard him passing on the instructions to other men who had been waiting at the side of the house. Le Froy bent once more over Charity's body, then stood up abruptly. I also got to my feet – too quickly. Suddenly I found myself trembling. Although the sun was as hot as always, my hands were cold. I felt lightheaded and wondered if this was how women felt before they swooned and fainted. I fiercely wanted it not to be the case but wasn't sure what I could do to avoid it. I had never fainted before so I wasn't carrying anything like the tiny bottle of Axe Brand Universal Oil my grandmother sniffed as a cure-all or the little blue bottle of Revivo, the scented smelling salts that Miss Nessa always had with her. I felt dizzy and it took all my willpower to subdue the nausea rising inside me. Even with my eyes shut, I could see Charity's closed eyes in her cold face. Had she closed them in terror or had someone closed them when they arranged her, as Le Froy suspected? The dead Charity did not look terrified, but surely she must have been.

I dug my fingernails hard into my palms and swore that if I got through this without throwing up or passing out I would never again mock English novels featuring women who swooned and fainted. I dispatched fervent prayers to God or Guan Yin, promising a cash tithe (the Christian God likes money) or a dozen joss sticks (Buddhist and Taoist gods prefer incense) to preserve my dignity. I was proud of being the tough, no-nonsense Chen girl, who had taught herself to face all problems calmly. I reminded myself that a dead body was just one more problem, and if I crumpled on my first day at work, I would deserve to spend the rest of my life hiding in the Chen family home.

Even though it meant moving towards the body, I stepped closer to Le Froy as if sheer proximity to him could protect me. He seemed to be studying the area around which Charity's body lay and trying to work something out. To distract myself, and my stomach, I focused on what he was looking at. A forked branch had been torn off the tree and lay beside Charity, sap already dry. I couldn't tell if her fall had caused the damage. Then Le Froy walked slowly around the driveway. I followed, looking up as he did into the sheltering trees, through the open doors to the dim rooms, then making a slow round of the garden, with its border of bushes, and again peering up through the branches of the frangipani tree to the balcony from which Charity had apparently fallen.

'Sir Henry Palin says it must have been an accident.' The policeman was back. 'He wants to see you, sir. He said to tell you he is waiting.'

37

'Yes, of course.' Le Froy looked from the balcony to the ground, then back up at the crown of the tree. Frangipanis are relatively small, soft-wood trees, with branches that bend easily. No one, not even a child, would think to climb one.

I suspected that if the acting governor had not asked Le Froy to take a personal interest this would have been dismissed as an accidental death. But what about the apparent knife wound in her side? Could a jagged branch have caused it? Something was not quite right there. It was like the pairs of pictures we were given in school to teach us to pay attention to detail: each pair would be almost identical, except for subtle differences we had to spot – a girl would have an apple in one picture and a ball in the other. I had hated them. No matter how many differences I found (and usually I found them all) I was always sure I had missed something. The scene under the tree that day made me feel the same.

'They are waiting for you inside, sir.'

Le Froy made his way into the house as though he knew it well. I hesitated, then scuttled after him. I could move quickly when I had to, but not for long. I kept up with him down the dark corridors and was by his side when he paused in the open doorway of a large room.

Two white men were silhouetted against the light bamboo blinds of the drawing room – as I learned later to call it. They were standing by the doors leading to the veranda that ran around the house. The older man was wearing a white *tutup*, the cotton-drill business uniform of older colonials, while the younger sported a modern Western suit. They were broad-faced men, alike enough to be father and son, though the darker-haired but greying older man had the ruddy, florid complexion of a long-term planter, while the pale skin under the reddish brown hair of the younger marked him as a civil servant who never went outside without his sola topi. Indeed, he was holding his white sun helmet now, playing nervously with its curved neck extension as his father stepped forward, 'Le Froy! Good of you to come. Confounded business, this—' He caught sight of me and stopped.

Miss Nessa had drummed into us that one of the greatest strengths of the British Empire was the etiquette that guided civilized beings through all conceivable situations. Sir Henry Palin epitomized this as he extended his hand to me. 'How do you do? Henry Palin. Thank you for coming.' His tone was earnest and sincere, and as I looked into his eyes, I knew I would do all I could to earn his appreciation and approval.

Like many of the British expatriates in the Straits Settlements, Henry Palin had come out years earlier to make his fortune in the East, and was co-opted into the colonial government. He was a thickset man with a tanned face and keen blue eyes. It was not difficult to see the independent, adventurous planter beneath the civil-service administrator's veneer.

Broad and tall, Sir Henry Palin was much the same age and height as Chief Inspector Le Froy but his bearing made him stand out while Le Froy merged into his surroundings.

'My son Harry,' said Sir Henry. I thought I heard a touch of wariness in his tone and studied the younger man with more interest. 'Chief Inspector Le Froy and . . .'

Harry Palin had bright nervous eyes, was slender in compari-son to his father, and affected a carefully cultivated air of world-weary sophistication. Yet I sensed he was the more shaken of the pair by the day's tragedy.

Le Froy, looking around the room with the air of a curious dog, made no attempt to introduce me. Fortunately, the door opened and Miss Nessa blew in, with her usual swift steps. 'Ah! Here you all are. What on earth has been going on, Henry? I leave the house for a couple of hours and come back to find policemen crawling through the bougainvillaea!'

'Chief Inspector, I believe you already know my sister Vanessa.'

'And you brought Su Lin here. Chief Inspector, this is not at all what I had in mind for her. Think of the shock to the poor girl, especially given she knew poor Charity!'

'You knew her? Were you two young ladies close friends?' There was a suspicious note under Sir Henry's jocular tone that surprised me.

'Su Lin is one of our best workers at the Mission Centre,' Miss Nessa said abruptly, before I could respond. 'We are trying to find her employment. Whether or not she was a friend of Charity is irrelevant. I'm sure you agree, Chief Inspector?'

Le Froy looked so blankly impassive that he might have been deaf or mesmerized. Soon I would learn that was a mask, which signalled furious thought was taking place beneath it, as though all his energy were directed to his brain, leaving nothing to spare for polite expression. But I didn't know that then.

'I hardly knew Charity. She came to the Mission Centre only a few times.'

'Of course. Nessa's little project in town. Of course.' Even in the cool, dark room the man's forehead was beaded with sweat and I could almost smell his nervousness.

'What happened, Henry?' Miss Nessa asked.

'Girl was upstairs. She fell over the balcony and broke her

neck,' Sir Henry said. 'I was coming up the drive. I heard her scream and saw her fall.'

'I saw her fall too.' Harry's voice trembled. He glared at his aunt and father, then addressed Le Froy: 'You're going to take her away, I hope? I've been here long enough to know you can't leave things like that too long, not in this climate.' He gave an unapologetic laugh and lit a cigarette with a flourish.

Le Froy gave him a grave nod. 'Did you close her eyes, sir? Someone did. Who was it?' He looked around enquiringly. 'Your servants wouldn't have taken it upon themselves to do so?' He fixed his eyes on Sir Henry, but it was Harry who answered.

'Thought it best. You know what it's like here. One dead bird on the ground, flies and ants everywhere. And they always go for the eyes first.' His own were mocking as he turned to me, challenging me to show signs of upset. I kept my expression calm by running through the twelve times table in my head. I hoped Harry was disappointed, and reminded myself that what he thought of me didn't matter.

'Anyway, it was clear straight away that nothing could be done for the poor girl.' He looked at the cigarette between his fingers as though surprised to find it there. 'So, if there's nothing else, will you take care of things from now? If there are any expenses I'm sure the pater will be only too glad—'

'Your men can wait outside, Chief Inspector. This is a private family room,' Miss Nessa cut in abruptly.

I noticed that the junior officer standing by the door waited for Le Froy's nod to dismiss him before he left. I was sure Miss Nessa had noticed too and would consider it nothing short of insubordination. It would be in her character to make sure Le Froy disciplined the man, or she might make etiquette lessons for police officers her next project.

'This is an unfortunate situation, very unfortunate. However, we must thank Providence that things turned out as they did. What measures have you taken to control the information?'

'There is no information to control,' Le Froy answered drily. 'And what there is, I doubt can or should be concealed for long. Concealment may well be a motive here.'

'It is our responsibility,' Sir Henry Palin said. His genial smile seemed to be the default expression his face assumed in repose and he beamed weakly at Le Froy. 'And yours as well, of course.'

'So that this matter is not blown out of proportion,' Miss Nessa insisted, 'the best thing for you to do is make sure the newspapers are informed that the Singapore police force sees this as an accident, a regrettable accident, that should not be discussed. In the opinion of the governor's office, that is the course you should take. There is no point in dragging this out, upsetting everyone and creating more gossip.'

Le Froy pointed out, 'The family, servants, doctor and several policemen are witnesses to the accident. It will make for far more gossip if your servants are told to say nothing. If we interview them and put their statements on record, they can rest assured that we are taking care of things.'

'Just the ticket! A man after my own heart!' Sir Henry's expression didn't change – despite the slight tremor in his voice, he seemed positively joyful at the prospect of khaki-clad policemen in his home talking to servants.

Miss Nessa's expression did not change either. 'All the servants are reliable, responsible people. I don't want them upset, and I won't have you planting ideas in their heads. Regardless of what they may think they saw or heard, they may have been mistaken. Isn't it obvious? The unfortunate girl fell to her death. It was an accident. How could it have been anything else?'

'How would you know, Aunt Nessa? You weren't even here. Won't you allow the chief inspector a little excitement? How often do you think he gets to investigate the governor's household? Anyway, it wouldn't have been very difficult. Charity liked to sit on the balcony railing, leaning against the upright. All it would have taken was "Here's your tea, miss", or "Here's a sandwich", then one good push.' Harry Palin mimed daintily holding a cup (little finger extended) in one hand, plate in the other, then executed a fierce two-handed push, flailed his arms and gave a soundless scream.

Sir Henry laughed. Miss Nessa glared.

'There is one other thing,' Le Froy said quietly. 'There is a wound in Charity Byrne's side, a knife wound,'

A stunned silence greeted his words, interrupted by a shrill voice from the couch in the corner of the room: 'The girl was stabbed?' I had not realized anyone was there until now. The back of the couch concealed the woman who had been lying on it with her feet up.

'She had a stab wound to her side as well as a broken neck,' Le Froy said. He inclined his head in the direction of the woman now sitting up, a token bow. 'Lady Palin.'

I had seen the two sofas in the conversation corner but mistaken Sir Henry's wife, Lady Mary Palin, for a pile of cushions. I knew Lady Palin by sight, of course. There had been photographs of her and Sir Henry in the illustrated papers when they had first arrived in Singapore and when they had opened the Christmas ball at the Tanglin Club. The Tanglin Club ball – for Europeans only, of course – was the highlight of the Singapore expatriate season. Lady Mary was a good deal shorter than her husband and looked rather like a fluffy white hen. She didn't seem to hear Le Froy as she stood up and fussed with her hair, which was thin, light brown, and falling out of the inexpert knot in which it was put up.

'My wife is naturally upset.' Sir Henry spoke stiffly. He looked as though keeping his eyes off her took some effort. 'The point is – let me get this straight – you're saying somebody stabbed the girl? Killed her? With a knife? It wasn't an accident?'

'There is a knife wound in her side,' the chief inspector said. 'I assumed you sent for me because you saw it yourself,'

'I wasn't sure. I thought . . . I didn't know what to think, frankly. I assumed – I hoped – it was some freakish accident, a branch perhaps. But now you're stating the poor girl was murdered under my roof?'

Miss Nessa was staring with her mouth open, which she had told us repeatedly ladies *never* did. I stared too, at both her and Lady Palin, who came across the room looking grumpy and suspicious.

Miss Nessa had brought her sister-in-law to the Ladies' Mission a couple of times but it had not been a success. Lady Palin had found the room too hot, her tea too cool. She had criticized women who could barely afford clean clothing for not dressing as respectable Christian ladies should. She had also complained that none of us showed proper respect 'to the wife of Sir Henry Palin'. She had criticized the Mission's goal of educating girls and training women in skills they could use to support themselves. 'The Great War made it necessary for them to work, but the war is over and a decent woman's place is in her home. You should not be taking jobs away from men who need them. By training for jobs you are destroying the traditional family.' It had been apparent to all of us that Lady Palin disapproved of spinsters in general and of her husband's unmarried sister in particular.

'The tropical climate doesn't agree with poor Mary,' was how Miss Nessa had explained Lady Palin's subsequent absence. Looking at the woman now, I was inclined to agree. Poor Mary Palin was a fair, plump, petulant woman, who seemed determined to find everything disagreeable.

'Ah, Mary. You are feeling better?' Sir Henry did not wait for her reply before turning to Le Froy. 'My wife was shocked. Ladies are sensitive, you know, not used to people dying on the premises without warning.' There was an apologetic note in his voice. Was he apologizing for his wife? When news came that the acting governor was moving into the Residence with a second wife, much younger than he was, the local gossipmongers had predicted a seductive Greta Garbo or Gloria Swanson type.

'Mama says the film star she resembles most is Mr Hardy of Laurel and Hardy,' Parshanti reported. Parshanti's mother, Mrs Shankar, took in sewing from society ladies who didn't mind giving her work as long as they could pretend her Indian husband, Dr Shankar, didn't exist. 'Mama says Lady Palin could afford all the best Indian cottons and voiles but she wants to wear only silk because she thinks it's more aristocratic. But she's so large and she perspires so much that the fabric keeps ripping and she blames Mama for bad sewing. Mama told her it was the fabric's threads that shift and tear but she wouldn't believe it and wanted her money back. Now Mama lines all her dresses with silk organza, which holds better but makes them hotter.'

'Charity wasn't much use here,' Lady Palin said.

There were sweat patches under her arms, and I could see why Parshanti's mother had imagined her as the tubby half of the comedy act.

'Always complaining about the heat and the mosquitoes and wanting to go into town to flirt even though the only reason she was here was to make things easier for me.'

'The girl is dead, Mary!' Sir Henry said sharply.

'So we should call her a saint? Don't be absurd. What's the hold-up?' she demanded of Le Froy. 'Why are you all standing around talking and wasting time? I have a good mind to complain to your superiors!'

Miss Nessa did not look at her. The island's gossip network had made clear that she did not get on with her brother's second wife, though it also suggested she had arranged the match. Unlike Miss Nessa, who had accompanied Sir Henry all over India and Malaya since his first wife died, Lady Palin had come out to the Straits Settlement to marry a planter, who had died before she arrived. She had married Sir Henry in Kedah immediately after it was announced he was being sent to Singapore as acting governor.

Lady Palin might have been younger than her husband but (as happened to many white women in our climate) the sun and the humidity had conspired to make her look older and wearier. She spoke in a breathless, high-pitched, little-girl voice

46

that might have been winsome when she was five years old, but was tiresome thirty years on. If I had been a man in search of a wife, I would have preferred the efficient Vanessa Palin, in her smart, sober cotton shirt-dresses, with her brisk low voice. But Mary Palin was a married woman and Miss Nessa was not, so men evidently felt differently.

I admired Mary Palin's clothes, though this was more a tribute to Mrs Shankar. They were fashionable enough to be on the pages of the *Lady's Realm*. Her pink pearl-beaded knee-length dress was somewhat crumpled from being stretched unevenly both above and below the banded waist (that she was wearing a loosened corset was obvious from the three rolls of flesh moulded by the stylish silk stretched over it), while the longitudinal frills had wilted in the damp heat. With it she wore a matching clustered-pearl necklace, the pearls in ornate slightly tarnished silver settings, and more make-up than was necessary for a woman of any age at any time of day.

'Mary dear, I believe you'll find Chief Inspector Le Froy is probably superior to anyone else in the police here, hah? Very good of him to come over himself to see about Charity.' The apologetic note was in Sir Henry's voice again.

'Very kind of you.' She did not even try to sound sincere. Her eyes moved over me with obvious distaste. 'Your girl can wait for you outside. There are valuable things in here.' She lowered her voice: 'You don't know how fast her kind can pinch things.'

I was used to this attitude but I sensed Le Froy stiffen beside me. I was well aware that many *ang moh*s in Singapore saw themselves as superior in brains, manners and morality, distrusting all Asians as either sly and dishonest or honest but stupid.

Lady Palin was probably worried I would use her pristine porcelain bath as a urinal. I was not offended, only surprised that she chose to be so openly rude to Le Froy, who had brought me there.

Then I realized she was watching him for a reaction – like an old empress trying to provoke a new concubine into behaving badly enough to be banished. Excitement, suspicion and anticipation shone in her eyes. If Le Froy said nothing, she would dismiss him as weak. If he responded, she would accuse him of not knowing his place. In either case, she was looking forward to the put-down.

'May I use the outhouse?' I asked. If I had really needed it, I would have been too embarrassed to ask, but I needed to get my distracting self out of the room. I didn't want Le Froy to find me a liability before I had even started working for him.

'Outside. Round the side of the house,' Miss Nessa snapped briskly, without looking at me. I could tell she felt much the same as I did about Lady Palin. She waved towards the side doors that stood open to the sheltered veranda that ran round the house. 'You can go out there. And down the steps.' Before I could leave, she turned and asked, in a lower voice, 'Do you require necessaries?'

'No, thank you, Miss Nessa.' I was touched by her consideration.

Le Froy looked thoughtfully between her and me as though he were working through a new idea.

As I walked towards the doors I heard Sir Henry tell his sister, 'Apparently the poor girl was stabbed before she fell. Not just an accident, hah!'

'I don't see how that proves anything—'

Sir Henry said curtly, 'We must do all we can. Charity is with God now. She needs nothing more from us. It is the living the inspector is concerned with. Le Froy, you must investigate this thoroughly to prevent any gossip or talk of a cover-up. In your hands, my friend.'

I heard nothing more before I slipped out of the room. Of course, I paused out of sight to listen, but they were discussing resources and manpower. I wasn't sorry: I had been surrounded by other people since very early that morning and my secret Henrietta Stackpole reporter side was overwhelmed. I was glad to have some time to myself to digest all that had happened so far that day, and I was interested in exploring the grounds. I was even more interested in exploring the inside of the house, but that would have been harder to justify. I would pay a quick visit to the outhouse, just to make sure I knew where it was, then look around. Also, I suspected everyone would be more comfortable if I waited for Le Froy outside. I just hoped he wouldn't be too long.

First, though, I went to have a closer look at the thick clumps of night jasmine bordering the slope. There was a bush in my grandmother's courtyard and I loved the scent but I had never seen such masses of it.

Finding Dee-Dee

———◆———

There was a token strip of lawn around the circular driveway, bordered by the low jasmine bushes, with larger clumps of red and orange hibiscus flowering behind them. Beyond was the tangle of undergrowth that the rows of shrubbery were designed to hide. Because we were at the highest point of Frangipani Hill, I could see the canopy of trees falling away below us in all directions in a hundred hues of green with red and yellow accents. Surely the long, curving road we had driven up to get there could not be the only access to the house. That would mean anyone without transport was practically trapped, and I could not imagine local servants putting up with that. I walked further and saw people moving around the outside kitchen: a houseboy, who looked at me curiously, and a very tall, very thin Indian cook, who kept his eyes on his terrifyingly rapid cleaver. I walked on towards the outhouse in the clearing behind the house, and when I glanced back, the houseboy had lost interest.

The outhouse was basic but clean, which spoke well of the order in the house. I would have expected no less of Miss Nessa.

The back of the house was almost flush with the sloping ground and a dirt track beyond led to steep steps cut into the side of the slope. Zinc roofing was just visible through the riotous red, pink and purple hibiscus blooms. It had to indicate the servants' quarters.

No one had emerged from the house and the few policemen I could see were squatting in the shade. Chief Inspector Le Froy would probably spend some time with the family, and no lady reporter would stand around waiting while she could explore. I was sure the earthen path that continued on the other side of the level clearing was the most direct route down the hill and I was curious to see where it led. I always tried to find the shortest, fastest and most efficient way to do things to make up for my limp.

Short wooden posts marked the rough trail, and a little further down there was a clearing with a row of wooden shacks – the zinc roofs I had seen earlier. The door of the first stood open. I looked in and saw a single low bed, some open shelves and a rolled-up prayer mat. The area in front contained gardening equipment as well as bicycle parts and what looked like a bicycle under construction.

The doors to the other three shacks were closed, but towels and wooden clogs were spread in the sun around them. These were clearly the servants' quarters. At this hour they would all be up at the main house, and the area was deserted but for a large tabby cat with white paws sprawled in the sun. It lifted its head to watch me but showed no alarm. It was not afraid of humans, which was another point in favour of the people who lived there.

Several semi-stray cats lived around my grandmother's house,

51

coexisting peaceably with the semi-feral dogs that guarded the premises. Why did I find life there so dull while a single cat in a strange place was interesting? Looking back, I see that, like all young girls, I had thought I wanted excitement and adventure, but maybe all I really needed was a change. I had not realized how privileged I was until I stepped out of the bubble in which I had been protected.

I know the exact moment the bubble burst: it was when I decided to follow the rough path a little further down rather than return to the house to wait for Le Froy in the shade. The big step was not my asking to work as housekeeper to Chief Inspector Le Froy. Even if he had been King of England and Emperor of India, my being hired to wash his socks and sweep beneath his bed, under Miss Nessa's supervision, couldn't be called a life-defining moment. But when I found a dirty young woman sitting on the side of the trail that curved around Frangipani Hill, my life changed for ever.

I had been right about the beaten-earth track being a shortcut down the hill. It was what the Chinese call a 'desire line', the shortest path carved out by people's feet, regardless of official routes. And that was where I found the young white woman. She was large, but sat on the dirt track with her legs spread out, like a tired child. Her eyes were red and she must have pushed her hair back with grubby hands because there were streaks of dirt on her face. She gave off the air of a panicky animal that might bite if it felt threatened.

'Hello, what are you doing here?' I asked in English.

'Sitting.' Her answer was scornful. I nodded acknowledgement. A child was speaking in a woman's voice. She looked very different from the few times I had glimpsed her but I guessed this was Deborah Palin.

'I'm thirsty.'

'Let's find you a drink,' I suggested. 'We'll go home and get you one. What's your name?' There were few enough white families in Singapore, let alone white families with a child-woman like this one, but it was not in my nature to take anything for granted.

'Dee-Dee. I'm very, very thirsty.'

'Come along, then. Your mama and papa will be worried about you.'

'My mama's dead,' Dee-Dee said, paused long enough for me to say, 'You poor little thing,' then continued, 'And now Charity's dead. I don't want to go home. But I'm thirsty and I want some pop.'

'My mother is dead too,' I said.

The child-woman studied me as she thought about this. Apparently I passed muster, because she scrambled to her feet and let me straighten her skirt over her underwear. She was wearing a tunic of light blue material, with tiny white spots echoed in the white collar and cuffs, over a long navy underskirt and bloomers.

'I'm tired. I'm hot.'

'Come on, then. We'll go home and find you a glass of pop.'

Dee-Dee looked sulky. She whined softly, 'I want to go into town for pop! I want ice cream! Nobody loves me, nobody pays any attention to me, and my mama's dead!' I recognized the build-up to a full-sized tantrum. I had to distract her fast.

'Come on,' I said, turning away from her. 'Race you back to the house! Loser is a pig's tail!' Supervising children at the Mission

53

Centre had taught me that a challenge often worked where reason failed.

Dee-Dee made it back up the trail first, of course. When I had turned and limped away from her up the slope, she had gaped for a moment, then given a shriek of excitement and was soon pushing past me. I took her hand and let her pull me along – it slowed her down a little but she seemed not to mind. Soon the house was in sight and Dee-Dee was dancing along, with gleeful shouts of, 'Pig's tail! Pig's tail! You are a pig's tail!'

We were spotted by two policemen standing in the shade. 'Excuse me, this is a restricted area,' one of the constables said. He did not address me as 'miss', which would have been polite, but luckily for him I wasn't the sensitive sort. Since I was holding the white child-woman's hand, he probably took me for a servant. 'Police business here. Move on, please.'

'She lives here.' I indicated Dee-Dee, wondering if she had been missed yet. 'I'm just bringing her home.'

They looked at each other but then, with perfect timing, I heard Miss Nessa's voice coming from the open kitchen: 'Of course you were supposed to be watching Deborah! What do you mean you haven't seen her? Never mind the tea, go and find her!'

'Come on!' I encouraged Dee-Dee. Given how tired and thirsty she was, I wouldn't be able to distract her from a second tantrum. 'Let's go and surprise them, shall we? Race you!'

Alerted by Dee-Dee's little squeals as she trotted up the steps, Miss Nessa appeared round the corner of the house. 'Dee-Dee! There you are! We were so worried! Oh, you bad girl! We thought you were safe in the kitchen with Cookie! You naughty, naughty girl! When we sent for tea we discovered they hadn't seen you!'

Dee-Dee preened in the attention, not seeming to mind the interspersed scolding. I guessed Miss Nessa was less strict with her niece than she was with her students.

I followed them into the drawing room, Dee-Dee still holding my hand possessively.

'Dee-Dee, the next time you decide to disappear mysteriously you might leave a note,' Harry Palin said. 'Poor Mary was absolutely frantic with worry.'

I could tell he was teasing. Lady Palin was the only person in the room who did not look relieved to see Dee-Dee.

Sir Henry smiled at me. 'I see you've found my daughter. Thank you for bringing Dee-Dee back. We were all getting a little anxious. Now, how about some tea? Mary, could you ring—'

Dee-Dee shrank back against me as her stepmother ignored him and came over to grab the girl's arm. 'Come here, you idiot child!' Dee-Dee whimpered and held on to me painfully tightly as Lady Palin tried to pull her away. 'How dare you hide and worry everyone now? Of all the times to choose! You are going straight to your room and I shall lock you in until you learn how to behave. No tea for you. And no dinner. It seems I'm in charge of you now and you are going to learn some manners.'

The mention of meals reminded me that I had not had any lunch. And now I was thirsty as well as hungry, though probably not as thirsty as Dee-Dee.

'Oh, please, Lady Palin, she didn't mean to worry you. She got lost and she's really sorry. Can she please have something to drink? It's hot outside and she's very thirsty.'

Dee-Dee struggled loose from her stepmother and flung her

OvIDIA Yu

arms around my waist from behind, holding me like a shield. 'I hate her! Don't let her lock me up!'

Lady Palin turned on me. 'How dare you? Do you know who I am? Inspector, will you do something useful and arrest this woman? She tried to kidnap Sir Henry's daughter.'

This was alarming, even though I was pretty sure Le Froy wouldn't believe me a kidnapper. Besides, a kidnapper would have taken the girl away and demanded ransom, rather than bringing her home and asking for her to be given a drink. 'I found her sitting on the side of the trail down to Bukit Timah Road,' I told Le Froy. 'She said she was lost. I asked her name and found out she lives here so I brought her back.'

Harry held out his arms and Dee-Dee left me to run to him. As he gave her a squeeze, she giggled and snuggled against him, gratefully hiding her face. He was clearly fond of his sister, not as cold and supercilious as he tried to appear. 'The chief inspector will be better occupied looking into what happened to Charity rather than worrying about who's offended you today, Mary.'

'That silly girl was always larking about. She went too far, fell and broke her neck.' Lady Palin plumped herself into the nearest upright chair. 'It's unfortunate but, if you ask me, she had no one to blame but herself. It's no use you trying to invent a murder to justify your salaries!' Her speech was slightly slurred. Suddenly I realized she was drunk.

'She's dead and you killed her,' Dee-Dee said tearfully. 'You and Charity were fighting upstairs. I heard you shouting at Charity. I heard Charity shouting at you. I hate you! I wish you were dead instead of Charity!' She smeared tears across her cheeks, then clutched at her skirt. She appealed to me: 'She hated Charity. She

56

hates me too. She killed Charity. You have to kill her back or she'll kill me now!'

Lady Palin stared at her. 'Rubbish,' she squeaked.

'I heard you shouting,' Sir Henry said slowly to his wife, 'when I was walking over from the office. I heard shouting upstairs. You and Charity. Took a detour to look at the sundial, didn't want to interrupt female business. Then I heard Charity cry out.'

'What did she shout?' Le Froy's voice was low and matter-of-fact, barely curious.

'It sounded like "No, Mary."' Sir Henry looked uncomfortable, 'At least that's what I think I heard.'

'Rubbish,' Lady Palin Said

———◆———

'**R**ubbish,' Lady Palin said, into the silence. 'I gave the girl some instructions, and she was being impertinent as usual. She raised her voice at me. I left her and went back to my room. I was nowhere near her when she fell.'

Le Froy studied her, as though he were trying to analyse her.

'That idiot child is a liar – ask anybody. She wouldn't know the truth if it hit her on the head! And Sir Henry is half deaf, if you must know. You can call him till you're blue in the face when he's sitting not five feet from you and he won't hear you. Ask him how he came to hear something that never happened when he wasn't even in the house!'

Lady Palin was calling her husband, the acting governor, a liar? Well, a death in the house would probably make more seasoned diplomats than her forget their manners.

'You may have been mistaken, Henry,' Miss Nessa suggested, in her low, steady voice.

Sir Henry nodded. 'Get a ringing in my ears sometimes. Don't know what it's all about. I may indeed have been mistaken.

Shock of the moment, what? But I could have sworn I heard the girl cry out.'

I saw Le Froy look at him, at Dee-Dee, then back to Lady Palin. 'You were in your room when Miss Byrne fell?'

'With the door closed. Couldn't see or hear a thing.'

'I hate you!' Dee-Dee said again. 'You're the liar! You hated Charity and it's your fault she's dead. I hate you!'

'You see what I have to put up with?' Lady Palin sounded triumphant. I could tell she was performing now, glad to have witnesses to Dee-Dee's behaviour, but it was her own that surprised me. She did not fit my idea of an English lady. But then, of course, my idea of the perfect English lady was a less authoritative version of Miss Nessa in more glamorous clothes. Lady Palin was nothing like her sister-in-law. If she hadn't been married to the acting governor, I would have thought her behaviour 'common', which Miss Nessa had always warned us against.

'Charity had no idea of how to discipline a child. She let Dee-Dee get completely out of hand. If anything, her behaviour is worse now than before that so-called nanny came. The only reasonable solution for Deborah is to send her somewhere she can't hurt herself or anyone else.' I sensed Lady Mary had slipped into a long-running argument. 'For her own good. There are some very good institutions in England, and if only you would put the good of your child ahead of your career—'

Apart from Dee-Dee, no one looked at her. They were all uncomfortable, but carefully acting as though they had not heard her tirade.

'She killed Charity,' Dee-Dee repeated, perhaps sensing she had lost our attention.

'Then you should go to the police,' I said to her calmly. 'Do you know where the nearest police station is?'

It was perhaps ten minutes away from the base of Frangipani Drive. Le Froy had pointed it out to me on our way in. It was more of a shed, built of lath and plaster, its roof woven from the dried leaves of *attap* palm. It was just large enough for one desk and a cupboard for files, but since Le Froy's mass overhaul of the police force, people had been taking the officers seriously and a telephone line had been installed.

Dee-Dee shook her head. 'They wouldn't believe me. Anyway, I don't want to tell them. It's my secret!'

'It's good to keep secrets,' I told her.

Dee-Dee nodded. 'It's my secret,' she said again.

'My daughter Deborah, secret agent,' Sir Henry said, with a wry smile. She punched him lightly and he restrained her with playful but firm familiarity. They were obviously very close. 'It's been a traumatizing experience for her. No, Dee-Dee. Sit. Now stay.' He might have been talking to an untrained but beloved dog. 'You have to get cleaned up, darling. Look at what you've done to your dress. Mary or Nessa, can you do something about her—'

'I want to stay with Su Lin!' Dee-Dee wailed.

'I'd like to see you in a clean frock,' I told her quickly. Dee-Dee frowned in an effort to consider this. 'May I help her wash?' I asked Miss Nessa quietly.

She looked surprised. 'I know Miss Blackmore sent some girls for nursing training. Were you one of them?'

'No, Miss Nessa. I trained in household management and as a mother's help, and I worked with the children in the Mission kindergarten. Dee-Dee reminds me of the seven- and eight-year-olds. They're sweet children but they haven't learned patience.'

Miss Nessa looked at her niece, the child-woman now chewing one of her straggling fair plaits. Her eyes softened. 'Deborah was seven when she caught the fever. And you're right. She's been seven years old ever since.'

'Seven-year-olds can be taught to look after themselves quite well.' I spoke from experience. I looked up at Dee-Dee, who was a good head taller than I was. 'Do you like ribbons? If you promise not to chew your hair, I'll see if I can find you ribbons for your plaits. We can pin your hair up like mine, to get it out of the way. Would you like that?'

'Oh, yes – yes, please, I mean!' Dee-Dee's eyes shone.

'Come with me,' Miss Nessa decided. 'Bring Deborah with you.'

She ignored Lady Palin's loud whisper-hiss, 'Don't leave her alone with anything valuable!'

Leading Dee-Dee by the hand, I followed Miss Nessa across the hall, past a wide black-wood staircase that turned a right angle on the landing, then continued to the second floor and into the dining room beyond. This was my first visit to a government official's home. Except for servants, local people were not allowed in. Along the hallway and lining what was visible of the walls there were more stuffed animals, with photographs of grinning hunters posing beside dead ones and framed collections of jaws and teeth forming a macabre scorecard of victims. I saw several monkeys, a large lizard, a mongoose and a tiny bedraggled tiger, which still had the round baby face of a frightened cub but had been arranged in a ferocious pose. There were also mounted displays of rifles and Oriental knives along the back staircase, which Dee-Dee was bounding up. 'I want to show you my room!'

It was upstairs, and there was a bathroom with a full cistern of water at the end of the corridor. I filled a basin and wiped the worst of the mud off Dee-Dee's arms and legs, then helped her to change. The girl really needed a bath but that would have to wait. There were several scratches on her arms and legs and I asked Miss Nessa for some iodine and sticking plaster.

'I'm afraid I don't know where everything is.' She rummaged helplessly in the bathroom cupboards. 'Mary likes to run the house herself – not that she's any good at managing the servants – and I keep out of her way as much as I can. The servants will know but the police are questioning them and we were told not to interrupt. I really don't know what I'm going to do about luncheon – it's way past time, isn't it? Sandwiches, I suppose. If I can find enough bread somewhere.'

'Dee Dee and I can make trays of sandwiches,' I offered, 'and see what else is in the kitchen. They must have been preparing something before the accident happened.'

'Would you really? Thank you, that would be much appreciated. I'll leave you to it, then.' It was clear Miss Nessa was eager to get back to the conversation going on downstairs. Either she trusted Miss Blackmore to have taught us girls not to steal or there was nothing in Dee-Dee's room worth stealing, I thought. The latter was probably true: a seven-year-old child with the strength of a seventeen-year-old woman could throw tantrums with great force and the furniture showed signs of repeated damage.

I had taught seven-year-olds at the kindergarten run by the Mission Centre, though, and I knew they were often capable of far more than people realized. I was sure the seven-year-old child inside this woman was no different.

———◆———

The chicken sandwiches, halved hard-boiled eggs topped with cold ham, and sliced fruitcake with which we returned to the drawing room were gratefully received. Even Lady Palin had no complaints beyond wishing the crusts had been cut off the bread and decrying the lack of hot soup. There had been no sign of Cookie and the other kitchen servants so I guessed they had either run away to hide or were being questioned by Le Froy's men. Le Froy himself was eating an egg in the corner, so unobtrusive that they seemed to have forgotten he was there.

'Never thought it was so difficult to run a household,' Sir Henry said jovially, in my direction, 'but once the servants are out of action, everything falls apart, doesn't it?'

'Don't blame me,' Lady Palin said automatically, without looking round. 'I'm not responsible for this mess.'

'Dee-Dee seems to like this Chinese girl.' Sir Henry was still looking at me, serious now.

'You should warn the child to keep away from strangers. What do you intend to do with the girl's body?'

'I beg your pardon?' Miss Nessa's voice was gentle, as always, but the steel beneath the velvet was very close to the surface.

'When the police have finished with it. You should decide where and how the girl is to be buried. She has no family here, and surely we cannot be expected to ship her remains back to England.'

Sir Henry chose not to hear the warning in his wife's voice. Perhaps it was his usual course of action. 'She has no family, I believe, neither here nor in England. The Church will take charge of the burial and I suppose we'll have to come up with expenses. Too bad she's not a native, eh? The Chinese temples are used to burying bodies for free, all the coolies and so on. We leave them alone to get on with it, and don't look too carefully into what they do with the dead blighters' possessions. They owe us something there.'

'Of course we'll deal with the funeral arrangements,' Miss Nessa said. 'I'll see to it personally. Deborah, please stand up properly. Your father is not a hat-stand.'

Dee-Dee was staring at her suspiciously. In other circumstances she might have been pretty, but now her eyes were red and her face was grazed. Sir Henry gave her a little squeeze and she snuggled against him, hiding her face from her aunt.

Le Froy recognized talk of funerals as dismissal and began to take his leave. 'I'll let you know what we learn.'

'Do be in touch if we can help in any way. And let us know when we can make arrangements for poor Miss Byrne—' Sir Henry was interrupted by his wife.

'She's not our responsibility,' Lady Palin said. 'Did you take responsibility for every native servant who died on your estates? I don't see what the difference is, why everyone is making such a fuss. Why not save your money to hire someone to care for the child if you won't find an institution for her? You might ask your sister to find us a woman. We can't wait another six months for the agency to ship someone out.'

'I want you to take me upstairs,' Dee-Dee left her father to come to me. 'I have itches here.' She was scratching under her skirt.

'I can't. I have to go now,' I told her. 'Do you have a maid to help you? You should have a bath and a good rest. You've had a very exciting day.'

'Why can't you stay with me? Charity's dead now. You can stay in Charity's room and look after me,'

'I'm sorry but I can't—'

Dee-Dee opened her mouth and wailed.

'Oh, Lord.' Lady Palin rolled her eyes. 'She's starting again.'

'You can stay a little longer,' Harry said awkwardly. 'I mean as long as Dee-Dee needs you – until she settles down. If the chief inspector leaves now I can run you back to wherever you like in the motor afterwards.'

'Why shouldn't you stay, Su Lin?' Miss Nessa asked suddenly. 'Chief Inspector, it would solve all our difficulties.'

'What's that?' Le Froy's mind had clearly already returned to his office and the work that awaited him there.

'The job for Su Lin. You didn't want to take her, you made that quite clear. Instead there's a place for her here and Deborah seems to like her. Why shouldn't she come here instead? Her family can't possibly object to her working in the governor's Residence.'

Le Froy looked at me as though he were trying to remember what I had to do with him. 'I signed the employment agreement.'

'I'll sort it out,' Miss Nessa said easily. 'The Mission Centre has more girls on their hands than they know what to do with. I'll tell them to send you another. Su Lin, I believe your friend Parshanti hasn't a husband yet either.' She did not ask me how I felt about the sudden transfer, but I hadn't expected her to. Miss Nessa was full of good intentions but for her this was no different from finding a replacement for a working goat that had died. Sir Henry was nodding his approval.

'What will she be expected to do?' Le Froy asked.

'Charity looked after Dee-Dee,' Sir Henry explained vaguely. 'She taught her – counting, drawing and singing – and she was company for her. She used to take her out for walks and–' A snort from the upright chair cut him off. 'She was good to Dee-Dee,' he concluded. 'Splendid idea, Nessa!'

Le Froy turned to me. 'What do you think? Would you like to work here for a while?'

The Palins looked as shocked as I felt. Asking a local servant what employment she preferred was unheard of. Miss Nessa gazed curiously at Le Froy, then at me and said nothing.

Lady Palin spoke up. 'All she has to do is keep the girl quiet and out of the way.' She turned to me and spoke very slowly and very loudly. 'You,' her finger jabbed at my chest, 'you keep Missy Deborah clean. You keep Missy Deborah quiet. You savvy? *Comprenez-vous?* Clean! Quiet!' Switching back to a normal tone, she asked Le Froy, 'Does she understand basic English?'

Before Le Froy could answer, I said quietly, 'Yes, madam. Thank you.'

'Well, then, what are you waiting for? Sunset?' She laughed at her own wit.

'If you could spend some time here with us, just till Dee-Dee gets over the shock, it would be a great help to us.' Sir Henry took his cue from Le Froy. 'Especially to my daughter. She likes you and she doesn't take to very many people. I would do anything for my daughter, if only I knew how.'

I could tell he was sincere. For a moment I saw him as a

worried father, instead of a powerful white man, and felt sorry for him. In the old days, the National Benevolent Emigration Society and the Female Middle-class Emigration Society had existed to send governesses and nannies into the world, but in the twentieth century, after the Great War, families like the Palins had had to make their own arrangements.

I held out a hand to Dee-Dee. 'Would you like me to stay and look after you?' Her shrieks of delight made Lady Palin wince.

'This is a crime scene, Su Lin.' Le Froy was still uncertain. 'And I am responsible for your welfare. I don't think this is a good idea.'

'I will be quite safe.' I almost said I would stay away from all verandas in the Palin house but was afraid it would sound flippant. It was a novel experience to have people as important as the Palins ask for my help and I didn't want to refuse. 'I like Dee-Dee and I would be happy to help her.' I lowered my voice so that only he could hear: 'And maybe I can help find out what happened to Charity.'

'Unfortunately not everyone in the household will think that a good idea.' He matched my low tone. 'Particularly if you find it was not an accident.' I noticed he did not veto my suggestion.

'Sir. There's this collection of knives on the wall by the stairs,' one of the policemen had come into the room with it. The knives were set on a dark green cloth backing, in a large ornate picture frame. 'It looks as though it's been tampered with. See? The glass is loose.' They had been going over the house, then, while the servants were questioned and Le Froy watched the family. I was impressed.

Sir Henry and Le Froy moved to examine it. They just looked

like a row of knives to me, but Le Froy said, 'That's the *khanjar*, the Indian dagger, a Tamil *bagh nakh* claw knife, and these are Kubrick daggers worn by Gurkha warriors. One of them is missing.' He turned abruptly to Sir Henry. 'Are your servants local?'

'I was in India and up north in Malaya before I settled here. Two of my men came from India with me but the house servants are local. They all say they didn't see anything.'

'I'll have to speak to them again, and I'll come back to see each of you individually tomorrow. At your convenience, of course.'

'You suspect us, then? Of taking that toy knife and stabbing her? This gets more and more ridiculous!'

'I did not say that, Lady Palin,' Le Froy pointed out. 'I would just like to get a clearer idea of what happened and perhaps an explanation – from all of the adults,' he added quickly, as Dee-Dee turned two very blue eyes in a still-grimy face in his direction. I noted that the fair skin showed the dirt much more than dark. Having fair skin must feel like wearing a white uniform everywhere. You have to be careful all the time because the least smudge shows.

'I'm sure we can clear up the mystery in two seconds.' Lady Palin went to the door and shouted, 'Boy! Come here! At once!'

One of the small houseboys appeared. Clearly Lady Palin in a temper outranked any police officer. Again, Le Froy melted into the background, waiting to see what would happen.

'Here!' She pointed to the cabinet. 'You dust – yes?' She mimed swiping a cloth over the surface. 'Every day?'

'Yes, yes.' The boy nodded and bowed. 'I clean now. I get cloth.' He seemed very relieved to have understood her meaning and in a hurry to get away from them.

'No, no, boy, wait. Stay. That's right – stay. These natives are so slow to grasp anything. I don't know why they can't learn to speak decent English!'

'Perhaps if we are so intelligent we should learn to speak Malayan,' Harry said.

'Harry, don't try to be clever and political. It's not becoming in a gentleman. As I was saying, the houseboy would have reported the knife missing if it was not there when he cleaned. Right, boy?'

The boy nodded, pleased to know the answer to this. 'Yes, yes,' he said.

'Then it was there this morning?' Le Froy asked.

'Yes, yes,' the boy said.

'So,' Lady Palin turned and glared at me, 'you are the only stranger who has been wandering around in the house since it disappeared. I knew there was something fishy about you forcing your way into our house.'

A squeak between a laugh and a cry escaped Harry. 'She thinks you stole it! Christ, Mary. This is a new low even for you.'

'It is a very valuable artefact. You heard your father say so many times.'

'Pa says all the rubbish he picks up is valuable! Well, it may be valuable to him but that doesn't make it valuable to anyone else. Why do you think this family is so poor?'

Lady Palin switched her attention back to the houseboy. 'How dare you lie to me?'

'I never take,' the houseboy said quickly.

'Mary, the boy had no reason to—'

'You would take the word of a useless houseboy over your wife?' She left the room.

We were all silent for a moment, hearing her heavy step going up the first flight, dulling slightly on the landing, continuing ponderously, then crossing above our heads to her room. When we heard the door being shut heavily – as good as slammed – there was a sigh of relief.

'I never take,' the houseboy repeated, almost tearful.

'No, no,' I answered in Malay, and smiled at him. 'They aren't saying you took it.'

'That would tie things up very nicely, wouldn't it?' Harry Palin said. 'Blame it on the servants. Easy to pick on them because they don't speak English and can't defend themselves.'

Sir Henry murmured, 'I have to get back to the office,' as though comforting himself with the thought. 'About that knife collection. Mary was asking me about it just recently. How much were they worth and so on. Wanted to look at them out of the case. Don't know why I mention it. Probably not relevant.' He turned to Le Froy, 'This accident – what happened to the poor girl – it happened under my roof. That makes me responsible. And the servants may know things they're afraid to tell my lady wife or me but may tell you. I would dearly like to get to the bottom of what really happened.'

'You may not like what we find out,' Le Froy said. This time I thought his 'we' might include me but it was possible he was thinking only of his men.

'If one of my household is responsible I would rather know it than go on suspecting all of them.' Sir Henry seemed both earnest and sincere. He offered his hand to Le Froy and nodded to me before following his wife out of the room.

'What do you think of the governor?' Le Froy surprised me by asking.

'I like him. It's not easy for important men to ask for help,' I said honestly, thinking of my uncle. Uncle Chen wanted so much to be seen as powerful and capable that he refused to ask for help from anyone. But Ah Ma, who asked other people to do everything wherever possible, was a good deal more powerful. 'I think he really wants to know what happened to poor Charity.'

'You don't think it best to call it an accident and move on?'

I could tell he didn't believe that himself. 'It would be like ironing dirty laundry,' I said. Ironing laundry that is not completely clean sets the dirt in the fabric, never mind that it might look presentable for a while. As far as I was concerned, sending Charity Byrne off in a respectable coffin without clearing up how she had died would have much the same effect.

I had not expected Le Froy's nod of agreement. 'You must do what you believe right, but be careful. One girl has already died here. I can still take you back to your own home, you know. Your family may not like you coming to a house where someone has died.'

He had no idea. My grandmother, Chen Tai, was notorious for being very particular about luck. If a maid returned to work after going home to attend a funeral, she had to wash in the courtyard before entering the house to make sure any dregs of bad luck or dross from evil spirits was removed. If the luck was particularly bad, say a death from cholera or tuberculosis, well-water alone was not considered enough and the girl would be soaked in a carefully assembled concoction of dried flowers and herbs, with a pair of scissors to cut off any bad luck that might have attached itself to her. It was a testimony to how much she had loved my late father that she had kept me in her house.

'I would like to stay.' If anyone was immune to bad luck it would be me.

Le Froy nodded. I could tell he had reservations, but all he said was, 'I'll tell your family you've been appointed teacher to Miss Deborah.'

He was right. My family might be unschooled but in the best Confucian tradition they all, even Uncle Chen, held teachers in respect.

I felt sorry for Deborah Palin. Having lost my own parents, I was only too aware of how it felt to be the object of everyone's pity. The least I could do was ask the kitchen to provide us with a tub of hot water and give her a good scrubbing. I have observed it is difficult to feel miserable when you are thoroughly clean.

Somewhat to my surprise, I found I also felt sorry for Lady Palin. I knew Sir Henry's wife was not much liked by the towns-people, but I was surprised to see how little regard other *ang mohs* seemed to have for her – even in her own household. Even if much of it was her own fault.

First Night

———◆———

I admit my main reason for wanting to stay at Frangipani Hill was the chance to make a good impression on Miss Nessa. Le Froy might be more important, but I knew that writing about crime as a lady reporter was only a dream. In real life, if Miss Nessa was pleased with me, she would be more likely to help me get a teaching certificate.

After Le Froy had left without me Miss Nessa did seem pleased. In fact, she patted me approvingly on the shoulder, as if I were a puppy worth grooming for dogfighting. Things might not be too bad after all.

Harry had given Dee-Dee a bottle of pop and she offered it to me now. 'Share half?'

She was a generous child, I thought. 'No, thank you.'

Harry produced a second bottle for me. 'Give this to Su Lin, then.' He passed it to Dee-Dee without looking at me. He didn't seem to like me, though I hadn't done anything to antagonize him beyond existing as an Asian female in his presence. I was used to people like him and it didn't bother me. Nessa made herself a cup of tea and Sir Henry had a medicinal Scotch and water. With Le Froy gone, Sir Henry seemed to have forgotten about returning to the office.

After a whispered consultation with me, Dee-Dee handed round a tin of Huntley & Palmers biscuits.

'We missed tea. Cookie will be cross,' Miss Nessa said, helping herself to a milk and honey biscuit. 'He doesn't like disruptions.'

'Cookie will blame the police,' I guessed, and was pleased when Nessa and Sir Henry both laughed.

'Cookie doesn't like the police, white or black,' Sir Henry said. 'He's going to be in a mood after today! You any good at cooking, girl?'

'Su Lin's not here to cook. She's here for Deborah.' Miss Nessa turned to me. 'You can take Charity's old room. No silly super-stitions, I hope. Get your things. Is that all you have? Harry, watch your sister.'

I still had the carpet-bag I had packed to take to Le Froy's house. Miss Nessa led me upstairs and showed me Charity's room. Of course, Charity's things were still in it, tossed and tum-bled around, which said something about her. The police had come to look over the room but it was unlikely they had had anything to do with the unmade bed. Of course, when she'd left her room that morning, Charity could not have known she would never return. I was not as superstitious as my grandmother, but the thought of sleeping there surrounded by a dead girl's belong-ings made me uncomfortable.

'If you can just put her things aside for now we'll decide what to do with them later,' Miss Nessa said. 'It's best and easiest if you stay here because Deborah's room is just next door. We had the locks removed from the doors to the corridor after Deborah locked herself in and Harry had to use the gardener's ladder to climb through the window. You don't have any silly notions about ghosts, do you?'

I was less worried about ghosts than about sleeping in a strange house in a room with no locks, but I said nothing.

Miss Nessa pushed open the connecting door between the two rooms to show me Dee-Dee's. I had already seen the sad mess in there, clothes and toys strewn all over the place, when I'd come up to help her change. I would enjoy bringing some order to this. But even as I picked up a limp cloth doll with one hand and a stained frock (with a pretty broderie-anglaise trim that I would try to salvage), it became obvious that Miss Nessa had other things on her mind.

'What did Le Froy want with you?' she demanded. The way the question burst out of her made me think she had been holding it back until we were alone. 'Why did he want to talk to you on your own in his motor-car? Did he ask about employment papers?'

'He wanted to make sure I was not a runaway *mui tsai* and he asked me about my family. And I think he wanted to practise talking in dialect,' I added, 'or show me how well he could. He's not bad, but he talks like a sailor or a trader – his accent is low class.'

That seemed to convince her. 'Men can be so stupid. Even the most useful ones. Don't trust him. Even the best-intentioned men get strange ideas in their heads. You must be sure to tell me anything he asks of you.'

'Of course.' I could not imagine Le Froy asking anything improper.

'Especially now that he seems determined to find out who stabbed the poor girl.'

Looking back, I realize I didn't want just to please Miss Nessa, I wanted to impress her as well. Not because she might help me towards a job, but because she might help me become more like her. Seen through my girlish eyes, Vanessa Palin was the perfect lady, accomplished, independent and respectable, although she had remained single.

'Charity was not stabbed to death, Miss Nessa.'

'I beg your pardon?'

'I saw the body when we arrived. There was a stab wound but very little blood. I would guess one of the policemen stabbed her after she was dead to give them an excuse to search the house. But it was done before Chief Inspector Le Froy arrived because that was when I saw it.'

'Have you studied the medical sciences?' Miss Nessa was not challenging so much as verifying my observation.

'My grandmother taught me to cook,' I explained, 'which means I had to learn to kill chickens. Once a chicken is dead there is very little bleeding.'

Miss Nessa's face froze, her eyes fixed on me with an expression I couldn't read. I knew at once that I had said something wrong. I must have been too eager to show off, I thought. Chicken killing was not something Mission-educated young ladies were supposed to be aware of. No doubt proper young ladies in England believed chickens grew on menu cards.

'I'll leave you to get settled,' Miss Nessa said, and was gone.

Charity Byrne's presence was still so strong in the room that I felt like an intruder even while I was looking for somewhere to put down my bag. Thanks to Dee-Dee, I already knew the small washroom at the end of the corridor by the door to the outside stairs had a cistern that was filled every morning and I paid it a visit. The small square of mirror above the washbasin showed that my encounters with Dee-Dee had left their mark and I quickly made myself presentable.

When I had finished I could hear voices downstairs. Lady Palin sounded upset about something. I decided not to go down straight away, just in case I was the something she was upset about. Besides, with the family downstairs and the servants still absent, it seemed a good time to get my bearings of the second floor.

Another corridor, on the opposite side of the rectangular stair well, skirted the main staircase and led to the other bedrooms: the large one that Lady Palin occupied alone, the dressing room where Sir Henry slept and, finally, Miss Nessa's at the rear of the house on the other side of the door opening to the outside stairs. Sir Henry and Lady Palin had another bathroom off the dressing room but Miss Nessa shared the one at the end of the corridor with Dee-Dee and myself. Harry's room was downstairs, where the only indoor lavatory was.

I had learned from listening to the police officers reporting to Le Froy that, in addition to the family, two houseboys and Cookie lived in. Like the gardener, they occupied the servants' shacks I had seen. Two maids, a washerwoman and a driver came in daily. It struck me as a strange way to run a household. Most of my grandmother's servants lived in during the week, to save the time and expense of travelling. Like the black and white *amah jies* who did not have families in Singapore, they took a longer period off once a year to visit their relatives. But the (other) servants were not my concern. I was there to care for Dee-Dee . . . and to find out what I could about the late Charity Byrne.

When I finally went downstairs, I found Dee-Dee and her brother alone in the drawing room. Sir Henry and Miss Nessa had walked across to his office in Government House, Harry said, adding nothing about where Lady Palin might be. I checked the sofas just in case, but there was no sign of her.

'They've taken away Charity's body but the police are still talking to the servants. Now you've finally decided to come down, I'll hand Dee-Dee over to you. Charity used to take her outside for a bit before dinner.'

'I hate going outside!' Dee-Dee said. 'I hate all of you! I want Charity!' Crossly she tugged at the fabric of her frock. 'I hate Mary Contrary. She killed Charity!' The child was genuinely upset, not just shocked. I could tell she didn't want her brother to leave. Automatically responding, I took Dee-Dee's hand, giving the thick, sticky fingers a reassuring squeeze as she looked round, startled.

'Mary Contrary?'

'Charity came up with that. It was either "Mary Contrary" or "Poor Mary".' Harry smiled slightly at the memory, then winced. 'Dee-Dee, you didn't really see Poor Mary push Charity, did you? What did you see? Was Poor Mary really on the balcony with Charity when she fell?'

'She killed her,' Dee-Dee repeated stubbornly.

Harry shook his head, and I guessed he was remembering

how Charity's body had looked on the ground. 'No,' he said softly. 'It's another of your stories, isn't it?'

His sister turned to me. 'I want to go outside to play.'

'You shouldn't make up stories about your stepmother,' I told her.

'Why not? She's not my mother,' Dee-Dee said mutinously, glancing at Harry for support. 'That's what Clumsy Charlie says!'

Harry remained impassive.

'Who is Clumsy Charlie?'

'She's a storyteller, our Dee-Dee.' Harry rose and started to walk towards the door. 'You can't believe anything she says.'

'He's the one that's a liar! Ask him where he sneaks out to at night!'

It was a strange conversation, carried out across the room at high volume, neither party looking at the other and ignoring everyone else (well, ignoring me, the only other person) in the room. It was almost like a modern telegraphic communication carried out across the sea, I thought.

'It's the way we talk.' Harry startled me by seeming to read my thoughts. 'You'll get used to it. You'd think we were talking to the Lord God Almighty, wouldn't you?' He rolled his eyes Heavenward and I laughed without meaning to. Harry looked pleased. 'Except you don't get answers when you talk to God! Do you know whether you'll be sleeping in the house?'

'Miss Nessa said I could use the room that was Charity's. It's next to Dee-Dee's.'

'Next to my room!' Dee-Dee echoed.

'Ah. That used to be my room but we shifted things around so Charity could have a room in the house near to Dee-Dee. It's not a conventional arrangement but not improper either.'

'Does Dee-Dee need help with anything at night?'

79

Harry snorted a laugh. 'Not till Mary Contrary told her there were bats in the house and probably bats in her room so, of course, our little princess wanted to sleep with her papa, and we had the circus in town every night until I offered to swap rooms with Charity so she could keep Dee-Dee company. After that everything was all right.'

'There were bats!' Dee-Dee protested, 'You saw them too!'

'I did not. I just told Poor Mary I did. But it all worked out for the best, didn't it?'

'Because now you can sneak out at night without anybody knowing!' Dee-Dee crowed.

I could just imagine how Lady Palin must be feeling at having a local girl sleeping upstairs in her house, right next to Dee-Dee's room. My opinion of Sir Henry rose. It was not easy to hold public office, but must have been even more difficult to do so with domestic problems.

'It's a state of constant warfare here between Dee-Dee and our *belle mère*.' I jumped. I had loosened and was reweaving one of Dee-Dee's plaits, and Harry had sidled over to stand just behind me without my noticing. He held out a cigarette case. 'You'll get used to the constant warfare if you stay but you'll have to pick a side. Do you smoke?'

I sensed he was offering a truce, perhaps even an alliance.

'No,' I said, 'but thank you.'

I joined the family for dinner that night. The servants reappeared and served unobtrusively while Miss Nessa talked about training

local girls to be teachers and nurses and, looking at me, mothers'
helps. Lady Mary's comments ran along the lines of how no
decent woman ever worked outside the home. She reminded me
of a fat, stubborn chicken, one of those hens that pushed in and
gobbled up grain faster than any of the others but refused to lay.
She would have been one of the first in the pot. But maybe I was
prejudiced against her for saying things like 'Allowing Chinamen
to move freely all over the island is begging for trouble. They are
a walking time bomb.' Lady Palin also told me several times that
I was useless, and hopeless at teaching Dee-Dee table manners,
even though I had not yet had a full day with the girl, and Miss
Nessa had commented that Dee-Dee was behaving very well. But
perhaps Lady Palin just wanted to show that her standards were
set high . . . far too high to eat with a backward child or a Chinese
girl at the table.

'Deborah doesn't usually take dinner with us,' Miss Nessa
explained. 'Usually Cookie gives her hers earlier in the kitchen.
But after all the excitement today we thought it would be good
to sit down to a meal together.'

'Mary thinks only adults should be allowed at the table,' Harry
said. 'No children, no farting, no belching.' Lady Palin, who had
just failed to suppress a bubbling burp, glared at him. He smiled
at her.

Still, Miss Nessa was right. There was something about sharing
food that was comforting, I thought. Nothing had changed since
the terrible discovery that morning but sharing food reminded
people they were still alive and not alone.

As the family adjourned to the drawing room for coffee, I
stayed to help clear the table. Previous courses had been moved

to the warmers on the sideboard and old Cookie came with the two servant girls to see how the meal had gone. I greeted him and was glad to find he spoke English.

'I'm sorry, I took some things from your kitchen to make sandwiches for lunch.'

'Oh, it was you. I must thank you, girl. The bleddy police got so many questions I am stuck there. If the people here all starve to death what will happen to me? I will lose my job!' He studied me appraisingly. 'You are the Chen girl, right? Chen Tai's precious granddaughter? The one she sent to English school? I see you and I know you, with the funny leg like that.'

I was surprised. Locals might know my grandmother but Sir Henry's Cookie had come with him from India. The tall old man clicked his tongue, pleased to have surprised me. I suspect he would have spat if he had not been inside the Residence but he swallowed instead. 'A good cook knows where to get good supplies. I am the best cook so I know where to get the best supplies. You should have made them fried eggs. Very easy, very fast, my eggs are the best. Give your Ah Ma my regards! And your uncle, that swindler, give him my regards also!'

—————◆—————

'I want to go over to the playroom!' Dee-Dee was saying, as I rejoined the family in the drawing room. 'The playroom in Papa's office. Freaky Freddy, Freaky Freddy, can't you take me over there to play?'

The elder Palins were discussing something by Sir Henry's

82

desk at the far end of the room so I sat beside Dee-Dee on the sofa and wondered about protocol. How soon could I take her upstairs to bed and effect my escape? Lady Palin and Miss Nessa had changed for dinner, and my best cotton frock, which had felt so smart and well ironed just that morning, was sadly limp, not to mention grimy from Dee-Dee's fingers.

'Who is Freaky Freddy?'

'Yours truly. Henry Charles Frederick Palin at your service, madam,' Harry executed a small bow before turning back to his sister. 'I thought you promised you wouldn't go over there any more? Didn't you?'

Dee-Dee pouted. 'That doesn't count now. I only promised not to go over there with Charity.'

'Promises count for ever.'

'No, they don't. Only "Till death do us part" and Charity is dead so that one doesn't count any more!' Dee-Dee shrieked with laughter at her own cleverness. She jumped up and ran over to her father. 'Papa! Precious Papa! Ask me about promises!' She was overexcited and I blamed the rich fruitcake and custard that Cookie had sent up for dessert. I suspected it was an emergency cake that had sat in waxed paper for some time waiting for just such an occasion and the thick sugary slices, with brandy-soaked fruit, had gone to Dee-Dee's head. The rest of the meal had been well and quickly put together – lamb chops, mashed potatoes and what seemed to be minced spinach. I had enjoyed the novelty but missed my daily rice and wondered what they were eating in the kitchen.

Dee-Dee seemed happy but a shrill note in her voice forecast tears before bedtime. I winced slightly. No, I did not want to be looking after Dee-Dee Palin for the rest of my life, no matter how appreciative Miss Nessa might be. What if this turned out to be the only kind of job I could get? Was I doomed to look after children, whether my own or someone else's? I was no closer to my fantasy of a fulfilling career here than I had been in the Mission schoolroom where reading about Henrietta Stackpole had put the possibility into my mind. I pulled myself together and straightened my slumping shoulders. I was tired. It had been a very long day with so many things happening. I would think about it after a good night's sleep. I just had to excuse Dee-Dee and myself from the company and get us upstairs . . .

Then I noticed Harry, who had not moved since Dee-Dee abandoned our corner. He was staring, frowning, and looked as though he was going to be sick.

'Mr Harry! Are you all right?' I touched his arm.

'What's it to you?' Harry jerked back to awareness. His eyes were wild, darting around the room as though he were looking for whatever he had been seeing in his mind's eye. 'Good God, what a nuisance you females are. Always fussing and nagging and bothering a man.'

I was more startled than hurt by the unprovoked attack. Harry slammed out of the room, and I glanced across to the other Palins but they were talking, oblivious. I was lucky, I told myself, to be shocked when someone was nasty for no reason. For some people it was a way of life.

Later, going to the kitchen to ask Cookie for Dee-Dee's warm milk, I saw Harry watching me. He was standing motionless at the far end of the corridor, as though he were waiting for me to do something wrong that he could pounce on. I ignored him, but felt the skin on the back of my neck tingle, like a cat sensing danger. I suspected I was not out of his sights just because he was out of mine.

It was not yet ten when I took Dee-Dee upstairs to wash before bed, but it had been such an exhausting day that she made only a token protest and was asleep before I had read her half of *Little Red Riding Hood*, which I had found under a heap of dirty clothes in her room. I looked forward to giving her room a good clean, but that would have to wait. It was with relief that I turned down the lights. Then, coming out of the bathroom after emptying Dee-Dee's dirty water out of the bowl, I saw Harry Palin watching me again. Or, rather, I saw a man's shadow on the landing. It ignored my greeting and went downstairs silently.

Then I was finally ready for bed in Charity Byrne's room. It was smaller than my grandmother's, where I slept at home, but pleasantly airy. Like the rest of the house, it had high ceilings and large windows, and I knew it would suit me very well once I had put away Charity's things and changed the sheets on the bed. Now, though, I felt uncomfortable, but not because of the sheets and clutter. It was the thought that if someone had pushed Charity over the balcony that someone was likely still to be in the house. It would be easiest to blame one of the servants, of course, but despite heavy questioning by the police and threats of dismissal, none of them had admitted to doing or seeing anything. And what reason could they have had to attack the foreign nanny?

No, if someone had pushed and stabbed Charity, Miss Nessa

was the only member of the family not under suspicion: she had been in town when it had happened.

Sir Henry and Harry had said they were outdoors, but there was only their word for it. If either of them had been upstairs, he could easily have run down the stairs and out of the house unseen. If Charity had already been sitting on the railing, it might have been no more than a joking gesture that had gone horribly wrong. Personally, I suspected Mr Harry. All evening, when he was not trying to entertain his sister, he had been silent and sullen. The police had questioned him at great length, wanting to know his whereabouts not only on that day but during his unexplained absences in town. At dinner Harry had blamed this on Lady Palin, who had told the police her stepson often spent evenings away from the house.

'Of course I didn't confess,' Harry had said, staring at his stepmother in a way that frightened me. 'I clear up my own problems.' If it had been me he was looking at, I think I would have run out of the house without stopping for my things. But no one else seemed to notice. Perhaps it was usual for Harry Palin.

And, of course, there was Lady Palin, whom Dee-Dee had accused of killing Charity. Dee-Dee didn't like her and she told stories, but Lady Palin had been upstairs with Charity: she could easily have reached out and pushed her over . . . but why would she have run down the stairs and stabbed her in the side? Or had that been someone else?

Exhausted as I was, I found it impossible to get to sleep in a strange house in the bed of a dead girl. Finally, I got up and moved the bedside table to the door where I wedged it under the handle to prevent it turning. The varnish on the top was scratched, suggesting Charity had put it to the same use. I did the same with a convenient shoe rack in Dee-Dee's room. Snoring lightly, Dee-Dee didn't stir. Then, finally, I slept.

Le Froy's Work

◆

Much later, Le Froy told me that Charity Byrne's death would probably have been dismissed as an accident if Sir Henry Palin had not called on him to take a personal interest in the matter. After all, people died every day, and the dead girl had been in the house only as a servant, even if she was a white woman, but Sir Henry had been insistent that the girl's death be thoroughly investigated.

'There must be no shadow of doubt. The young lady lived under my roof. She was under my protection and was therefore my responsibility.'

Le Froy assumed Sir Henry wanted to clear any suspicion from himself and his household. People would always talk, and the less that was said officially, the more was whispered. Sir Henry's role as acting governor, while Sir Shenton Thomas was on home leave due to his wife's health, was to keep things functioning. In the Crown Colony this meant keeping the natives quiet, content and in their place.

At eighteen years old Charity Byrne had been barely able to

read and write, but was brought over to Singapore at great expense as a nanny for Deborah Palin, the acting governor's backward daughter.

'Perhaps it was not surprising,' Le Froy said, 'that the qualities that made the girl willing to undertake a trip halfway across the world to live among strangers were the very qualities that made her unsuitable for her role once she got here.'

Charity's manners, Le Froy had gathered from Lady Palin, had been impossible. Back in England, Charity would probably have settled to work in a shop or done quite well behind the bar of a public house. But there had been nine children in her family and respectable places were hard to come by. Charity had known that and wanted to escape. Although she had walked out with the butcher's assistant a couple of times, and enjoyed teasing the blacksmith's apprentice with kisses, she had known her place. When I learned that, I could not help feeling that Charity and I had been in the same situation on different sides of the world.

On arrival in Singapore, Charity had suddenly found herself one of the few single white girls on the island. At home she had been a poor Irish girl, but in the Crown Colony she was considered 'White', as were all Europeans, and suddenly she was in demand. The island was full of single, or temporarily single, soldiers and travelling professionals, and all those invited to the governor's mansion were friendly and flirtatious. Charity was even reported to have teased and flirted with old Sir Henry, whom everyone else treated with respect. She had walked out with several soldiers in the town, who had related that she had laughed as she told them about her old mammy who had been so against allowing her youngest daughter to go so far from home, warning her against the darkies and Chinamen who did terrible things to decent Christian girls. It was clear that Charity had enjoyed the respect that her race granted her in Singapore.

Sir Henry urged Le Froy to pursue the investigation, even inviting him to drop in for a drink at the end of the day to update him and discuss possible avenues of future investigation. Le Froy had little to report, but took the opportunity to get to know the acting governor better.

'What exactly did you do up north, Sir Henry?'

Sir Henry would have considered this an offensively intrusive question if it had come from anyone other than a chief inspector. 'I managed things, smoothed things over and kept systems running. Let me give you an example. One year eight coolies were taken and eaten by tigers on an estate in Muar. The estate was under European management so I went to make sure it was a tiger doing the killing and got someone to hunt it down and shoot it. So, you might say I get rid of problems for people.'

'Eight people were killed by that tiger? Why did they wait so long to call you in? Why didn't someone just go after the tiger once they were sure that was what had happened to the first man?'

'Coolies are regularly taken and eaten from plantations. Probably even more from the native-owned estates but there are no records there. I suppose the simplest explanation is that labour is cheap. Labour is cheap therefore the labourers' lives are cheap and one man taken is one man fewer to feed, house and pay ... and there will be plenty more waiting to take his place. After a while you have to consider the cost of bringing in new workers. And when you have someone like me, able to take care of a problem ...' Sir Henry winked and pantomimed raising a rifle to

90

his shoulder and firing. 'A man has to be willing to take the necessary steps. Otherwise you might as well stay at home and make a living pulling teeth.'

Le Froy had also sent his men to find out more about Harry Palin.

'He might be seeing someone,' the sergeant explained to Le Froy. 'He spends enough time skulking around in town in places he has no reason to be. But if it's a white woman she's not single, and if it's a single woman she's not white. Unmarried white women are like gold dust here and we would know. It is the rule of supply and demand.'

In other words, there was nothing to go on, other than Le Froy's feeling that there was something funny about Palin Junior. All men act on unsubstantiated feelings to some extent. Le Froy was one of the few who tried to analyse what had given rise to such feelings.

'Ask if there are any stories about him in India and up north. Any stories about women especially. And find out where he went to school and follow up there.'

Le Froy had also enquired around the Mission Centre about Miss Chen Su Lin.

Miss Johnson, who oversaw the day-to-day running of the centre, was practical. Poor Miss Byrne's death was a tragedy, of course, no matter how her fall had come about, but that was no reason why Su Lin should not fill the now vacant position of nanny. Su Lin had always been good at teaching the younger girls and had helped regularly at the Mission kindergarten. No, Miss Johnson knew nothing about Su Lin's family background other than that the Chen family practised ancestor worship and, therefore, the sooner a good girl like Su Lin could be removed from their clutches the better. Miss Johnson saw no reason why someone else should not fill Su Lin's arrangement with Le Froy.

'We can send someone straight away,' Miss Johnson suggested. 'You should meet Parshanti Shankar. She's a great friend of Su Lin, speaks fluent English and can take messages. I can send her over to your office. Would you like to speak to Miss Palin or Miss Blackmore about her? I am sure they will give you the highest references.'

'No. Thank you.'

Chief Inspector Le Froy respected the good intentions of the ladies at the Mission Centre, even if their attempts to educate women in a country where few men could read made no sense to him. When he finally escaped he had learned little, other than that Chen Su Lin was well thought of there and many other young women were seeking employment. Le Froy had no intention of taking on a housekeeper. Su Lin's employment document still bore his name and signature and he felt responsible for her taking the dead girl's place at the governor's Residence, even though she had made the decision to stay. After all, if he had left her at the Mission Centre instead of transporting her to Frangipani Hill, the issue would not have arisen.

Perhaps what troubled him most of all was that he had a feeling Su Lin had sensed something not quite right about the situation at Frangipani Hill and had chosen to stay because of that. She had certainly won over the Palin girl. And perhaps Le Froy was just a little disappointed he had not had the opportunity to probe the intelligence he had sensed under that damned Chinese reserve.

Settling In

———◆———

My first few days at Frangipani Hill passed rapidly in a confusion of learning and adapting to the domestic routines
there. In addition to caring for Dee-Dee and keeping her calm,
clean and quiet, I had to learn for which meals she joined her
family and which were brought up to her in her bedroom, which
also served as a day nursery. There was a small corner table and
two chairs, more suitable for the average six-year-old rather than
a seven-year-old in the body of a large seventeen-year-old. As
always, the most difficult adjustments were the small things every
household takes for granted, to the extent that they are considered
sacred yet not mentioned to newcomers. However, Cookie and
the kitchen staff were quite agreeable when I suggested Dee-Dee
take her meals in the kitchen, instead of alone in her room. It was
a cheerful, noisy place and this arrangement saved the houseboys
carrying food trays up the narrow outside staircase.

It was in the kitchen that I learned Sir Henry spent most nights
sleeping in his dressing room or in the guest room next to his
Government House office. Since he usually walked back across

the lawn to Government House after dinner, this could hardly have been because he was caught up in work. It was something the Palins made a point of not noticing, but the maids, who had to make sure there were clean sheets on all the beds, told me it was because Lady Palin frightened him away from the room they were supposed to share.

'She doesn't *look* very fierce,' I said, using the Cantonese word for 'she-demon'. I was more fluent in the Malay that Sihat, the gardener, and his houseboys spoke, but I understood the Cantonese and Hokkien dialects they used in the kitchen. Fortunately Cookie, who had accompanied the Palins from India, spoke the King's English.

'No need to be fierce! That kind of woman kills husbands by talking, talking, talking until the man dies or goes deaf!'

Lady Palin was clearly not popular with her servants. They mocked her behind her back, although they were careful to treat her with the subservience she required when she was around. Yet the servants struck me as good people because they treated poor Dee-Dee gently. They could have nothing to gain from her but they let her follow them around and played little games with her when no one else was watching. I saw they were suspicious of me at first because, although I was a Straits-born, I slept inside the house with the *ang moh*s rather than in the servants' quarters behind the kitchen. After watching me with the *sor nui* ('silly daughter'), as they called Dee-Dee, they accepted me. The term 'silly daughter' was affectionate and Dee-Dee was always welcome (and remarkably well behaved) in the kitchen, where treats were produced for her at all hours. A seven-year-old was old enough to help in the kitchen, I decided, and when we were there, I set

Dee-Dee to topping and tailing bean sprouts, which she took to with great glee.

Most mornings, Miss Nessa and Sir Henry walked across to Government House after breakfast. From there, the car took Miss Nessa into town, where she spent most of the day seeing to her various projects and good works. Lady Palin said sourly that, despite her sister-in-law's reputation for good works, she didn't lift a finger in the house . . . not that Lady Palin did much either. I suspected Miss Nessa deliberately stayed away because of Lady Palin's *sotto voce* comments about 'sponging spinster relatives' whenever they were in the same room.

Most mornings I gave Dee-Dee her lessons in the kitchen instead of at the tiny table in her room. While we were down-stairs, the servants could clean her room and I could leave Cookie to watch Dee-Dee while I nipped upstairs to tidy my own. The washerwoman, who came daily, gave me fresh sheets in exchange for Charity's but I washed my own clothes.

Lady Palin was the only family member at home for lunch, which she usually had in her room on a tray, so Dee-Dee and I ate in the kitchen with the servants. After that, I took Dee-Dee for a stroll around the gardens. It was hot, far too hot to play games then, but as though she had stepped out of Noël Coward's 'Mad dogs and Englishmen', she could not settle quietly until she had burned off some energy. Fortunately, the trees along the driveway offered some shade and I made sure we stayed beneath them.

One of Le Froy's men was always on duty by the gate at the foot of the driveway, a discreet man in the not-so-discreet black *songkok*, khaki shirt and shorts, black puttees and ankle boots of the local police. Strict regulations concerning starching and ironing produced a cardboard-like material, which stood out as unnaturally as the man himself.

Le Froy had explained his presence as a courtesy to the Palin family, under the excuse of deterring curious trespassers from becoming a nuisance, though I suspected the real reason was that he wanted it known the police were still watching. After all, if he had really wanted Frangipani Hill protected from intruders he would have had to station men in the undergrowth on the slopes surrounding the official buildings, not to mention the servants' shortcut down the side of the hill.

Later, when Dee-Dee was having her afternoon nap, I would sit on my bed and look around Charity's room. It still felt like hers because most of the things in it were hers. Lady Palin had reminded me she wanted to go through Charity's things personally before anything was removed, but so far she had not found time. I had made space for myself by packing as many of her things as would fit into her steamer trunk, which stood beneath the windows, and pushing the rest under the bed. I had not gained much of an idea as to who Charity had been from her things. I was curious about her but all I had learned was that she must have had a great many admirers since there were many little gifts, and that she had not done much mending – which I could understand. Most of my time was occupied with Dee-Dee and I had *her* mending to catch up with. It looked as though Charity had simply pushed Dee-Dee's torn frocks and knickers to the bottom of the cupboard and left them there. And Charity had had a mountain of stockings. If I had had any chance at all of looking elegant in stockings, I would have been so tempted by them, which shows that even polio comes with warped blessings.

In the afternoons I prepared Dee-Dee's lessons. I found she enjoyed learning to read and could do basic arithmetic so I made up simple lessons, with counting and adding games, for her.

'The Mission School trained you well,' Miss Nessa said approvingly, when she found me disguising a jagged rip by sewing it into a flat pleat while Dee-Dee coloured a picture beside me. 'Some day you will make a good mother.' I knew she meant it as a compliment, though it felt like a dismissal of all hope of a career.

The person in the house I found most difficult to get on with or even understand was Harry Palin. I didn't know why any young man would go out of his way to provoke me when I had nothing to do with him. Did he really? Or was I imagining it? All I had to complain of was that when he was at home (which was not often) and in the same room all he did was stare and glare. He directed his baleful looks at his stepmother if she opened her mouth, and at me if she did not. He seldom spoke to me but, then, Harry Palin did not seem to have much to say to anyone other than his sister, who clearly adored him, and his father, who also was seldom at home.

Next to Harry, I found the dinners at Frangipani House the most difficult. Dinner was the one meal everyone sat down to together and seemed to be Lady Palin's attempt to recreate England in the tropics. There was usually a five-course meal – that night, for instance, we sat down to brown Windsor soup, fish, which Cookie had picked up that morning in the market, roast lamb, bought by Lady Palin from Cold Storage in town, a limp lettuce salad, Cookie's miserable attempt at boiled jam pudding and some doubtful-looking cheese and biscuits.

Because Lady Palin had said Cookie's houseboys were not trained to serve at the table and she couldn't stand the sight of the maids' dirty faces while she was eating, the dishes were all sent up from the kitchen at the same time and set on warmers on the sideboard. The diners helped themselves in turn to the lukewarm food. I was appalled.

'His first wife was clearly hopeless at managing a household,' Lady Palin said, 'and his sister was supposed to be running the house but I took over, only to find the servants don't know anything and refuse to learn. It's impossible to teach them even the most basic service etiquette and table settings.'

'The food was better then,' Harry observed, to no one in particular.

'Because she left it all to servants. I shudder to think what you must have been eating! Curried dog and stewed horse, no doubt!'

'We should not rush into saying things like that,' Sir Henry said. He picked up his fork and prodded the stodgy pudding on his plate, then put it down again. I noticed the self-conscious glance he gave his wife at the other end of the table. 'I'm putting on too much weight.'

'So am I.' Harry stuck out his flat stomach and burped, making Dee-Dee giggle and Lady Palin sniff. He was always better-natured when Dee-Dee was around.

As long as I was with her, and felt I was doing her good, I was happy to be there. It was only at night that I found myself almost painfully homesick. I found it surprising because I had always thought myself out of place in the Chen household. And it was not my narrow bed in the corner of my grandmother's room that I missed. Here at night in Charity's old bedroom I had all the quiet and privacy I had once longed for, but I found myself missing the atmosphere of people in the vicinity, the nosy, noisy, provoking, demanding people I was used to. In Chen Mansion there were always people visiting. Talk, laughter, mock-quarrels and the clatter of mah-jong tiles floated through the open windows at all hours. My grandmother was well known for her kitchen skills: she had trained her daughters-in-law and servants rigorously because it was taken for granted there would be extra people at all meals. Uncles and aunts invited friends, acquaintances and potential business partners to the table, and the guests usually stayed on after dinner to repay the hospitality with stories and gossip. Aside from her servants, they were my grandmother's main source of information. Full of Miss Nessa's instructions on ladylike deportment, I had despised their raucous anecdotes, especially re-enactments of confrontations they had supposedly had with *ang moh*s – standing up to Europeans was considered daring and reckless, given the law was almost always on their side. Now the reserved, well-bred silence of my British employers left me feeling isolated and lonely. I was glad to be distracted by Dee-Dee waking to demand a drink or another story. Sometimes she seemed the most normal person in that household.

After Dee-Dee had fallen asleep, I sometimes took out my brush and ink stone and practised my calligraphy. When my grandmother had arranged for me to attend the Mission School, she had asked me to promise two things: first, that I would not forget the Mandarin in which I had been so laboriously tutored (Ah Ma spoke only Hokkien and Malay though she could follow gossip in Cantonese, Hakka and even English), and. second, that I would not marry a Christian Englishman. I would have promised her anything to study at the Mission School and, so far, I had not broken my promise.

Scones and Photos

———◆———

One morning about a week into my stay at Frangipani Hill, just as Sir Henry was preparing to leave for Government House after breakfast, Dee-Dee tugged at me and said, 'I want to go to Papa's office today. Charity takes me there to my playroom. I want to go now with you!'

Sir Henry laughed. 'Not today. A man has to work, you know. Affairs of state!' He winked at me and left the dining room.

'I want to go to my playroom in Papa's office! I want to go now!'

'There's no playroom,' Miss Nessa said to me, ignoring the building tantrum as Lady Palin rolled her eyes and shook her head.

'When Pa's not too busy he sometimes lets Dee-Dee visit but it's not a good idea. She isn't like other children,' Harry said stiffly.

As though I might not have noticed she was different from other children! But I thought I understood his need to say it. Miss Nessa was very protective of her niece and part of that meant treating Dee-Dee as she would any other seven-year-old child and refusing to let anyone say any different. She was the only one to address Dee-Dee by her given name, as though jealously protecting what little dignity the child-woman had.

'Why don't we make a surprise for your papa?'

'A surprise?' Dee-Dee was intrigued but suspicious.

'We can bake something. What do you think he would like? Maybe some biscuits?'

The distraction worked. 'I want to make him scones, picnic scones, like in *Piggy's Little Picnic!*' That was the current favourite.

'Scones!' Lady Palin said scornfully. 'It's impossible to get a decent scone out here. They don't know the difference between a scone and the Rock of Gibraltar!'

That was a challenge no Mission School student could have resisted. Domestic science as taught by various homesick expatriate Englishwomen had covered scones and teacakes as well as roast chicken, roast beef and Yorkshire pudding. I would not have dared try any of their recipes in my grandmother's household, but surely nothing could be worse than the puddings served at Frangipani Hill!

'This afternoon we'll make scones,' I promised Dee-Dee, 'but first we have to tidy our rooms and do our sums. If you get a star, we'll make raisin scones!' That would give me time to check that Cookie had all the supplies we needed, plus raisins.

Miss Nessa touched me lightly on the shoulder as she left the dining room. I knew her smile meant either 'thank you' or 'good luck'.

'Come on! Hurry up! We have to tidy our rooms and do our sums!' Dee-Dee headed for the stairs.

I had assumed Harry would be as cynical about scones as he was about everything else, but for once he was smiling. 'Excited about sums, Dee-Dee? So that's where the brains of the family went!'

That afternoon we made raisin scones. All of the ingredients had been in the kitchen except the baking powder, which Cookie swore he had in stock and which Miss Nessa finally produced from her room. 'Baking powder has so many useful purposes,' was all the explanation she gave.

After I had chopped the butter into the flour, baking powder and sugar, Dee-Dee proved surprisingly skilful at rubbing it in with her fingertips. 'Is that enough?' she asked.

'Smaller bits. Like bits of sand, if you can.'

'Of course I can!'

Cookie seemed quite happy to heat up the oven. I suspected he was far better at his job than the victuals he sent up to the table under Lady Palin's directions might demonstrate. Meals eaten at the kitchen table always tasted far better than those served in the dining room.

'Why are they taking so long?'

'If you wait until they cool down they'll taste better,' I said diplomatically.

'I like them hot.'

'And if you wait until teatime there will be butter and jam to eat with them.'

'No clotted cream?' Harry Palin came in through the open kitchen door. His tone was sarcastic as usual, but the hand that stroked his sister's hair was gentle. 'There's no point in eating scones without clotted cream, don't you know?'

I was getting used to Harry. At first I had been hurt and confused by how he alternately ignored me and delivered a barrage of cutting comments but I had come to see that was how he treated everyone in the house, except his younger sister. It was just how Harry was. In fact, he treated me with far more consideration than he did Lady Palin.

'I want to eat them naked.' Dee-Dee said. 'Naked with nothing on. Then I'll eat all the clogged cream and jam.'

I coughed to smother a laugh and focused on transferring the fragrant scones, glossy with egg glaze, from the baking sheet to the waiting plate. Despite my confidence in the recipe, I was relieved to find I had remembered the proportions correctly.

'Why are you wearing your hat, Harry?'

'I've finished my film,' Harry said. 'I'm going into town to leave it to be developed. Do you want to come out for a ride?'

'Oh, yes! Yes! Yes! Can we have some ice-cold pop?' It worked. Dee-Dee was immediately distracted.

'After Miss Chen has made raisin scones for your tea?'

Dee-Dee hesitated, torn. 'If you put some in a basket I can eat them on the way.'

'What were you photographing?' I asked, to distract Dee-Dee from what she was doing. If Harry had meant merely to distract Dee-Dee until her scones cooled, he had opened the wrong can of worms.

'Oh, the usual. Just plants, birds and bugs. Not like Charity's artistic shoots.' Harry raised his voice slightly and darted a sly glance in my direction that I did not understand.

'Come, Deborah,' Miss Nessa said abruptly, from behind me. 'You should wash before tea.' As Dee-Dee protested, she continued, over the girl's wails, 'You spend far too much time down here with the servants. No, you are not going to town with Harry.

Su Lin, you might bring the scones up to the drawing room. I will see if Sir Henry can come back to join us for tea.'

'What's going on?' I demanded, irritated enough to forget my manners. I could hear Dee-Dee's protests as she dug in her heels all the way up the stairs with Miss Nessa. She had been having such a lovely time that it was frustrating for it to end in tears again. I knew Miss Nessa had been upset by what Harry had said, and suspected he had done it on purpose. I just didn't know why she would mind him talking about photography.

Harry laughed, not unkindly. 'Don't worry. Dee-Dee will have forgotten about it by the time her hands have been washed. And she'll enjoy the scones at teatime. I'll take her to town for pop tomorrow morning and we'll all live happily ever after. That's what people like you want, isn't it?' Cookie and the houseboy, politely deaf, started clearing up the mess Dee-Dee and I had made.

'What did you say to upset Miss Nessa?' I rejected the distraction Harry offered. I placed a bamboo cover over the plate of scones to keep off the flies and took the slab of butter out of the refrigerator to soften. I guessed Harry would shrug so I was careful not to look at him. If he didn't want to answer, all he had to do was leave the kitchen. Anyway, he had no business there while I was seeing to the tea. Family meals were not my responsibility, of course, but Miss Nessa had approved my scones for the drawing room. I sliced squares of butter into a bowl.

'Aunt Nessa doesn't like cameras,' Harry said, lifting the food cover and helping himself to a scone.

'Really?' I was surprised by this. 'Is she superstitious about photographs?' That idea belonged to my grandmother's generation.

'Of course not. That's absurd. Aunt Nessa isn't superstitious about anything. Anyway, any spirits would be terrified of her! I'd like to tell her you called her superstitious and see what she says!' Harry was provoking me again. I smiled vaguely, as though humouring his sister, and turned my eyes back to the butter I was creaming to make it easier to spread. As I'd suspected he would, Harry continued.

'I photograph plants, mainly,' he said, through a mouthful of scone. 'I'm documenting them. Did you know the banana tree is related to plants like ginger, cardamom and arrowroot?'

'Really?'

'Extraordinary, isn't it? I'm cataloguing everything I photograph. It's a scientific process and it's easier to photograph plants *in situ* than to draw them. I'll show you my pictures, if you like. When they're developed, I mean.'

'Why doesn't Miss Nessa like cameras?' I asked, turning to him again. I had finished my preparations. The servants would already have set up the tea service in the drawing room, and Cookie had almost finished the *otak* sandwiches he had only started making when he'd heard Sir Henry would be returning to the house for tea. The remaining *otak*, a savoury grilled fish cake to which Sir Henry and Miss Nessa were partial and which Lady Palin said was 'disgusting', were kept warm over charcoal for the servants' meal. Dee-Dee and I normally took our tea in the kitchen with the servants and I wondered whether I was expected in the drawing room. I had set aside several of the too large or too small scones for Cookie and the other servants to sample.

'Aunt Nessa doesn't mind cameras,' Harry said dismissively, as though the suggestion had not come from him. 'She even likes my photographs. She just doesn't like cameras being treated like toys. That was what she said when she found out Charity had borrowed mine. She got so upset, saying it was valuable and if I was serious about photography I should look after the tools of the trade ... The next day the pater went to town and bought Charity a little Kodak Brownie for herself. It's not like the one I use. My camera is a Leica – it's what all the top newspaper photographers use. That should have been the end of that but I think Aunt Nessa felt Charity had made a fool of her. Some women are like that, you know. Hey, why don't you come up and have tea with us? Charity always did, even when Dee-Dee didn't, so I don't see why you shouldn't. And these scones are pretty authentic, I must say.' He took another.

'It's my off time,' I said lightly, but I smiled to show I appreciated the invitation. When Harry forgot to be sullen I glimpsed a sweet boy. 'I can practise my Cantonese if I eat down here.'

'Oh ...' Harry looked awkward. 'I forgot you're not – I mean, you speak English so well ... Oh, dash it, I don't know how you do it. I had to study French and Latin at school but if you asked me to spend a day, or even an hour, speaking one of them I would say, "Just kill me now."'

I suspected the other servants understood much more English than they let on. Although neither Cookie nor I said anything, it was clear they all knew that I had been invited to have tea with the family but had preferred a low wooden stool in the kitchen to the floral upholstery of the drawing room. There was extra condensed milk in my hot, sweet tea, and the first of the fresh rambutans was not only pressed on me but peeled for me. The rambutans were to be kept secret for now, Sihat the gardener had made clear. The *ang moh*s owned all the fruit on the trees in their garden, of course, but there would be plenty for everyone as the season wore on, and if they didn't look up to notice the red appearing among the clusters of green fruit, well, they wouldn't know they were missing anything. The translucent rambutan flesh was sweetly tart and juicy over the woody pit, and eating them out of their hairy half-shells was like tasting little mouthfuls of happiness.

'Have you seen Mr Harry's photographs?' I asked casually.

'Boring, nothing to see,' one of the maids said. 'Only leaves and trees, not even flowers. Not so interesting as Miss Charity's!' They all giggled, even the timid houseboys.

'Don't talk so much!' Cookie glared at the girl, who subsided, unabashed.

Another spoke up: 'Yah, what. Just because somebody is dead doesn't mean cannot say anything about her, right? Miss Charity liked people to take photos of her. Sometimes without clothes on! So dirty!'

The others laughed, even Cookie, though he shook his head disapprovingly. It was clear this was not news to anyone except me.

'But Miss Charity was not dirty for three months.' It was the houseboy, who had not understood a great deal of what had been said. He was one of the 'outside' servants who came daily for the heavier cleaning. He usually grabbed a piece of bread and ate by himself under a tree, but today he had been drawn inside by the fragrance of baking and had stayed.

'Not dirty for three months?' I coaxed, offering him another buttered half-scone, 'What do you mean, Tanis?'

'Her monthly "dirty",' explained the child, who cleaned the bedroom chamber pots. The Residence was equipped with a modern indoor chain-flush toilet but since there was only one – downstairs off the drawing room – each bedroom was provided with a potty for use in the night. I had been emptying my own and Dee-Dee's but clearly Charity had not. Cookie shook his head and scolded the boy for being lazy, telling him he was useless and if he didn't get back to work he would not get paid. I knew his threats were just for show, probably for my benefit. After all, I had seen him slipping the houseboys leftover food, neatly packaged in banana leaves, to take home to their families.

I left the kitchen soon after Tanis went back to work, saying I had to check on Miss Dee-Dee. I found the houseboy digging manure into a pile of earth. The grass lawns favoured by *ang mohs* needed constant maintenance.

'Did you like Miss Charity?'

'I don't know . . .' The boy looked uncomfortable. 'I don't know how to say, I cannot say . . .'

It was probably nothing, I thought, already sorry I had started this. The silly child had probably had a pash on Charity, like most of the silly men whose paths she had crossed. Still, I had started so I went on, in Malay, 'What you just now said about Miss Charity? What did you mean?'

Neither of us was Malay, but we understood enough Malay to communicate in it. And Tanis seemed more at ease speaking a language not understood by his white employers.

'I am the number-two boy,' he explained. That was the lowest position in the house so it was his job to empty all the 'dirty' containers. But when it was that time of the month for women

109

of the house, he got his sister to come in and help him since, as a male, he could not touch a woman's monthly blood—

I froze.

'I got permission!' the boy cried, misunderstanding my expression. 'Men cannot touch such things! I am a man!'

'No, no. That's all right,' I said quickly. 'I am only thinking they should not have asked a man to do such a job.'

'I am not offended,' Tanis said graciously. '*Ang moh*s don't understand such things.'

———◆———

That night, after Dee-Dee had finally fallen asleep, I remained in the chair by her bed, thinking. It had been a tiring day. The scones had been a great success but Dee-Dee had overexcited herself, eating too much jam, and had been more difficult than usual. She loved sweet things but, despite her constant demands, she wasn't allowed to indulge very often and, today, had made the most of it. Now she was asleep I still couldn't decide what I should do.

It might make all the difference to Le Froy's investigation if Charity Byrne had been pregnant but, then again, the information Tanis had innocently let slip might not mean anything. Even if it was true, what made it important was what made it difficult for me to discuss with Le Froy. I knew the facts of life, though this was no thanks to my well-meaning Mission School teachers. You don't grow up around pigs, goats, chickens and ducks without discovering that a male of the species is needed to trigger the event. But Le Froy was an *ang moh lang* and, apart from the difficulty of bringing it up with him, I didn't have the English vocabulary necessary.

'What are you doing?'

I gasped, startled. Lady Palin was leaning against the open doorway.

I lied automatically: 'Dee-Dee was having trouble getting to sleep. I just wanted to make sure she didn't wake up again.'

'Oh. Poor girl. It's this bloody weather.' Lady Mary made her way across the room. Either her eyesight in the dim lighting was none too good or she was drunk. She sat down at the foot of Dee-Dee's bed, fortunately not waking her. 'You still haven't cleared out Charity's things. What's taking you so long?' Her slightly slurred voice had lost the cultured accent she usually affected.

'Lady Palin, you told me not to sort through Charity's belongings unless you were present.'

'I did? Of course I did. Never mind. You're a good girl, not like that other one. Just tell me if you find anything that shouldn't be there. The girl came here without a penny. Shouldn't be anything valuable among her bits and pieces.'

With that settled, Lady Mary made no move to leave. She was desperately lonely, I realized, painfully so. But I was hoping Dee-Dee would not wake. Finding her stepmother in her room would trigger another crying fit.

I stood up. 'Would you like me to bring you a hot drink to help you sleep?'

'She looks so beautiful when she's asleep, doesn't she?' Lady Mary said, gazing down at Dee-Dee. She rose to her feet and followed me to the door. 'Such a waste. If only I'd had her looks, what a life I would have had! I thought I was coming out here to marry a very important man, and I was ready to do my best to be a good wife to him. I even prayed about it. Publicly and privately, I would be the best wife I could. Instead I'm married to some twopenny-ha'penny civil servant who's under his sister's thumb!'

I closed Dee-Dee's door quietly behind us. 'Sir Henry is the governor, the most important man on the island.'

'Acting governor. He's just a man with no ambition who's meant to keep the seat warm till the real governor's wife dies and he comes back or until they appoint someone else. "Don't make any changes!" That was the one directive they gave him. But I would still do what I could if that sister of his didn't make clear how useless I am.'

'I'm sorry,' I said, meaning it.

Lady Palin shook her head and said, not looking at me, 'Such impudence! How dare you feel sorry for me?' but that was just out of habit. I could tell her heart wasn't in it. 'I made up the story of a wonderful husband and wonderful life for myself. That's a failing we women have. I dare say Charity Byrne did the same. She was a shameless little flirt, but likely she thought she was living an adventure or a romance . . . and look where it got her. At least no one will ever flirt with you.' She looked at my withered leg and I understood she meant it as reassurance rather than insult. 'Men have no imagination. They don't bother with stories and projections. All they want is facts.'

———◆———

Ironically, Lady Palin had helped to resolve my dilemma. I sent a note to Le Froy early the next day. The houseboys regularly took the mail to the post office, and I told Tanis if he carried mine directly to Le Froy at the police station in town and answered any questions the chief inspector might ask, I would give him the three cents that a stamp would have cost. Of course, I worried that was not the way the police did things, but Tanis appeared happy enough to run the errand.

Later I learned that mine was one of two relevant notes Le Froy received by runner that morning. But he was kind enough to send word that the questions I suggested he ask Tanis had helped.

Le Froy's Information

◆———

The other note Le Froy had received was from the mortuary asking him to 'drop in' around six for a chat. It was a dry, matter-of-fact communication, with no sense of urgency, and Le Froy did not try to second-guess what had been found, just wondered why they had not sent a standard laboratory report with it. Even hospital laboratories got overwhelmed with records and paperwork, though, and the dying took precedence over the already dead. He let himself get caught up in work, and it was just after five when he stepped out of his office wondering if it was too early to head to the mortuary.

He was feeling tired and, as so often happened, he had not had lunch. Although Chief Inspector Thomas Le Froy had adapted to the equatorial climate he never had much appetite in the midday heat. When his work demanded all his attention he neglected his meals, and when he was not working there seemed to him little reason to eat. But it had been a long, tedious day and he was hungry. It was far too early for dinner and Le Froy had never found afternoon tea and cake appealing. He was

114

on the pavement outside one of the Navy shops, deciding between walking to a more local part of town where he could buy a hot bowl of noodles from a street hawker and a couple of sticks of *otak* from a roadside stand when he was hailed: 'You need a wife,' Miss Blackmore said, taking him by surprise. She was one of the older Mission ladies, who spent most of her time at the school. 'A wife who will feed you better meals than you get on the street!'

She had two young local girls with her and they chorused, 'Good afternoon, sir.'

'Good afternoon, madam. Ladies.' That made the girls giggle. 'May I treat you to an *otak*?' They giggled even more as he offered each of them a stick of the fish cake. Other men might find it flattering to be the object of girlish attention but Le Froy found himself thinking of, and preferring, Su Lin's calm, assessing gaze.

As though she were reading his thoughts, Miss Blackmore interrupted them: 'And how is Miss Chen getting on?'

Now she, as well as the girls, was watching him with an attention that made him uncomfortable. One was a dark young woman who looked vaguely familiar.

'Well, thank you. Very well.' Le Froy was not sure whether the woman knew Su Lin was helping at the Palins' rather than at his house. It was ridiculous that a spinster teacher could make a man who had faced down savage killers uncomfortable but there was something about Miss Blackmore that reminded him of his grandmother, though Miss Blackmore was probably closer to his age than Granny's. They had the same soft faces surrounded by silvery grey hair and there was a similar impression of tempered steel within their softness.

115

'Su Lin is a great help. So efficient and so . . . quiet. If you will excuse me, I have an appointment at the hospital.'

Which was why Thomas Le Froy arrived at the mortuary with his thoughts and footsteps slightly agitated.

He was surprised to find Dr Leask and Dr Shankar in the tiny cluttered office next to the mortuary. Dr Leask was the young resident doctor at the St Andrew's medical dispensary. Dr Shankar, though experienced and armed with degrees from the Imperial College School of Medicine and King's College, London, found most European patients didn't trust an Indian doctor. Since most Asian patients were still wary of Western medicine, regardless of who dispensed it, Dr Shankar ran Shankar and Sons Pharmaceuticals and Photographic Prints and assisted in the hospital's pathology department. Le Froy was even more surprised by the excitement on their faces.

'Fortunately my son's friend Prakesh was on duty,' Dr Shankar was saying to Dr Leask. He continued, with one eye fixed (not very subtly) on Le Froy, 'He was not at the Palin house but he saw the report and talked to the men who went over and they say it may not have been an accident. The girl Charity quarrelled with Lady Palin earlier in the day. Just before she fell, she screamed, "Mary!" which is Lady Palin's Christian name. Sounds like she may have been pushed.'

'Anything's possible.' Le Froy said noncommittally. 'She had a stab wound in her side, didn't she?'

Prakesh Pillai was one of Le Froy's most reliable sergeants. He wouldn't have thought the man would discuss police business outside the station. Several people – one of the maids, who had been in an upstairs bedroom, one of the gardener's boys, who had been trimming the driveway bushes – claimed to have heard Charity's last cry, but Le Froy was not certain they hadn't just echoed what they had heard Sir Henry say. Also, it would not be easy to conduct an investigation into the acting governor's wife.

The Palins were European, which was enough to turn what might otherwise be an unfortunate domestic mishap into an ugly scandal. There was already a small movement of resentment against the white colonial overlords – not so much the handsome new King Edward VIII but his representatives, who treated all natives with the disdain of royalty. And, though Sir Henry had not been in Singapore long enough to make himself unpopular, it was no secret that his wife certainly had.

'But now that we know the unfortunate girl was expecting a baby—'

Le Froy nodded, then turned on Leask: 'I asked you to do a quick examination when the girl was brought in and you told me she had never been intimate with anyone.'

'You asked if she had been interfered with and I said no. I assumed you were asking about non-consensual relations, not whether she was *virgo intacta.*'

'Chief Inspector,' Dr Shankar stepped in, 'I believe what my esteemed colleague meant is that the deceased had not been assaulted or interfered with immediately prior to her death. In the most basic terms, she was not raped or assaulted before she was pushed. Gordon, in such a case you should have informed the inspector that the deceased was not a virgin even if he didn't ask. Then it would not be such a surprise to him to learn that she was at least three months pregnant.'

That was the problem with gentleman doctors, Le Froy thought. Certain activities could not be mentioned in polite society but might have deadly consequences, which had to be resolved.

Dr Leask recovered: 'My initial examination did not go beyond cause of death.'

'Do the Palins come to you for medical care?'

'As the official physician for Government House I am responsible for Sir Henry and his staff but he's had no need of my services so far. I believe Mrs Palin – Lady Palin gets her powders from Dr Farley at the General Hospital at Sepoy Lines in Outram Road,' Dr Leask said obligingly.

'And the stab wound in the girl's side?'

'Investigation suggests it was made by a very sharp waved blade, very likely a *keris*. For a weapon of its size and weight the *keris* inflicts greater damage than a standard Western blade, severing more blood vessels and creating a wider wound. Often poison is applied to the blade but no trace was found in the wound.'

Something in Dr Leask's manner made Le Froy probe further. 'You found something else in it?'

'No, not at all. That's why I called Shankar in. It appears the girl was stabbed after she fell. It suggests someone wanted to make sure she was dead.'

Le Froy remembered Su Lin's words. But that did not mean it was not murder – just not murder by stabbing . . .

Thursday Evening

◆

I was playing clock golf with Dee-Dee on the lawn along the driveway in the cool evening when Le Froy's now familiar car appeared at the gate. I had discovered that, as is the case with small children and big dogs, Dee-Dee was much easier to handle in the evenings if she was allowed to play outdoors until she was physically exhausted. Dee-Dee told me Charity had taught her to play hide-and-seek and I found badminton racquets, a croquet set and the golf game, with clubs, in the storage area beneath the house.

We had already finished an early dinner of rice porridge, stir-fried water spinach and fried fish in the kitchen and I had meant to keep Dee-Dee outside until it was time for her to join the adults in the dining room when Cookie sent up the pudding.

When she saw the car slow down, Dee-Dee shouted, 'Race you!' and dashed up towards the house to announce the visitor. Le Froy was driving himself and he slowed down for me to step up and stand on the running board as he rolled on up the driveway.

'Are you quite sure that's safe?'

'Safer than hanging onto a bullock cart. Your car won't kick and there are no dung bombs to dodge. What are you doing here?' I hadn't realized how rude the question would sound until I heard myself voice it. 'I mean, they're not expecting you, are they? They're still at dinner. If you wait a little you can go in with Dee-Dee and have coffee and cake.'

'I wanted a word with you.'

Dee-Dee had already reached the house and disappeared inside.

Le Froy slid the old black car onto the grass at the side of the drive. I hopped off and he got out, looking even more glum than usual.

'Is something wrong?'

'I just received the autopsy results for Miss Byrne.'

'And?' What was there to be so mysterious about? 'I already know about the knife wound in her side. It didn't kill her, did it? Was it to make sure she was dead?'

'Charity Byrne was pregnant when she died.'

Le Froy paused, watching me. He clearly expected me to be shocked and, for a moment, I considered trying to look surprised so as not to disappoint him but I wasn't quick enough.

'You already knew?'

'No. Well, I didn't know, but I wondered. That was what I was trying to tell you in the note I sent with the houseboy. One of the servants mentioned Charity missing her time of the month and I thought it was possible she was going to have a baby but I didn't know for sure and I didn't know how to tell you. Did you talk to Tanis? Do you know who the father was?'

Le Froy ignored my questions. 'Given the circumstances, it's possible Miss Byrne chose to take her own life rather than face the consequences of her condition. Do you see what I mean?'

I did, and it irritated me. 'I'm certain that Charity Byrne did not kill herself because she was pregnant. There are women she could have gone to see if she didn't want to have the baby. Besides, if she had wanted to kill herself, she wouldn't have just climbed over a balcony rail. She would have gone up to the roof at least.'

Later Le Froy told me how shocked he had been; not by what I said but by how easily I spoke of Charity's pregnancy. He had not been able to find a term that would be understood but not offensive. It was his first inkling of how tough a practical female can be.

'Since I'm here,' he said, 'is there anything else you want to tell me? In plain English, please. No social conventions that go round in polite circles.'

'Not about whom Charity was walking out with, no. Apparently she used to have huge fights with Lady Palin. They had one on the day she died, in fact. The servants say so and I believe them. But it's no use you asking them again. I don't think they'll talk to you.'

'Well, I'll talk to them,' Le Froy said, heading towards the front door. 'Someone must have an idea, must have seen her with somebody. I'll have to talk to everyone here again.'

'Not now. Do you really want to walk into the middle of their dinner?'

He stopped, looking surprised. Apparently the law did not observe mealtime etiquette. 'Of course. I realize . . . it's been a long day.'

'If you wait until they've finished they'll be full and happy, and you'll get better answers out of them than if you charge in now. Have you eaten?' He looked as though he had missed his lunch and probably breakfast, as well as his dinner.

Le Froy dismissed my question with a shake of the head and looked towards the house uncertainly. Fortunately, Dee-Dee appeared at that moment. 'Banana pudding! And Aunt Nessa made custard! Come on, hurry up!'

———◆———

Le Froy ate two helpings of banana pudding with custard poured over it. And when, after a word from me, Cookie sent a houseboy up with a warmed-up plate of shepherd's pie for him, Le Froy ate that too, barely seeming to notice what he was doing.

'Even if Miss Byrne was little more than a servant here you must, of course, investigate,' Sir Henry said. 'Charity was out here under our protection, the poor child. And now it seems that not one but two innocent lives have been lost.'

'Innocent!' His wife snorted. 'Henry, did you hear what the man said? The girl was expecting a bastard of her own. I warned you about taking in strangers. That kind of bad blood runs in families.'

I noticed both Le Froy and Lady Mary dart suspicious glances at Harry, who sat silent, looking shocked. For once he made no sarcastic comment.

'Can I have a word with you in private?' Le Froy asked him.

———◆———

Later, on his way out, Le Froy looked into the drawing room where I was playing draughts with Dee-Dee on her father's board. 'Su Lin, get your things. You're coming with me. I'll wait by the car for you.'

Miss Nessa started to say something, then stopped when I shook my head. Le Froy hadn't mentioned anything to me about leaving, and I certainly hadn't, and wouldn't have, agreed to go.

I could just let him wait outside, I thought. But that might make things worse. I followed him out onto the driveway. 'No, sir.'

'No?' This made him turn to me in surprise. 'I'm responsible for you.' He did not sound angry. 'And I'm afraid of what your uncle and the ladies at the Mission will do to me if anything happens to you. I met one of them in town and she made quite clear my responsibilities regarding you.'

His tone was deadly serious but I suspected he was not, so I dared say, 'I'm not the Mission's responsibility and I'm not yours either. But I am responsible for Dee-Dee now. I can't leave her with no one to look after her.'

He studied me impassively, as though waiting for something more.

'And I feel responsible for Charity's sake too. I want to find out what happened to her. She was not much older than me, all alone here and having a baby.' I could tell he understood even if he did not approve.

He nodded. 'Part of independence is being allowed to choose what risks you take. That note you sent was good. You will let me know if anything else occurs to you? If anything or anyone makes you feel uncomfortable, if you need to leave for any reason, you will let me know? The Palins treat people well, but they don't consider you and me "people".'

'Of course, sir.'

I went back into the house to find Dee-Dee, feeling warm with Le Froy's trust and approval.

Sir Henry and Miss Nessa had disappeared and only Lady Palin and Harry were still in the drawing room with Dee-Dee, who was seated at the grand piano.

'Where were you? You're supposed to be caring for the girl and keeping her quiet!'

Without looking at her stepmother, Dee-Dee touched a note on the piano and started singing, '"Row, row, row your boat, gently down the stream . . ."'

'Will you be quiet!' Lady Palin snapped. 'You give me such a headache.'

Dee-Dee gazed at her. I knew that, left to herself, she would have tired of her song in less than a minute, but annoying an irate stepmother was interesting enough to keep her going for some time. She tapped another note and 'Row, Row, Row Your Boat' started up again in a different key. She had a gift for carrying a tune. It occurred to me Dee-Dee might enjoy singing lessons. She also had a natural, almost animal, gift for getting the better of Lady Palin.

'"Life is but a dream . . ."' Dee-Dee sang. She was watching Lady Palin expectantly.

'Dee-Dee, can you run and tell Cookie that Inspector Le Froy sends his thanks for the excellent pudding?' I suggested.

'I'll go,' Harry offered. 'Cookie likes me.'

'No! Cookie likes me better! Anyway, she asked me first! I'm going!' Dee-Dee dashed off.

Lady Palin didn't try to hide her relief: 'Thank you. It's such a pity you're not one of us. You would have made a good teacher – or mother.'

For a woman who did not set out to be offensive, Lady Palin certainly managed it.

'Some of the ladies at the Mission suggested I train as a teacher. I've been helping teach the younger children but they can't pay me because I don't have a teaching certificate.' Gaining one had once represented the pinnacle of my dreams, but as I spoke I realized that I did not want to spend my life as a teacher any more than I did as a nanny.

'They are training local teachers? To teach in English?'

'The Mission needs more teachers at the girls' school as well as the kindergarten. There's a great shortage of them.'

'It will be the blind leading the blind.' Lady Palin shook her head sadly, then lost interest in me and turned on Harry. 'That inspector suspects you, you know. Clearly everyone will think it's you – you must have got Charity with child and then you killed her when she threatened to tell your father. It's obvious, isn't it? If I were you I'd get away while you still can.'

Harry raised his eyebrows. 'You fell for it, then? Le Froy was just trying to distract and confuse you. I'm in the clear and so is the old man. Remember that when it happened I was coming up the driveway on my motor steed and I saw Father on the link path, walking towards the house. I stopped and waited to give him time to go into the house before I did, so we as good as alibi each other.'

'Why would you wait?' Lady Palin asked.

'Why? You don't think I have any filial respect? All right, I wasn't so keen to go into the house because I could hear you shouting at Charity upstairs. And Dee-Dee tearing out of the house and hiding.' Harry laughed gently, remembering.

'Was she scared? Upset? Did she say who she was running away from?' I asked.

'Oh, no! She wasn't scared. I remember I called, "Where's the fire?" and she laughed, as if it were a huge joke. She was up to some mischief. The last time I saw her looking like that was when she had just put earthworms inside Mary's special tin of tea leaves. Mary scolded her for playing with the tin, which had been specially shipped out for her from England, so Dee-Dee put worms in it.'

Lady Palin's mouth twisted. Obviously she remembered. But Harry hadn't finished.

'I'd say they're working on the jealous-female motive. There's always some of that in these arranged marriages, you know – oh, you don't know?' He feigned astonishment. 'We Westerners have arranged marriages too, but it's not done openly and above board like you people do it. Your way makes a lot more sense, I must say. "If you want my daughter, you must build a house with an upstairs toilet for her and I will give you two goats, a pig and a dozen chickens." That way you're really setting up the new family, aren't you? Making sure both sides provide. But when Mary first arrived in Singapore it was Aunt Nessa who arranged for Father to marry her.'

'Really?' I wanted to hear his version of events.

'Oh, yes. My *belle mère* came out east to marry some other fellow, but he died of the fever before she arrived and she didn't have the passage back. I would guess Aunt Nessa told Father he ought to marry her for Dee-Dee's sake, told him he'd be giving Dee-Dee a mother. Aunt Nessa had been calculating the cost of shipping out a proper housekeeper and nanny. She must have thought he would get the same services from a wife – and without having to pay salaries. But there are worse reasons for marrying. My mother was dead. Dee-Dee needed supervision. And Miss Mary Lowell was frankly coming to the end of her shelf life and desperate to be married. But even out here, where single white women are precious as gold ingots, there were no takers. Really, Father did you a favour by making you an offer, didn't he, Mary? Or was it Aunt Nessa who made the offer?'

For a moment I thought Lady Palin was going to hit him. Instead she turned and walked out of the room, bumping into the doorframe as she passed through it. I heard her trip and stumble as she started up the stairs.

'That was cruel of you.'

Harry shrugged, but I saw he looked abashed. The excitement generated by Le Froy's visit had spent itself in his recital. 'Mary is officious and condescending and she wants to send Dee-Dee away to an institution. Father would never stand for that and neither would I. If there's a murderer in the house I'm surprised he didn't kill Mary instead. You think she treats you badly? She was much worse to Charity, making comments about her background and her class . . .'

'But she doesn't treat me badly. Anyway, I don't mind. I don't care what she says to me. Lady Palin just says those things because she's unhappy. I'm sure Charity didn't care either.'

Harry shrugged. *He* had cared what his stepmother had said

to Charity, I thought. He hadn't attacked the woman on my behalf but to defend Charity Byrne. Had he cared for her enough to father her unborn child?

Bedtime

———◆———

Dee-Dee, energized by the tension in the grown-ups around her, was whiny and petulant, and it was only with difficulty that I got her upstairs, then washed and changed for bed. Even then we had a minor fight over a cache of sweet papers that Dee-Dee had pinched downstairs and carried up with her. Usually I closed my eyes to the girl's habit of collecting anything she found – there were bottle caps, buttons and thimbles stashed away in various corners – but I drew the line at wrappers. It wasn't just the ants I was worried about. In Singapore, it was ants, cockroaches and other insects.

By the time I had got Dee-Dee into bed and read her to sleep, I was exhausted. It didn't help that the confirmation of Charity Byrne's pregnancy was buzzing around in my head, like an irritating housefly. Until now it had been mere gossip-fuelled speculation – I had thought fit to pass it on to Le Froy but knew he might disregard it. After all, maids and slaves who didn't get enough to eat also missed their monthlies. I thought of Charity dealing with Dee-Dee night after night, so far away from home, and I could not help feeling for the dead girl. What must she have been thinking, feeling and fearing? What plans had she made? Who might she have confided in? It was clear Dee-Dee had liked her very much and that made me like her too. I had been looking forward to getting into bed, the one place in that house where I had some privacy, provided Dee-Dee didn't wake in the night, and having a good think about who Charity might have taken into her confidence. But pushing open the door that separated Dee-Dee's room from my own, I saw that wasn't going to happen tonight.

Lady Palin was standing at the wooden dresser. One drawer had been emptied onto the bed and she had clearly gone through my underclothes and monthly rags. Now she was rummaging in the second drawer, where I kept my carefully ironed and folded daily shirts and skirts, and my Sunday dress.

'What are you doing?'

Lady Mary barely glanced up. 'I want to go through Charity's things. What have you done with them? Where did you hide them? Did you take them away? That's stealing, you know. If you don't show me where they are immediately I'll have that pompous idiot of a policeman lock you up for the rest of your life.'

Without answering, I stooped and pulled out Charity's trunk and boxes from beneath the bed where I had pushed them. There had been nowhere else to put them.

Lady Palin started to go through them. I could tell she had no idea what she was searching for. She had already set aside several of my letters and two exercise books, and now she shook out Charity's novels to make sure nothing was hidden inside. Lady Palin was already in her nightdress, with her hair combed out. I could smell alcohol and guessed she had had a few drinks in her room, tried to sleep and failed. Now she was just drunk and belligerent enough to want to take on all challenges. Her large pale arms were covered with ginger freckles and mosquito bites, and wings of soft flesh flapped as she pawed through all the worldly goods Charity had left behind. It was not much to show for a life, especially one that had begun with such hope and determination.

'It wasn't my fault, you know,' she said aggressively, as though I had just accused her of something.

I guessed at once what she meant, but I waited for her to go on. She would hardly have come to my room in her nightclothes unless she wanted something, and just then it looked as though she wanted to pick a fight. Well, I was not going to fight back.

'That stupid girl dying. It was not my fault. I had nothing to do with it. I had already walked away from her when she fell. I was far away from her, back in my room. The door was shut – slammed. I slammed the door on her. Now everyone thinks I killed her.'

'Who says you killed her?' I asked, in the tone I used to steer Dee-Dee away from a temper tantrum. 'What exactly do you think they are saying? That you pushed her over the balcony wall? I haven't heard anything.'

'No one says it directly to me but they are all whispering behind my back. Everybody is! Why do you think I can't go into town? I'm not going to give them the pleasure of staring at me and whispering. All the *hoi polloi* whispering about me! And I know who started those stories.'

'Nobody in town is looking at you, Lady Palin.' I felt like Miss

Nessa conducting one of her proper-deportment-in-public sessions.

As though sensing this Lady Palin raised her voice: 'You believe whatever she tells you, don't you? You stupid natives believe anything the wonderful Miss Palin says because the governor's sister wouldn't lie, would she? Oh, no. I could tell you things about that one and about her precious brother too – governor, my foot!'

She came across to me and jabbed a finger painfully into my shoulder to emphasize her points. The servants say we quarrelled before she fell and I pushed her. That's not true. The police questioned me. Such insolence. They treated me like a criminal in my own house! And I know they would never have dared to without my husband's permission. He's behind it. He's the one persecuting me!'

'I'm sure they questioned everyone.' I moved away from her. Her breath was sour, suggesting bad teeth and poor digestion, combined with her secret supply of whisky.

'Now the servants say they see her ghost and refuse to come upstairs at night so I've got no one to help me. I am not respected in my own home and it is all because of that damned Charity Byrne!' Her voice cracked slightly as she glanced around with hostile eyes. She seemed ready to kill Charity, had the girl still been alive.

Something about her hopeless anger struck me as pathetic. 'Lady Palin, people will always gossip, but it will pass. They will find something else to talk about. I'm sure the police are doing all they can. They have to show they are making an effort to investigate.'

'It's not fair, you know.'

Again she reminded me of Dee-Dee. 'No, it's not fair. But you've got a beautiful house to live in and food on the table. A lot of people would be grateful for such things.'

For a moment I thought she was going to snap at me for using nursery talk to her. I took another step away in case she tried to slap me. Instead she nodded and seemed to deflate, sinking onto the nearest surface, which happened to be my bed.

'Nobody likes me here. You all hate me. You're all on her side.'

'I don't hate you. And I'm not on anybody's side. I don't know what Charity did to upset you but I'll try not to.'

'Charity was here as a servant, but she didn't see herself as one. She ate with us.'

I ate with the family too, sitting next to Dee-Dee and watching her manners, according to Miss Nessa's instructions: I was to have my meals with Dee-Dee; if Dee-Dee ate downstairs with the rest of the family, I did too.

'I'm sorry if I offended you by eating with you.'

Lady Palin looked surprised, as though she had forgotten I was in the same servant class as Charity. 'It's not the same thing at all!' she said impatiently. 'If my husband had people in for drinks, Charity would come and join us. All dressed up, bold as brass, as if she were a guest herself. I told Henry he let her take too many liberties but he never listened! She would sit down with us as though she were our equal! I blame that sister of his for giving her ideas above her station. Vanessa did it just to irritate me, talking to her about books and women's education, as though anyone cares about such things! Vanessa is always pushing herself forward. She forgets I'm the wife of Sir Henry Palin, I'm the one who should be making conversation. She is only the spinster sister, living with us on sufferance because she can't find a man to marry her!'

For a moment I thought Poor Mary – Harry's teasing nickname seemed more and more appropriate – was going to burst into tears. But apparently women of her class did not cry.

'I'm sorry,' I said softly.

'Don't be impertinent.'

'What do you want to do with all of this?' I tried to direct her attention back to Charity's things.

Looking at the mess she had scattered all over my bed and floor, I now saw that Charity had had some good-quality things. There were two – no, three elegant little bags made of fine silks with beaded embroidery. One even had little gemstones and feathers worked in. I had made my own bag out of good cotton scavenged from worn bed sheets and had been proud of the pockets I had created by sewing cloth scraps into the lining. Charity had also had high-heeled shoes and elaborate dresses made from vividly coloured fabrics, luxurious to the touch, in addition to the five gingham ones that had probably served as her work attire.

'How could Charity have afforded such things?' I asked, as Lady Palin opened an enamelled tin and emptied out a collection of decorative combs, a hairbrush and lipsticks. There were jars of Satin Skin Cream, Satin Skin Powder (in 'flesh', 'white' and 'pink') and a bar of Colgate's Cashmere Bouquet toilet soap. There were also two packets of Cigarettes Saphir, one of them half empty, and several packets of Chiclets, the sugar-coated chewing gum that was brought in by American sailors.

This was what temptation felt like, I thought. It was in the soft new fabrics, the feather-shaped combs, an oval looking glass and, the greatest luxury of all, the privacy of a room of one's own to store it all in.

Lady Palin smiled wryly, looking almost friendly for once, but did not answer. We got to work, sorting everything into piles – clothes, shoes and accessories. Perhaps it was just as well Lady Palin was with me to block temptation. I had to remind myself that Charity was dead and to be pitied, but a small covetous kernel remained, along with the possibility that whatever Charity had done might, after all, have been worthwhile for a time at least.

At the bottom of the suitcase I found a small case that clicked open revealing what looked like a tiny rubber bowler hat.

'What have you got there?'

I showed her. I didn't have a clue what it was, but it had been tucked inside a pair of white cotton underpants, which suggested Charity had wanted to keep it hidden. 'Some kind of monthly necessary,' I suggested.

Lady Palin smirked as she took it from me. 'It's a Dutch cap, you ignorant girl,' she said. But the curiosity with which she studied the little bowler hat told me she hadn't seen one before either. 'They're all the rage in America, don't you know? That awful Margaret Sanger woman has engineered a court case, "United States versus One Package of Japanese Pessaries". She will corrupt all the married women of America. It's in the newspapers!'

I had not seen any newspapers since moving to Frangipani Hill. Sir Henry and Miss Nessa probably saw the *Malayan Times* at Government House, and Lady Palin kept her old copies of *Woman's Weekly* and *Ladies' Home Journal* safely in her room.

Anyway, I didn't need newspapers to tell me the Great Depression was still hanging over us. The number of men queuing hopelessly for day labour since the Malayan tin and rubber market had crashed was reminder enough.

But if Charity had an immoral Dutch cap in her possession, how could she have found herself expecting a child? 'But she . . . the baby. How?'

'The wicked will be punished,' Lady Palin said, with relish.

The connecting door opened. 'What are you doing?' We had woken Dee-Dee. 'What is Poor Mary doing here? Why aren't you sleeping? I want some water.'

'I can't get to sleep,' Lady Palin answered honestly, as though speaking to another adult. 'I can't sleep out here in this God-forsaken place. Back home I sleep like a baby with my powders.'

I doubted Dee-Dee understood but she nodded and said, 'You look tired.'

Lady Palin did look tired. 'It's the Singapore weather. Even Veronal, sent over specially from England, doesn't work here. I even tried some native concoctions but they just made me fat. I have to take three or four times the dose before there's any effect, and even then it takes so long to work.'

'You could try eating Papa's special chocolates, Aunt Mary.' Spoken to as an adult, Dee-Dee responded like an adult. 'I always sleep after one of Papa's special chocolates.'

'Thank you.' Lady Palin sounded surprised and a touch suspicious but not unwilling to accept the overture. It made me wonder if someone, whether Charity or someone else, had been deliberately fuelling Dee-Dee's dislike of her stepmother.

With Poor Mary finally returned to her room and Dee-Dee resettled in bed, I looked at the mess around me and, for a moment, wished I had accepted Le Froy's invitation to leave the Palins to solve their problems. Ah Ma would have told me to mind my own business and let them mind theirs. So why had I stayed?

I was staying because I wanted to know what had happened to Charity Byrne. All my life I had wondered what life was like as one of the privileged, and I had thought of Charity as privileged. Well, this had been Charity's life. And since she had come all the way from Ireland, travelling thousands of miles instead of across an island fewer than fifteen miles wide, it must have been far more difficult for her. And she had been carrying a child in secret . . . Despite what I had told Le Froy, could she possibly have killed herself? No. Now I had looked through some of her things I was even more certain of that. Charity had been young and driven, probably vain and self-centred. I could imagine her trying to abort the child she carried but she would not have killed herself. I really wanted to know what had happened to her – not to write it down as a reporter, just to know.

It was more out of habit than fear that I wedged the bedside table under the door handle that night. There was also a clothes horse that I suspected Charity had used to block the connecting door to Dee-Dee's room, but I did not want to shut Dee-Dee out. Sometimes there were nightmares that could lead to bedwetting. I did not want to add further complications to the poor girl's already confused life. I checked on Dee-Dee – blessedly fast asleep – and used the clothes horse to block the handle of the door connecting her room to the passage.

Neither Sir Henry nor Miss Nessa had paid Dee-Dee any night visits, so this would not discombobulate them. And although Harry made a point of spending time with his sister he never came to her room at night. Only Lady Palin might find herself inconvenienced, if she tried to return, but that night I could take no more of Poor Mary.

As I drifted off to sleep I realized I was different from Charity in one very important way. She had been alone in Singapore – alone as in without any family and friends around to help her. I had family, however hard I tried to detach myself from their control, and it was about time I made their nosy, interfering busy-body ways work for me instead of against me.

Father of Her Child

———◆———

'**M**iss Chen! What are you doing here in town?'

Fond as I had become of Dee-Dee Palin I found her tiring. Like many young children, she was either bursting with energy and running in all directions or fast asleep. But at the same time, being much larger and stronger than a young child, she was harder to control and capable of doing far more damage. That morning, for example, she had thrown a piece of buttered toast at a large housefly and, after being reprimanded, had flung the butter dish at Lady Palin, who had grabbed me and hit me repeatedly with it. Which was why Dee-Dee was in the kitchen with Cookie, supposedly in disgrace, though I knew she would enjoy her time there, and why, in compensation, I had been sent in the car to town to get Lady Palin's shoes mended and given a whole dollar to spend on myself.

From Le Froy's tone I might have been a maid he suspected of running away.

'I'm on an errand for the Palins. To the old cobbler.'

'I'm impressed by your sense of duty. Why?' He was staring

at me, at my face. If Thomas Le Froy had been the kind of man to flirt, I would have thought he was trying to do so. Most men who want to flirt tease and ask provocative questions in an effort to catch your attention and get you to answer them. But Le Froy was a police officer, who seemed genuinely curious.

'Why do I have a sense of duty?' I opened my eyes – small, sly, slanted Oriental eyes, as Lady Palin described them – and faced his curiosity with my own. 'At the Mission, they told us a sense of duty was the most important thing we could learn in school.'

'Why do you have bruises on your face? What happened?'

'A little tantrum at breakfast,' I said succinctly. It was unfair to Dee-Dee to imply that she had hit me but, to be fair, she had started it. Lady Palin would not have lashed out unless provoked.

He nodded. 'Education is a dangerous business.'

I suspected Chief Inspector Le Froy, like many other men, might not have approved of education for women but I had seen him salute Miss Nessa and our lady teachers with respectful nods when encountering them on the street. Of course, he did not slacken his pace in case they took this as an invitation to stop and chat – he clearly dreaded the huge amounts of time women could chatter without passing on any useful information.

Today, though, he was the one stopping to ask me apparently pointless questions.

'Surely there are others, more physically able than you, to run errands in town and to take charge of the unfortunate girl.'

So, he had not forgotten my polio limp. I felt hurt – after all my efforts to show that I was not handicapped and could cope with anything life and Dee-Dee could throw at me!

'I offered, actually. Lady Palin's shoes need resoling and I know where to get them done cheaply.' Since people started switching from clogs to Western-style shoes, stalls that replaced worn-out soles and heels had sprung up. But Lady Palin was terrified of driving into town alone and of speaking to locals.

'Are you waiting for the shoes to be finished?' Le Froy fell into step beside me.

'Yes, and I was going to call in at my uncle's shop,' I admitted. 'Just to let them see me and know I'm all right.' When he returned home that night Uncle Chen would say, 'Ma, Su Lin came into the shop today and asked after you. She asked me to give you this dollar.' And, though my grandmother had more money than I could ever earn, the filial gesture would make her very happy.

'Ah. Very good.' Still he continued at my side, adjusting his usually long stride to my much slower step. I didn't try to make conversation. If he wanted to spy on my doings – did the man suspect me of pinching some of Lady Palin's precious teaspoons or salt-shakers to sell to an illegal pawn shop? – he was welcome to spend his time trailing me around town. I slowed my pace even further, exaggerating my limp.

'Is there any deformity of the spine or pelvis?'

'What?' I used my surprise as an excuse to stop.

Le Froy proffered a supporting arm, bending it at the elbow and holding it horizontal so I could hook a hand over it, as though it were a railing. 'You had poliomyelitis, didn't you? Is it just the muscles of your leg that are affected or your spine? Or the pelvic region?'

Now it seems ridiculous that that question shocked me. But I had grown up in a family where my childhood polio was considered the worst of bad luck, so extremely dangerous that even naming the disease aloud would curse both speaker and hearers – the deaths of my parents were proof. Even my grand-mother, who had refused to allow me to be given away, always referred to the cause of my limp as an 'accident', and at school Miss Blackmore, Miss Nessa and the other teachers had been so determined not to let me see my limp as a handicap that they had refused to see it at all.

I winced as I remembered Miss Johnson bellowing, 'Effort conquers all!' and 'Attitude is ability!' across the lawn while I struggled, always last, through physical education classes. I would gladly have been labelled 'handicapped', if it had got me out of those lessons. And now, as long as Dee-Dee was quiet and happy, the Palins didn't seem to notice any physical difficulty on my part. Looking back, I must admit that I could keep up with Dee-Dee only because of Miss Johnson's physical-education torture, but adult gratitude cannot erase the memory of childhood misery.

I was also shocked because I had never heard anyone say 'pelvic region'. Indeed, I only knew the term because of the dia-grams in the single tattered copy of *Maidens' Monthly Blessings* in the locked drawer of the Mission Centre's office.

We were walking again and Le Froy was watching my legs. If he had looked concerned or apologetic, I would have filed him away as someone with bad manners and left it, but he seemed genuinely interested in the mechanics of walking on a weak leg.

'Just the muscles in my leg. Why do you ask?'

'Sears Roebuck and Company in the United States make wheeled skates – a kind of wheeled platform you strap to the bottom of your shoes and roll along on. If a strengthening brace could be mounted on one of those skates, it would support your weight, add enough height to keep your pelvic region balanced, preventing additional back strain and pain, and you might find it far easier to step and glide, rather like using a kick scooter than . . .' For a few steps he mimicked my lopsided gait. 'You see?'

He had been lost in his subject until he caught sight of the expressions on the faces of two people passing us in the opposite direction and dropped my arm so abruptly that I was caught off balance and almost fell. There was still mud and some puddles from a brief storm during the night and the wheels of bicycles and bullock carts had left muddy tracks, making the road uneven.

'I apologize.' He spoke so awkwardly I barely recognized the words. I had seen the looks on their faces too: disapproval of me for walking so familiarly with a white man and disapproval of Le Froy for mocking a limping cripple. I realized something else too. He wasn't sure how much he might have offended me. A wrong word from me now would put me firmly into the drawer labelled 'Female: best avoided'.

'You're interested in wheeled skates?' I asked, as though nothing had happened.

'Yes. I proposed them for our foot patrols. Just imagine the advantage it would give them on paved roads.'

'As long as the people they're chasing stay on even surfaces,' I pointed out. 'There are not very many paved roads in Singapore.'

'True.' He held out his arm to support me again. 'To your uncle Chen Tou Seng's shop?'

'Yes.'

143

Le Froy had clearly been checking up on my family. If I had had time I might have been cross, but I wanted to get there quickly and moved faster with Le Froy's arm for support.

Uncle Chen, whom Le Froy had previously encountered aggressively demanding my return, appeared perfectly willing to welcome my white police abductor to his store. A Singaporean is always practical.

'Small Boss Chen!' Le Froy said in Hokkien. 'Have you eaten yet?'

'Police Demon, why have you chased me here? I eat too much already. Have you eaten yet?'

Their offhand familiarity surprised me. Uncle Chen, broad and tanned in his singlet and old knee-length shorts, was a simple man who tended to keep *ang moh*s at a distance. Though he had become the official head of the Chen family after my father, his only brother, died, he still went to work every day in the small shop that had been set up for him when he married Shen-Shen. Everyone called him 'Small Boss', even though he was such a large man.

Uncle Chen's shop had begun as a tools and mechanical bindings shop that had flourished in the construction boom after the Great War. He had added construction materials and equipment – you could see samples in the shop but the stock was kept in enormous storehouses elsewhere – cookware, and now he sold everything from shoes, dress materials and hat-trimming supplies to dried medicinal roots, century eggs and tontine tickets. This last, along with the informal (i.e. illegal) pawn shop and money-lending business, was run strictly under the counter or, rather, from the room upstairs. Customers needing such services were ushered up the narrow wooden staircase, ostensibly for a cup of tea. I was sure Le Froy had never been invited upstairs. I was equally certain that he knew exactly what took place up there.

Outside the back of the shop, a sheeted cubicle contained a giant earthenware pot of water and a scoop where workers could pay to wash themselves. Shen-Shen collected their coins and sold scoops of rice, curry and *achar* on banana leaves to take away. It was a thriving business.

'Su Lin, you are here also?' Uncle Chen barely glanced at me. He opened one of the giant biscuit tins and poured a generous scoop of Biskut Ais Jems into a paper bag. Ever since I could remember, my every visit to his shop had been marked with a gift of Little Gem biscuits with their pointy swirls of bright green, pink, yellow and white icing.

'From your grandmother,' Uncle Chen announced, handing the paper bag to me.

'Please tell Ah Ma I said thank you, and give this to her for me. How is she?'

'Eating too much for an old woman!'

I wondered if Le Froy got Uncle Chen's subtle boast: that he was a man who could afford to house and feed his old mother well. Miss Nessa would have missed the point and gone into a diatribe on filial respect, but Le Froy looked suitably impressed and murmured, 'Please give Chen Tai my regards.'

'The old woman will want to know why the Police Demon came to look for me!'

'I just wanted to ask after her.'

Uncle Chen clearly did not believe this any more than I did.

'Actually I was hoping to talk to your wife.'

I was taken aback, although that was precisely why I was there myself. Uncle Chen looked worried. 'I don't know where Shen-Shen is,' he said, ignoring the sound of her voice coming from the back of the shop.

'I have to go and collect Lady Palin's shoes.' I tried to distract Le Froy. 'Will you come and help me?'

Le Froy ignored us. 'I only want to make sure your wife knows that Su Lin is all right. I'm told she keeps in touch with everybody in town. Can I talk to her?' Shen-Shen was every bit as nosy as my grandmother and, being in town every day, she had more opportunity to exercise her skills.

Uncle Chen didn't seem happy about it. I could see him wondering whether someone had complained about the bath-house out at the back. 'I will go and call her.'

'What do you want? I don't know anything.' When she appeared Shen-Shen sounded aggressive, and I knew she was uncomfortable. If she had known a white man was coming she would have dressed up but, caught off guard, her solid, stocky form was in an old floral cotton *samfoo*, a loose cotton blouse and trousers, already stained with dirt and sweat. She looked suspiciously at me. 'You want to send her back now? I told you, once a girl goes to work in a white man's house, no respectable man is going to marry her. What happened?' This last was directed at me. 'What did they do to you? Who was it? That boy with curly hair? I will tell your uncle to go and *hantam* him!'

'I wanted to come and thank you . . .' Le Froy said. He was speaking gutter Hokkien. You could tell he had not been brought up with the politeness he would have learned in a Hokkien-speaking household but I wouldn't have been able to tell his accent from that of any man on the street. '. . . for bringing up Su Lin so well. The governor's family is very happy with her. She is very good at taking care of the governor's daughter. Somebody had to teach her how to look after children and prepare food to feed them and I'm sure you taught her all she knows.'

Le Froy was in full flattery mode and I saw its effect on Shen-Shen. It was almost like watching a magic trick, the way her face twisted and changed: it was as if she was trying to work out what expression to put on – trying on different faces like she would try on different outfits.

'I may have taught her some things.' Shen-Shen's nonchalant mask didn't entirely succeed in hiding the triumphant smile. 'When my girls were small I showed her the right way to look after babies. I showed her how to clean them and make their food.' In other words, I had been her unpaid slave once the confinement nurse had left. Helping to care for my cousins, among other things, had fuelled my determination to see more of the world before I was tied down to a husband and children for ever.

'I taught her everything she knows!' Shen-Shen preened. Tonight she would go home and tell everyone in the family that the white police boss had called on her to thank her. 'In fact, after her parents died, I was the one who took charge of bringing her up!'

Uncle Chen had returned to sorting nails into heaps of different sizes, but I saw a satisfied grin on his face. Shen-Shen would be easier on him for the rest of the day: he would be allowed all the beer and cigarettes he wanted, and he didn't care what Le Froy said to her now.

'Mrs Chen, did you know the girl who was looking after the governor's daughter before Su Lin went to work for them? Her name was Charity Byrne. She used to come into town quite often. Did she ever come in here?'

A shifty look came into Shen-Shen's face. 'The girl who was murdered by the governor's wife?'

'We don't know Charity Byrne was murdered. It may have been an accident,' Le Froy said smoothly. 'But please don't worry about Su Lin. She is not in any danger.'

For a moment Shen-Shen looked blank: she had forgotten I had taken Charity's place. If I had been a sensitive girl, I would have been hurt. Instead I was eager for her answer.

'Do you think that girl just fell down by herself?'

'We're looking into it, Mrs Chen. Charity Byrne used to come here to shop, didn't she? Did you know her well?'

So that was why Le Froy was here! And I had thought I was the only one who had access to Shen-Shen's gossip sources! Stupidly, I had thought he was following me to make sure I was all right.

'Oh, she came in here to get her sewing things. I didn't know her very well.'

'Did she have her own money to spend or did she buy things on the Palins' account?'

'That girl always had a lot of money. She was very careful with it. When she bought ribbons or trimmings she would insist on measuring them herself. As though she didn't trust me! I don't know how much they were paying her up there.' Shen-Shen darted a speculative look in my direction. 'How much are they paying you? Now you are working, you should give money to your grandmother, you know. So many years she supported you for nothing! Paid your school fees, even. Anybody else would have sent you away to be a *mui tsai*!'

'Oy! Woman! Don't talk nonsense!' Uncle Chen shouted. Selling extra daughters as *mui tsai*s was now illegal under colonial law although, of course, informal arrangements were still conducted. Throughout my childhood, I had lived with the threat, made mostly by Shen-Shen. It was generally the poorest families who had to resort to selling daughters into indentured labour. I didn't know whether Uncle Chen objected out of family pride or fear that Le Froy might decide to take Shen-Shen seriously.

But Le Froy was not interested. 'They were not paying Charity much. She must have been getting money from somewhere else. Did she have a young man in town, do you know? Was she seeing one of the soldiers, maybe?'

I was listening with interest. Lady Palin had hinted that Charity was wild and immoral, but I suspected she said the same of me behind my back. Charity had certainly left some nice things behind, but I had never thought about how she had paid for them.

'There were a lot of men after that one, always somebody following her around. Admirers. They would ask her to go and have tea with them. They would ask her to go for walks and to movies. They would offer to pay for her things here. But as far as I know she was not walking out with anyone.' Shen-Shen looked as though she would have liked to say more. I knew – and I suppose Le Froy knew – that if there had been the slightest whisper of scandal Shen-Shen would have been onto it.

In fact, all she could tell him was that Charity had seemed a well-behaved young woman. There being so few single white girls on the island, no one would have been surprised if she had walked out with one or more of the young men, but she had kept them all at arm's length. Of course, she had spent far too much money on dress materials and trimmings. Charity's spending benefited Uncle Chen's business, but Shen-Shen disapproved on principle of young women having their own money.

'Did you ever see her with Henry Palin Junior? Harry Palin? Did Charity spend time with him?'

Uncle Chen laughed. 'Mr Harry was definitely in town when Miss Charity was, just not with her. Why would that boy be with her?'

'And not by coincidence?'

'Don't talk about that Harry boy!' Shen-Shen cut in. 'If he was a local man, the police would have thrown him into prison and whacked him upside down. But because he's a white man your policemen didn't even see him! If you want to know about funny things and funny people, you should ask about that one!'

I wanted to hear more about Harry but Le Froy asked mildly, 'Did she seem afraid of him? Do you know if she was afraid of anyone? Man or woman?'

'Afraid? Nah. From what I could see, she liked getting attention. That kind of girl likes to be looked at but she behaved very well. I'm not just saying that because she's dead. She liked to have the men interested in her and she would smile and lead them on but she never let any of them touch her. But that was only in public, mind.'

'I beg your pardon?'

'Oh, nothing . . . I was just thinking that the last time I saw the poor girl she was in the printing shop leaving a film to be developed. That was just a few days before the terrible accident.

I heard they were very interesting photos but, of course, old Shankar wouldn't say what they were of.' It was clear from Uncle Chen's sly wink that they had been 'naughty' pictures. 'I wonder whether the poor girl ever saw her pictures. Chief Inspector?'

But Le Froy was backing away towards the door. 'Thank you, Mrs Chen. Good day, Miss Chen, if you don't need help getting back to Government House . . .'

Before I managed to say I would go with him (photographic films were developed at the Western pharmacy, run by Parshanti's father), Le Froy had left the shop. From the door I saw him speeding down the narrow pavement in the direction of Shankar and Sons Pharmaceuticals and Photographic Prints, one hand pinning his hat firmly to his head.

'Police business, I suppose,' Uncle Chen murmured. 'Or he is desperate for the toilet and dares not say. Should have told him we've got one here. We can even give him a discount on use.'

Shen-Shen turned on him: 'Old man, tell me! What were the photographs of?'

'How would I know? Shankar said he can get arrested for showing people photographs he is paid to develop.'

'But he must have shown you, right? Otherwise how would you know he can be arrested for it? Anyway, people take photographs so that other people can see. If you don't want people to see, why take them?'

Uncle Chen didn't trouble to answer. I knew he also sold under-the-counter camera flash bulbs and rolls of photographic film, even though Shankar's claimed to be the 'sole importer'.

'All men are crazy,' Shen-Shen muttered, returning to her domain.

What else could I do while the cobbler worked on Lady Palin's shoes? There was no point in returning to Frangipani Hill without them, and if I stayed at Uncle Chen's shop for much longer Shen-Shen would have me scrubbing out her cooking pots. It felt strange – and wonderful – not to have someone to look after or to tell me what to do, just for a little while.

'I have to leave you now.'

'Where are you going?' Shen-Shen demanded.

'Su Lin is a working woman. She has to go and work!' Uncle Chen said. 'You want some more sweets?'

'Enough, thank you.'

'Enjoy them. As I told you, they are for you from your grand-mother. I will give her your money.'

———◆———

I made it to Shankar and Sons Pharmaceuticals and Photographic Prints shop in time to meet Le Froy coming out of it. He seemed too frustrated to be surprised to see me. 'Too late.'

'They're closed?'

'Weeks too late!' He held out his arm as a support again. 'Miss Byrne left two rolls of film to be developed but she collected them before she died.'

'I'm going into the shop.' I reached for the door handle.

'Your friend Parshanti isn't there. Her brother said she wouldn't be coming in today. Dr Shankar isn't there either. He's over at the hospital.'

I was surprised enough to let him tuck my hand into the crook of his arm again.

'And there are some other things I want to ask you.'

I looked back into the shop window and saw Parshanti's brother, Vijay, watching us. I waved at him and he waved back. He looked nervous but there was nothing suspicious about that. Chief Inspector Le Froy bounding in to ask what they had done with a dead woman's photographs would have made anyone uncomfortable.

'You know him?'

'You aren't suspecting Vijay of bothering Charity, are you? He wouldn't have. He's not the sort. You can't go around suspecting everybody of everything.'

'Suspecting everybody is my job and I don't like it. That's why I have to find out who is really responsible, so I no longer have to suspect all the others.'

Even though he did not say so, I knew he wanted to find out who had been the father of Charity's baby. I did too. Whatever I had been taught at the Mission School, I did not believe in immaculate conception when it came to Irish nannies.

He turned to me. 'Your shoes won't be ready yet. We'll go back to my rooms first. I want a private word with you. And you can see where you were supposed to be working before all this happened.'

Le Froy's Rooms

———◆———

O f course, it would have been far more proper for me to go back to Uncle Chen's shop to wait until Lady Palin's shoes were ready but I already knew Uncle Chen's shop inside out and surely any lady reporter would choose to visit a policeman's rooms instead. I believe you can only truly understand people when you see how they live, especially when they have no house-keeper to cover up the evidence.

Unlike most other colonial administrators, who lived in large bungalows outside the city, Le Froy had a traditional Peranakan home in Emerald Hill. The terrace houses had been built for previous generations of new town dwellers in the 1860s over former nutmeg plantations. It was said you could still smell the spicy, woody scent of nutmeg oil in the air there. All of Le Froy's neighbours were local families and the stucco decorations – flowers, dragons, birds – and brilliantly glazed tiles were familiar to me. He had kept the *pintu pagar*, or swing-ing doors, opening off the 'five-foot' way, the sheltered passage mandated by Raffles on Singapore's first town plan to provide pedestrians with protection from equatorial sun and torrential rain. From the outside, his house looked no different from those on either side and it was impossible to tell that a white man lived there.

I felt a great relief stepping through the dark entryway into the light and airy open courtyard where the kitchen and the lavatory were located. It was especially refreshing when I compared it to the heavily shaded rooms on Frangipani Hill.

'My research and storage rooms are on the third floor. I sleep up there too. Much safer, as the stairs squeak. You would have your privacy on the second floor, if you came to stay here.'

'Your stairs squeak because they're coming loose. You can tighten them quite easily. Or you can ask Uncle Chen to send someone with the tools.'

We looked at each other.

'You want squeaky stairs so that you'll know if someone's coming,' I realized.

'I prefer to hear any unannounced visitors in advance. Of course, if the stairs trouble you, you can have the room next to the kitchen.'

At Frangipani Hill I was going up- and downstairs all day after Dee-Dee, but I was touched. I was also touched that Le Froy was making the effort to show me I would have my privacy, should I come to him as housekeeper after all.

'I probably won't be coming to work for you here. I appreciate you agreeing to give me a job, but Miss Nessa says that once they get a proper nanny for Dee-Dee she will try to get me into a secretarial course.'

'If Charity Byrne was not meeting some man in town,

someone in that house fathered her child. It's not safe for you to stay there alone.'

Le Froy reminded me then so much of Uncle Chen that I laughed. 'I'm never alone there! Look, if I were a white girl I might be at risk. And if I were an ignorant local girl with no English whom no one would believe, I might also be at risk. As it is, Miss Nessa keeps an eye on me and I am quite safe. She wouldn't let anything happen to me.'

He nodded. But not, I thought, in agreement.

'You don't like Miss Nessa?'

'Miss Nessa has good manners and is gracious with her time. But I would say the woman has a strong practical streak.'

'I'm practical too.'

'That's different.'

I looked at him expectantly, and he continued, 'Miss Nessa has a ruthless streak. All her good works are grandiose, abstract schemes.'

He sounded like one of those men who still wrote letters to the newspapers denouncing suffragettes, as though the Great War hadn't changed anything.

'Well, Miss Nessa couldn't have killed Charity. She was at the Mission with us when the news came. And I don't believe Lady Palin could have killed Charity either. She's more scared of blood than Dee-Dee! And one of them is always around so I'll be quite safe. I'll take a look around, if you don't mind, just to see what needs doing in case you'd like the Mission to send you someone else.'

Le Froy's rooms were not exactly dirty. I learned he had a cleaning woman who came in three times a week to do his laundry. She also scrubbed his floors, the indoor lavatory and the outdoor washing area. Madam Neo was the widow of a local police clerk, whose former employers made sure she had enough work to provide for herself and her children, but Le Froy's dislike of pointless conversation meant he avoided her, even leaving her wages for her on the table. Madam Neo bought cleaning supplies on his credit and I suspected he never questioned the bills. I am sure she was an honest woman who did her best, but in cleaning, as in anything else, it is difficult to keep up standards when ignored and unappreciated.

'I should be getting back soon.'

'I'll run you to your cobbler. Just let me look at a few notes first.' Le Froy headed for his cluttered desk where he got caught up in his work. It was at least an hour before he looked up again.

I made myself useful. Even if policemen didn't need to eat while working, I needed sustenance to face the long walk back up Frangipani Hill. I could not afford a trishaw since I had sent my dollar to my grandmother. I prepared us a simple meal of fried Indian mackerel, buying three through the back door from a boy who had hooked them that afternoon, long beans fried with prawn *sambal* and steamed coconut rice.

Le Froy, surprised, ate heartily. He had a second helping of rice, then sat and picked over the remains of his fish as we talked. 'I usually lunch at the office and make supper out of whatever is left over from the lunch my men pick up for me. Thank you. This is the best meal I've had in a long time.'

'The food here is one of the reasons Poor Mary wants to leave Singapore.'

'"Poor" Mary? You feel sorry for Lady Palin?'

157

'Oh, no. I mean I do feel sorry for her but that's not why. That's what they all call her at Frangipani Hill, even Sir Henry. I suppose I picked it up without being aware of it. Harry said Miss Nessa told them to be kinder to poor Mary and from then on Charity always called her "Poor Mary". Of course, Dee-Dee thought it was a huge joke.'

'Sir Henry talks to you? And young Harry? About leaving Singapore?'

'Hardly. They talk to Dee-Dee but I'm usually around. It sounds as if Poor Mary wants to leave Singapore. Last night they had another big fight.'

'Another? They often have fights?'

'Not like that.' I frowned in an effort to work out what exactly had been different. 'Usually Lady Palin is noisy but you can tell it's not serious, just her being cross because it's too hot or the butter's too soft or the milk's run out. She's like Dee-Dee – she has to let everything out and then she'll be all right for a while.

'The other night she came and took some of Charity's books and things back to her room. I don't know what she found, but after she'd looked through some of them, she got very quiet. Then she went and banged on Sir Henry's dressing-room door – that's where he sleeps when he doesn't stay at the office – saying she had to talk to him. She wasn't shouting but she seemed strange. Miss Nessa came out and asked what was wrong, but Lady Palin said she had talk to Sir Henry alone.'

'And?' Le Froy seemed not to think much of this. Perhaps eating had slowed the man's mental processes. In domestic science we were taught that feeding a man well was the most important factor in a happy marriage – not surprising, since the only bedroom matters discussed were the turning of mattresses, the laundering and ironing of sheets – but my experience suggested that people functioned better when slightly hungry and more alert. I knew Le Froy was not sleepy, though his eyelids were lowered and his eyes unfocused. In fact, I had seen enough of him to tell that he was thinking deeply, but an observer who didn't know him would have been forgiven for not seeing the difference between that and drowsiness.

'And that's all. Sir Henry refused to unlock his door and Miss Nessa made Poor Mary go back to her own room.'

'You found it strange that Lady Palin wasn't shouting?'

'Not really. I think it felt strange because she was serious about something. Usually she picks on little things to make a big fuss about but last night it was as if there was something so big she didn't have to exaggerate it. And she was pleased about it. Triumphant, almost.'

'And you have no idea what it was all about . . .'

'No. And this morning Lady Palin actually came down to breakfast. She usually has breakfast and lunch sent up to her room and stays up there until teatime. I had the feeling she wanted to catch Sir Henry before he left for the office, but then Dee-Dee had a tantrum and there was a fuss and Sir Henry and Miss Nessa had to go. She will probably speak to him tonight.'

'You didn't see any photographs among Charity's things, did you?'

'No. Why?'

'Just a thought I had. Since Charity Byrne had a camera. Odd, that there are no photographs.'

'Not really. She hadn't had it for very long.' I filled him in on the subject of Charity's camera, which led on to Harry's plant photography. Something in Le Froy's expression, or lack of it, made me say, 'Harry's not a bad sort. I don't know why he tries so hard to make people think he's nasty about everything.'

'Maybe it comes naturally to him.'

But I had seen how gentle Harry Palin was with his poor sister. Dee-Dee had the sound instincts of a child or animal. If she trusted Harry, I felt I could too. But Dee-Dee was unpredictable. She adored her brother and father and hated her stepmother but she seemed afraid of Miss Nessa, who did so much for her. Miss Nessa was the disciplinarian, taking on the role Dee-Dee's father would not.

'I'd like to come and talk to Miss Nessa and Lady Palin again. Sunday, perhaps?'

'Sunday is a very busy day for Miss Nessa.' It might be an official day of rest but it was a hectic day for anyone as involved in good works as Miss Nessa Palin. 'Why don't you tell them you want to pay a call on Monday evening? I'll try to find out what Lady Palin's secret is before then.' I didn't think it would take much effort. From what I had seen of her so far, Lady Palin was not very good at keeping things to herself.

'And one of the *keris*es from Sir Henry's collection is still missing. Remember the one he said might have been misplaced the day Charity died? It still hasn't turned up. He mentioned it again a few days ago.'

'But why the *keris*?' Le Froy had started pacing around the room but now threw himself onto a chair. 'Why that wound?' Though his thinking expression was familiar to me, I wondered briefly if he suffered from gout. I was about to suggest green papaya tea, boiled for hours and strained, when he said, 'For generations the *keris* has been the weapon of choice for executions in this region. You stabbed a man through a cloth compress on his chest right into the heart. Instantaneous death and no excessive bleeding. But why that girl? And why, if she was already dead?'

'Maybe it was a religious act,' I suggested. '*Ang moh*s keep statues of saints with arrows sticking in them. And there's St Paul with a thorn in his side and Jesus with a sword in his.'

'For show . . .' he murmured. Now he looked at me. I did my best to look less like a limping nanny and more like the forensic investigator he had always dreamed of having in the police force. But, given that I was not white, not male and not trained in the medical profession, I suspect I was less than successful.

'The doctors don't seem to think it was relevant to her death,' he said, with a touch of wistfulness.

'That doesn't mean it's not relevant to why she was killed,' I pointed out.

Dinner

———◆———

'We called them belly-button biscuits in school.' I found Dee-Dee with Harry in the drawing room, when I finally got back, and passed her the paper bag of Biskut Ais Jems. 'You can have just one now. It will be dinner soon.' Dee-Dee was intrigued, of course. I watched her lick, then carefully bite off a pastel iced tip as I had done as a child. Some things didn't change, I thought. As long as we didn't ask any more of Dee-Dee than that she behave as a seven-year-old, she was fine.

'The Labour Party's out, you know. The great Ramsay MacDonald who said Singapore was no more than a wild and wanton escapade – but now, even with the Conservatives back, rooting for Singapore as their naval base in the East, what have we got in Seletar? One iron fence and that's it.'

'I beg your pardon?'

'Ah, that's better!' Harry smirked as though he had just done something clever. 'You were looking all in the clouds just now, like you were walking around in a dream, and with those bruises on your face, I had to get you back down on the ground. There's trouble afoot.'

'What's been going on?'

'God only knows. Pow-wows. Mary Contrary just swept by and told me I would have to start earning my own living soon.'

He didn't seem very troubled by the prospect.

'And you and Dee-Dee are to have dinner with the family in the dining room tonight – if there is any dinner. There was this huge fight while you were out and Cookie's either walked out or been dismissed, depending on whose version you believe.'

'What? Why?'

'Poor Mary went down and gave him notice. Told him Sir Henry was leaving for England and he could pack up and start looking for a new position. The thing is, Father promised Cookie passage back to India as part of the deal for following him out here, so of course he thought he was being cheated and there was shouting, even some waving of the meat cleaver.'

'Oh, gosh.' I got back on my feet fast, intending to find Cookie. I winced – my back was sore from all the walking I had done in town.

Harry stopped me with a steadying hand. 'Where do you think you're going? It's no use trying to talk to Cookie. Aunt Nessa went down and explained it's all a mistake but now Cookie says he won't work for us as long as Poor Mary is in the house. So the fire's out – which also means there's no hot water.'

'Oh dear.' I looked at Dee-Dee, who certainly needed a bath. 'At least I can get the fire started . . . and see about something for Dee-Dee's dinner. Is Lady Palin in her room?' I held up the bag with two pairs of resoled shoes.

'You're a good girl,' Harry said. He looked serious for once, and I realized that whatever had happened that afternoon had shaken him more than he wanted to reveal. 'Charity was a good girl too – even if she did her darnedest to prove she wasn't. She couldn't help it. The dear old British Empire, educating savages to standards of honour and nobility even as her own people milk them for all they're worth!'

'That's not very fair to you British. At least you've built roads and schools and put in sewage pipes here. That's not taking advantage of people.'

'Did you know nearly a third of colony revenue comes from opium? The colonial government has the monopoly on opium importing. His Majesty's Government controls and runs all those dark, squalid Chinatown saloons that the good church people are always railing against!'

'Harry? Why do you stay here if you hate it so much?'

'Hate it? I don't hate it here. It's the only home I know. I'm certainly not at home in England. And Dee-Dee's never set foot there.' Harry seemed to mean this. 'Even if I did hate it here, where else would I go?'

I could think of nothing to say to him. He had no home but Singapore, yet could Singapore be a home to him? I was lucky, I thought, to know I was accepted where I felt most at home. Glancing at Dee-Dee, who was occupied in sorting her Iced Gems into piles of different colours, he lowered his voice: 'Our mother died out east just months after Dee-Dee was born. After that I was sent away to school. All the time I was in England I was longing to come back here. It was the closest I could get to where she once was.'

'I'm surprised—' I stopped myself.

'Surprised I came back? Where else would I go? Mother is buried here. Well, in Kerala, actually. But this is a lot closer than Devonshire. And a lot less cold. And if you think things are difficult for Dee-Dee here, let me tell you it would be much worse back home. You may not have the latest medical and scientific advances out east but people are more understanding and accepting. Your *kampong* people accept Dee-Dee as she is much better than those hopeless snooty city people can. If we lived in an *attap* house in a *kampong* Dee-Dee would be running around with all the other kids and chickens, and there would always be someone to keep an eye on her.'

It was true. The *kampong* spirit meant everyone in the *kampong*, or village, was family. I tried to imagine Harry Palin living in a wooden hut on stilts and couldn't help smiling. 'I'm sorry. I'm not laughing at you.'

'No, I'm sorry. You're right. I don't know what I'm talking about. I'm just realizing that if Poor Mary gets her way and we move out, I won't have a base to call home. Everyone here talks about England as "home" even if it's been ten, twenty or thirty years since they were last there. When I was sent away to school all I wanted was to go home. And this bloody hot island was what I meant by it.

'I didn't set out to torment Poor Mary, you know. In fact, I called her "Aunt Mary" from before she married Father. She asked me to. She was supposed to help with Dee-Dee – but then, of course, Dee-Dee started having her episodes and would scream any time Mary was in the same room. That was where Charity came in. She was wonderful with Dee-Dee.'

'Lady Palin seems to have hated her.'

'Poor Mary is the sort of woman who automatically hates all other women. It's just a habit with her. She hated Charity's names. Charity had names for everybody. Dee-Dee was Dee-Dumpling, I was Freddy the Frog or—'

'Why?'

'My second name's Frederick. If you're asking about "Frog", well, alliteration, I imagine.'

'The situation is changing in Singapore. Change is happening all over the world, but under the maverick Chief Inspector Le Froy, it's happening faster here. No special allowance for the ruling classes! In fact, let's haul them over the coals! In the old days if a servant had an accident, that was what it was seen as. An accident!'

Le Froy had telephoned to say he would be coming on Monday evening to ask a few questions and Miss Nessa was not pleased.

Everyone else was strangely polite over dinner, which I had prepared after Harry had helped me start the gas stove. There was no sign of Cookie or the houseboys, who must all have retired to their shacks. I served rice with curried tomato and aubergine, and a savoury omelette, all of which I knew Dee-Dee would eat without fussing. We used tiffin plates as Lady Palin had announced she had decided to have the good china packed, ready to be shipped to England.

'In any case they're too good to be used out here.' She had

been almost cordial towards me as she supervised the packing. She only said, 'Be careful. Those plates came from England, and I want them to get back safely,' three times, and I suspect more out of habit than anything else.

Sir Henry said nothing at the dinner table, toying with his fork and barely eating as Lady Palin chatted about various packing ideas she had. She seemed to be brimming over with some delicious secret that she could barely keep inside her.

'What will Dee-Dee do in London?' I asked quietly. 'She's learning a lot but she's never going to be able to look after herself.'

'Don't worry about that.' Lady Mary did not trouble to lower her voice. Fortunately, Dee-Dee was oblivious. 'Once we get out of this place and back to civilization she will have a professional examination and most likely we will find an institution where she can be properly looked after. Girl, why are you looking at me like that?'

It was not Lady Palin's prejudice that struck me now: the older woman had suddenly reminded me of one of the girls I had taught at the Mission's kindergarten. Little Pei Ling had slapped, shouted, even spat at and bitten the staff. Why? I had finally persuaded the child to explain: her brother had told her that if she let anyone think she liked being at the Mission she would be forced to stay there for ever and never allowed to go home again. Once that had been cleared up, Pei Ling had settled down nicely, and gone home after her mother had recovered. I suspected Lady Palin was labouring under a similar misconception.

Harry had been watching her in silent hatred throughout most of the meal. He had not eaten or said much more than his father but he spoke up when Miss Nessa wondered if Inspector Le Froy should be invited to come earlier on Monday evening and join the family for dinner.

'So has he finally decided which of us to arrest for murdering Charity?' He looked at me. 'You gave him a full report of all our doings this afternoon, I expect. What are the odds that he's coming to arrest me and take me away in handcuffs? Should I do a bunk tonight?'

I smiled, taking it as a joke. Harry, having directed the full force of his hostility at Lady Palin, had actually been quite pleasant to me since I'd got back, even helping me carry the dinner up from the kitchen.

'I don't want Freddy the Frog to be arrested,' Dee-Dee said. 'Tell them to arrest Mary instead.'

Lady Palin smirked. What surprised me was how she was lording it over Sir Henry. But neither Sir Henry nor Miss Nessa seemed to notice.

Sour Dreams

———◆———

D ee-Dee fell asleep halfway through her second bedtime
story. With the open book on my lap, I sat and watched
her steady breathing. Lady Mary had told me to pack Dee-Dee's
things, but I had not started yet. I would wait until I heard from
Sir Henry or Miss Nessa that they were leaving Singapore. So
far they had been noncommittal. I heard raised voices, and
though I could not make out what was said, I knew Sir Henry
was talking to his wife. Their footsteps went past Dee-Dee's
room and one pair continued down the stairs. Not long after
I heard Lady Palin calling, 'Help me, Henry. Why does no one
come? Someone come and help me!'

She sounded cross rather than in trouble, and although I
knew she would hardly be calling for me, I could not walk away
from a cry for help. 'Can I do anything?' I asked from outside
her room.

'Who's there? Open the door!'

She was sitting in bed, pouting and fretful. For a moment I
was reminded powerfully of Dee-Dee – perhaps indulgent *amah*s

were not the only reason for the girl's tantrums: she had learned her behaviour from her stepmother.

'What do you want? You have no business here. You shouldn't even be allowed upstairs! Get out!'

Perhaps because I had seen her as a child in the middle of an extended tantrum I was not intimidated. 'I'm sorry, Lady Palin. I heard you call and wanted to know if there was anything I could do for you. Good night, then.' I started to close the door but she called, 'I want my powders. Henry is such a brute. He doesn't consider my feelings at all. No one knows what I have to put up with, how he talks to me. Nobody cares. I need my medicine and there's nobody to help me. The servants are hopeless. No hot water for my bath, no tea by my bed. Henry could help but he's gone off and left me. Everyone just goes off and leaves me. I could call until I'm hoarse here and no one would bother to bring me so much as a glass of water!'

I glanced at the jug of water and glasses on top of the cabinet by the door.

'Don't look at me like that. If I get out of bed and start walking around now I'll never get to sleep tonight. My gout is killing me. I need my rest and it's too hot for a Christian soul to sleep in this awful country. And there are lizards about. I saw one by the door just now. Someone must have let it in. I'm very careful. I keep my windows shut always – I can't stand lizards – but the servants here, no matter what I say, they just don't care! No, you fool girl. I should knock some sense into your head. What good is giving me a glass of water without my powders?'

'Where are your powders, Lady Palin?'

'You should know! You servants with your nasty spying ways!'

Her sleeping powders were in the top drawer of the cabinet. There were several paper sachets inside a little glass bottle. 'Just one?'

'Bring the bottle to me, you stupid girl. You don't know what I need. They don't work like they should in this climate. And the damned mosquitoes are in the room again!'

'Shall I pull down the mosquito net?' The mosquito net, loosely knotted on its hoop above the bed, looked as though it had not been used for some time.

'Don't be ridiculous. I can't sleep under that ridiculous thing. I feel like I'm being smothered alive! Hurry up!'

I brought the bottle of powders across to the bed after pouring her a glass of water from the jug on the nightstand. I started to leave, but 'Stay with me until I fall asleep,' she said, again reminding me of Dee-Dee. 'Sit on that chair over there and talk to me.'

'Would you like me to read to you?'

'No. Just talk to me.'

But she was the one who talked.

I learned how Lady Palin had tried to prepare for her new life in Singapore. She had bought herself a little phrase book and learned phrases of Hindustani before coming out east and discovering Singapore was not part of India. When her Chinese and Malay servants did not understand her she suspected them of making fun of her and shouted at them, then cried, which of course confused them even more. She had always meant to have children of her own and still longed for them but Sir Henry had broken her heart, saying his two children were more than enough for him. She had not counted on dealing with an insolent stepson and a retarded stepdaughter. Charity Byrne had been supposed

OVIDIA YU

to help her and be a companion to her but Charity had made fun of her and encouraged the servants to do so too.

Lady Palin was one of those women whose minds seem to shrink as their hips and bellies swell. She had made it clear to me that she considered the admission of a local girl into her household on a par with the encroachment of cockroaches and other vermin. If I was sitting down – whether on the floor playing with Dee-Dee or at the table feeding her – when Lady Palin came into a room, she would stare at me, tapping her foot, until I stood up and apologized for being in her way. This was new to me because in my grandmother's household the servants were expected to carry on with their work when family members were present. But once I saw that all she wanted was acknowledgement, there was no problem. She needed to feel superior to someone, and since I was happy to be that someone, she had started to pop up wherever I happened to be with Dee-Dee.

If only Lady Palin had had other white women to listen to her righteous grievances and distract her with gossip, she would never have talked to me. But at present she was a pariah within the European community, which she affected to despise because they did not give her the respect she felt was due to the wife of Sir Henry Palin, so she suffered unheard, though not in silence.

'That girl called me names behind my back. She thought I didn't know but I'm not as stupid as they think. I got it out of that idiot child. And I have trouble with my knees. I know it's because of the climate but all those fool doctors say a hot, humid climate is probably better for me than a cold humid one, and I know they're laughing at me too. Me, a helpless woman alone out here!'

Harry had not helped matters by regularly pointing out that the amount of weight she had put on since coming to Singapore had probably damaged her knees.

'I should go and check on Dee-Dee. Can I fetch you anything else?' Lady Palin's was the largest room upstairs, and there was an old photograph of King George V in a British Army field marshal's uniform above the wide, lonely bed where she slept alone.

'Another glass of water. Fill it and put it by my bed.'

'Good night, Lady Palin.' I saw her reaching for her sleeping powders as I left the room, closing the door gently behind me – and jumped. 'Oh! You startled me!'

The dark figure peeled away from the wall just beyond the door at which I suspected it had been leaning and listening. It was Harry Palin. There was an intense look in his eyes, very different from his usual sneer.

'Were you listening?'

'What were you doing in there? With her?' The look in his eyes frightened me. For a moment I thought I might scream, but couldn't find my voice.

'Miss Chen?' Miss Nessa appeared at the end of the corridor. 'I was looking for you. May I have a word?' She looked coldly at Harry, who turned and walked away without a word. Normally Miss Nessa would have told him off for his manners, but she wasn't her normal self that night either.

'Oh, Miss Nessa!' I was so relieved to see her that my knees almost gave way beneath me.

'What did Harry want with you?'

'I don't know. I heard Lady Palin calling so I went to get her some water and when I came out Harry was there.'

Miss Nessa stared at Poor Mary's closed door and I saw venom in her eyes, 'You should go back to your room.'

She walked there with me and, by way of changing the subject, asked me what Le Froy was doing, and why he wanted to come over with more questions on Monday. When I told her I had no idea, she wanted me to tell her exactly what Le Froy had asked me in town and what I had told him. Had he seemed interested in anything or anyone in particular?

'You should learn to be more observant, girl. You can hardly expect me to believe the man showed as much interest in Deborah as in what Sir Henry has been doing . . . or myself, for that matter.'

'I did think he seemed to be more interested in you,' I said honestly, but half teasing.

Miss Nessa looked disbelieving. 'He said so? That he suspects me of some foul play? He is a confoundedly silly man!'

'Oh, no. I meant . . . in the way men are interested in women who are out of their reach. I'm sure he would never do anything to embarrass you. It's just that he kept saying you were sensible, not emotional like most other women.'

I felt bad for clumsily adding to the score against Le Froy. 'But I think he really wants to talk to the men here.'

'What? Why?'

I did not answer her. I knew that Miss Nessa was aware Charity had been pregnant when she died, but with all that was on her mind it was not surprising she did not immediately make the connection with Le Froy's inquiries. I saw the wince of pain on her face when she realised. Miss Nessa patted my shoulder and left the room without saying good night.

Another look into Dee-Dee's room showed her still fast asleep. Just as Lady Palin was, I hoped. It was sad that she and Dee-Dee were estranged despite living in such close quarters. In a poorer household, they would either have bonded or killed each other by now and perhaps either situation would have been preferable to this endless stalemate.

Dead Mary

◆

'I cannot make Lady Palin wake up,' Tanis, the houseboy, said, looking stubbornly dutiful. 'I must go and empty rubbish but she is inside. She locked the door and won't open.'

It was Cookie who, stony-faced, had brought the houseboy to the dining room. Miss Nessa had managed to persuade him to come back to work with assurances that he was not dismissed and, regardless of whatever Lady Palin might say, they had no plans to leave Singapore with or without him. But Cookie was still angry with Lady Palin and determined not to let her interfere with household routines.

It was almost noon by the time Tanis's complaint came to Miss Nessa's attention. In the damp heat of Singapore, rubbish bins and chamber pots had to be emptied daily as a matter of hygiene. No one had made anything of Lady Palin's absence at the breakfast table. Things were in such upheaval it was perhaps more surprising that everyone else was still present. Instead of going over to Government House that morning, Sir Henry and Miss Nessa had remained in the dining room, conversing in low, urgent tones since breakfast. And, because her father was there, Dee-Dee had insisted on staying too, with Harry and me to keep her from distracting them.

'I'll go and rouse her!' Harry headed towards the stairs. Dee-Dee shrieked with delight and leaped after him. Whatever mood Lady Palin woke in, those two would make it worse.

'I'll let you know when it's safe to go in and clean,' I told the houseboy, gathering and stacking Dee-Dee's colouring books and crayons before following them. 'Thank you, Cookie.' He nodded, and Tanis grinned, knowing he would not be scolded for sounding the alarm.

Sir Henry was still speaking to Miss Nessa, his finger repeatedly stabbing a point on the table, but her eyes were on the doorway Harry and Dee-Dee had just gone through. I suspected that her mind was on Lady Palin.

Upstairs, Poor Mary's bedroom door was still locked. After knocking and calling, with enthusiastic assistance from Dee-Dee, Harry tried to kick it in but failed, hurting his ankle. By this time the commotion had drawn the others. Miss Nessa summoned Cookie and Sihat, the gardener, and between them they broke down the door. As soon as I sniffed decay in the air, I knew something was very wrong.

Harry swore. There had been no love lost between him and his late stepmother – everyone knew that – but I could tell he was sincere. This was not something that should have happened, in Hell or anywhere else.

'Get Deborah out of here,' Miss Nessa said, 'and tell Sir Henry to come up – no, tell Sir Henry to call the police. Or you can get hold of that Le Froy fellow. Tell him to come at once, and to come himself, not send his minions. What are you waiting for? Harry, don't touch her! Go and get your father!'

It was not like Miss Nessa to become flustered but I could see why she had. Lady Palin was lying half on and half off the bed. It looked as though she had tried to get up then changed her mind and turned back towards the bed where she had fallen. There was vomit on the floor, and the smell in the room, with the stains on her nightdress, indicated that she had lost control of her bladder and bowels.

Tanis gave a little moaning squeal and fled. Cookie and Sihat stood as though awaiting instructions. Cookie, for all his confrontations with his mistress, looked as though he was going to be sick.

'Come on, Dee-Dee,' I said.

For once she came without a word.

———◆———

'It wasn't easy for her. She wasn't used to life out here,' Harry said. He looked unguarded for once and his face was grimly sober. 'It's different for us, I think. Being born out here is one thing. Or coming out because it's your life and your dream and you want to give it a go, like my parents did. But Mary came out as an adult and she hated it here. I'm not saying it was easy for my parents and Aunt Nessa, but at least they had a chance to learn the ropes together. And my parents loved each other, I'm sure that made a difference, just as Aunt Nessa loved her good works. Mary probably spent the last of her savings on her cheap, fancy London clothes, hoping to make a good impression, then found they no longer fitted after the voyage out. When she came down with dengue fever, she was sure she was dying but nobody took her seriously and nobody bothered to tell her all Europeans get it on arriving here. She was always yelling at poor Cookie, who's a good sort, but no cook likes to be yelled at because you've got nothing better to do. None of us tried to understand her problems and we blamed her bad temper on dhobi itch.'

'You were probably right about that,' Miss Nessa said wryly, joining us in the drawing room. 'I offered her some of the chemist's preparation I had left over from my own encounter. Poor Mary was so affronted, offended and insulted that I knew what I'd said had struck a nerve. Of course she refused it. She tried to do her own washing for a while after that but she couldn't get anything dry and didn't trust the houseboys to hang up her sheets for her and she couldn't do it herself. Poor Mary.'

'Poor Mary' was no longer a teasing nickname. It had become a fact.

She turned to me. 'Your inspector is upstairs now, poking about. I invited him to join us for tea here when he's finished. Make sure Cookie doesn't forget.'

'He's not my inspector,' I said, but when I went to order tea I asked Cookie for some sandwiches as well. I guessed Le Froy wouldn't have remembered his lunch. Come to think of it, none of us had eaten either. I was surprised Dee-Dee had not made a fuss, but she was dozing on the sofa with chocolate smears on her fingers and I suspected Harry had applied chocolate-biscuit treatment before heading upstairs to show the police where Poor Mary had been found.

We got through the rest of the day somehow. I can remember only parts of it, but a few points stand out. Cookie sent the houseboys up with tea and a generous supply of sandwiches, some filled with sardine and onion. Lady Palin had thought tinned sardines vulgar and raw onions disgusting, and I wondered if he had deliberately sent up something his late mistress would have objected to. Since she was not around to mind, where was the harm? Dee-Dee enjoyed her sandwiches and a tumbler of milk, and I couldn't help feeling that things would be simpler without her stepmother around.

Especially when Le Froy showed us the scrap of a letter he had found in her room. In her characteristically large, uneven handwriting it said, *God forgive me, I know what I am and I am guilty.*

'But at least this clears up everything else,' Sir Henry said. Ignoring the tea and sandwiches, he helped himself to whisky.

Le Froy accepted a cup of tea, put a sandwich on the saucer and promptly forgot them both. 'Her door was locked when you broke in? Where's the key?'

'It's open now. What does it matter where the confounded key is?' The strain showed in Miss Nessa's voice.

Le Froy persisted, sending his men back upstairs to search, and Miss Nessa had to go with them. It wouldn't have been decent for strange men to go through Lady Palin's room while she lay unchaperoned in a nightdress. Being dead was no excuse for impropriety. The key to the door was found in the little vanity box in Lady Palin's bedside drawer.

'You were the last person to see Lady Palin yesterday night?' Le Froy looked from me to Miss Nessa. 'Miss Palin, you confirm you saw Miss Chen leaving her room? Did you see or hear from Lady Palin after that?'

'I spoke to her this morning through the door,' Miss Nessa said. 'I just knocked and reminded her to take in her tray. It was on the stand by her door. It was a mushroom omelette and I knew if it got cold she would order another, making extra work for the kitchen.'

'Poor Mary likes making more work,' Harry said automatically. 'Sorry, I mean liked. Never mind. Ignore me.'

Le Froy did. 'What was on her tray when you found her?'

'The breakfast tray had been taken in and the toast was gone, but Mary did not seem to have touched her omelette or coffee. She must have had a bad night,' Miss Nessa said. 'She always had trouble sleeping. She must have taken another dose of her sleeping powders this morning. And if the dose from last night was still in her system . . . It was an accident, of course. No matter what her state of mind at the time, surely you can see that it must have been an accident.'

'And this morning she ate all her toast?'

'Why the—' Miss Nessa caught herself and started again. 'What difference does that make?'

'The entire family was in the house this morning. What if Lady Palin took her powders last evening, which would be the natural thing to do, and died during the night? Then any of you could have slipped into her room this morning to make certain she was dead and leave the suicide note. It is possible, no?'

'She was alive this morning,' Miss Nessa said coldly. 'We heard her voice through the door. She ate her toast.'

It was officially described as an accidental overdose. Lady Mary

Palin had died of an overdose of Veronal, which she had been
taking for insomnia. There was also a high level of alcohol in her
system, which made it difficult for tests to pinpoint the hour of
her death. But, given that she had responded to Miss Nessa and
taken in her breakfast tray, it was safe to assume she had woken,
eaten her toast, felt unwell and tried to go back to sleep with the
assistance of Veronal and whisky.

Of course, the gossip information system said Lady Palin had
been driven to commit suicide by the ghost of Charity Byrne,
who had returned to haunt her. It was proof, they claimed, that
she had murdered the girl. Even if the earthly court would not
condemn a white woman, there was no getting away from the
demon spirits of the unhappy dead.

There were indeed many demons in Poor Mary's room: a
profusion of pills and medicines in containers in her bedside
drawer, in a pill box in her handbag and more in her writing desk,
still in the brown-paper envelopes they had been collected in.
In addition to the sleeping pills and powders, there were laxatives
and purgatives.

———

'You're still not satisfied?' I said to Le Froy, after the body had
been taken away. 'I thought you'd be happy. This is much better
than having her arrested to stand trial . . .'

Le Froy had been looking out of the drawing-room window
directly below Lady Palin's bedroom, 'Was Lady Palin fond of
birds?'

'Birds? What do you mean? She ate chicken and turkey,'

'As in pigeons and crows. Did she feed them out of her window?' He pointed to where a few desultory birds were exploring the lawn.

'Oh, no. She hated them.' She had disliked sitting outdoors because she claimed birds deliberately relieved themselves on her. Harry had suggested that this might have been because she made the largest target.

'You're talking nonsense.' Miss Nessa said petulantly. 'Please get to the point or leave us to grieve. It has been a very traumatic day and my brother needs to rest.'

'My apologies. I really came to ask if any of you knew who was the father of the baby Miss Charity Byrne was carrying?'

Both men gaped. I got the impression that Harry Palin was trying to appear affronted without quite succeeding. Miss Nessa glanced sharply at me but I was relieved that she did not say anything.

'Are you sure? How could you know?' Harry Palin demanded.

Le Froy looked at him steadily but Harry's bravado held. 'We are certain,' Le Froy said. 'And we're looking for the father of her child.'

———◆———

It was with relief that I read Dee-Dee to sleep that night and returned to my room.

Out of habit I wedged the door handles on my room and Dee-Dee's. There seemed no real reason – Lady Palin, whom I had dreaded most in that house, was dead, and if her unhappy ghost decided to haunt the bungalow, blocked doors would not stop it. But the small action made me feel better. So many major upheavals were taking place all around me that my own little routines kept me anchored.

I did not know what time it was when I woke. The room was dark. The connecting door to Dee-Dee's room stood slightly ajar and I could hear the girl's regular breathing. I also heard what had woken me: the soft thud and scrape of the door handle against the dresser that blocked it. It released, then a slightly louder thud followed. I squinted eyes acclimatized to the darkness and saw the handle turn once more with greater force. But the bedside table was made of good solid wood and stood firm. A man – or woman – could have pushed it aside with little more effort than was required to turn the door handle but, working together, the handle and the table would keep out anyone trying to get in. I thought of Lady Palin coming back as a ghost and— But a ghost wouldn't worry about doors. It was a person. I thought of Harry and felt afraid.

'Hello—'

I couldn't identify the low, hoarse whisper. I couldn't even tell if it was a man or woman outside the door. I'm asleep, I told myself, willing whoever was lurking to believe it too. I'm asleep and I can't hear anything at all. I stayed motionless, measuring the time in shallow breaths. I couldn't tell when the would-be invader finally left, or when I fell asleep, but when Dee-Dee came to wake me it was daylight and there was no one outside either of our doors and no sign anyone had been there.

Calm After Storm

———◆———

'**P**eople do bad things and say it is bad luck.' Sihat the gardener stopped sweeping leaves off the driveway to let us pass. 'Next thing they will say, "Cut down the frangipani tree because got ghosts."'

'The frangipani trees are on Government House property,' Harry told him. 'They can't be cut down without official permission.' Sihat only spat (politely, away from us) and continued sweeping. The police vehicles and mortuary van had left tracks on the lawn where they spilled over from the driveway and he was in a bad mood.

'I don't understand what Poor Mary wanted,' Harry said. 'Sometimes she seemed pleasant enough. She picked up words and tried to like local food. I think she even tried to be nice in her way. But when it came to Charity, and they were in the same room, sparks would fly. They riled each other over and over again about the same things and they got upset over and over again too.'

'Some people find it very comforting to have set dialogues.

Repetition can be a game, like Dee-Dee wanting to hear the same stories even when she can recite them herself.'

'Like going to church,' Harry said. I saw what he meant.

'You think she killed Charity, don't you? And then killed herself.'

'What else?'

———◆———

Sir Henry and Miss Nessa were occupied with the police and official reports on what had happened. Thanks to my grandmother preparing me to run any household I might marry into, and Miss Johnson's Western-style domestic-science lessons, I managed to take over the supervision of the Palin servants and household without too much trouble. In fact, the floors were soon cleaner, the laundry more crisply starched and the meals better than they had been under the late Lady Palin's supervision and Miss Nessa seemed happy to leave things to me – to an extent that surprised me. Of course, Miss Nessa had her good works and Government House affairs to think about, but she seemed unusually preoccupied even when she was at home.

While I knew I did not want to spend the rest of my life managing a household, whether as mistress or servant, I found it surprisingly comforting to arrange and supervise a smoothly running system. It was how our colonial overlords felt, I supposed, as long as things ran smoothly.

I continued to look after Dee-Dee, who accompanied me down the back stairs to talk to Cookie and the servants about the day's tasks and what was to be ordered for meals. In all honesty, Cookie, who had been in Sir Henry's household the longest, functioned as unofficial housekeeper and was doing all the real work. My only real contribution was to approve all his plans and decisions. Lady Palin had tried to improve and educate Cookie in a mix of pidgin English and Malay phrases that Harry had written down phonetically for her ... and were full of vulgarities. Cookie, who spoke good basic English, having worked for several British masters in India before Sir Henry, had been offended and rejected her suggestions, leading to fights and cold food.

'It was all Dead Mary's doing, really,' Harry said. He had started following Dee-Dee and me around since his stepmother's death. Although he had an official position on his father's staff, no one seemed to object or even notice when he didn't appear at the office.

'Before she came here we had rice and curries and that sort of grub. Father and Nessa were always busy and never minded what was on the table, and Dee-Dee was too young to care, so it was pretty much up to Cookie, and he fed us whatever he liked. Good stuff too. When Mary came, she said she couldn't eat the food here, it made her sick – literally – and took over seeing to the meals. We went back to eating what she called proper food. Roast beef, roast mutton, roast chicken ... Cookie used to buy it from the Javanese meat sellers who came to the back of the house until one day Mary saw the whole bloody transaction and that was the end of that. She didn't know where the animals came from, she said. We couldn't eat that. Father told her we had been eating it for years but it was no good. From then on she ordered our meat from Cold Storage, guaranteed all the way from Australia.

Father says it was five times as old and tough and ten times as expensive!' With Lady Palin gone, Cookie chose his own meat and meals improved dramatically.

But there were other matters I could not leave to Cookie and the servants. Charity's things still had to be sorted, then given away or discarded, and now Lady Palin's things had to be gone through as well. Miss Nessa had glanced at her room in disdain and told me, 'Pack up her clothes and send them to the Mission. I'm sure they'll have use for the material. Give everything else to the gardener and tell him to burn it. Once all her things are cleared out, we'll see about getting the room in shape for Henry to move back in. Finally.'

While Lady Palin was alive, Nessa had strictly upheld the fiction that Sir Henry only slept in his office when there was enough work to keep him there all night.

'Won't you be wanting to keep some of her things?' I couldn't help asking. 'For Dee-Dee, perhaps. Or would her family want them?' Lady Palin had liked ordering goods from England, even things like underskirts and towels that could have been purchased more cheaply from India, and Dee-Dee had been scolded for showing too much interest in her stepmother's boxes. I supposed Miss Nessa might already have set aside what she considered worth keeping, but there were still so many good-quality items, some still in their original packaging and clearly never used.

'Mary had no family to speak of. Why else would she have ended up out here on her own, looking for a husband? And Dee-Dee? Of course not. Dee-Dee doesn't need anything. Oh, I'm sorry.' Miss Nessa pulled herself up short and looked at me apologetically, 'I didn't think of it. Of course you must take whatever you find useful. Or that your family might find useful.'

'Thank you.' I no longer even tried to explain that the Chen family did not need charity. Nor did I think about how horrified my grandmother would be at the idea of my taking a dead woman's leavings and all the bad luck that came with them. After all, Miss Nessa meant well, given her belief that all local girls were poor and desperate for hand-outs from rich white women. And, more importantly, I wanted to go through Charity's and Lady Palin's things and meant to take anything that might give me a clue of how their lives had led to such ends.

Miss Nessa also (finally) paid me for the time I had put in so far. 'From next month you'll get your wages at the end of the month when we settle the household accounts. But here is something to help you resolve any immediate needs.' And this despite all the upheaval she and her family were going through. I couldn't have asked for a more considerate employer, I thought.

The only time I had to sort and pack Lady Palin's things was during Dee-Dee's afternoon playtime by letting her play in her late stepmother's room. This suited me as well as Dee-Dee: the afternoons were getting too hot to play outdoors, even in the shade. Dee-Dee persisted in wanting to go back to her Government House playroom; she even said her father had told her to ask me to bring her over, but by then I was used to Dee-Dee's stories. She didn't set out to tell lies but she saw things the way she wanted them to be.

The still unemptied wastepaper basket by Lady Palin's bed was a glimpse into a pathetic, lonely existence. It was filled with discarded tissues and sweet wrappers. She must have spent her evenings alone crying and eating sweets. Her greed and loneliness reminded me of Dee-Dee. If only they had got on, things might have turned out very differently.

As I sorted, it struck me as curious that Mary Palin had no recent papers or any receipts from the start of the year. That was six and a half months undocumented, though she seemed to have kept everything scrupulously until then. She had been something of a hoarder, I thought. The sort who kept everything 'just in case', then forgot about it or couldn't find it if a need for it arose. The cupboards in her room were stuffed with old newspapers, bed sheets and pretty dresses – far too small for the size she had been in her last days. But her habits were not my problem. What I wanted to know was what had happened to her missing documents. Even the receipts from recent purchases I knew she had made were missing. Had someone taken them? It seemed such a ridiculously trivial matter but it bothered me. Years of going through my grandmother's accounts had made me particular about such discrepancies. Chief Inspector Le Froy had asked me to pass on anything odd I noticed, no matter how trivial . . . but surely this was too trivial even for that. To tell the truth, I suspected Dee-Dee might have had something to do with it. Dee-Dee often made off with things that caught her fancy, but they were usually shiny or pretty things. She had never shown much interest in paper.

I'd think about it, I decided. There was no hurry, after all. The papers and receipts might turn up. Le Froy's men might have taken them, the better to trace Lady Palin's movements before her death. Then again, if the papers did not turn up they would still be missing later, if I decided to mention it to Le Froy.

Something was troubling me, though: even if Lady Palin had been someone who would kill herself, she would not have done so just when she thought she was on her way home to England – just when she thought she had won.

There was one other small thing. Her rattan laundry hamper behind its modesty curtain appeared empty, but I ran my hand around it, a habit that came from years of accounting for handkerchiefs and other small items that girls were always losing in the laundry, and was rewarded with a scrap of paper caught in the woven cane. It was filmy waxed brown paper with traces of red markings from the sales chop, and resembled the packaging used by local grocers and market stalls. I would not have looked at it twice if I had come across it in the kitchen or storeroom. But what would something like that be doing in a white woman's bedroom? There were white patches on the paper, thanks to Singapore's ever-present damp. Whatever it was had been left in its wrapper for some time. I scraped at it with my fingernail. It did not feel like soap or talcum powder, as I had expected, and I automatically touched it to my tongue, thinking a moment too late of sleeping powders and poisons – but by then I knew what it was. Baking soda? Not just baking soda: a strange mix of baking soda and tapioca powder.

Tapioca powder was used in local kitchens as a thickener for curries and gravies. Tapioca cost about two cents per *kati* in the market but most people grew their own or cut down wild plants so it was a cheap ingredient. But I couldn't think of any reason why it would be mixed with baking soda.

'What are you doing?'

I jumped.

Dee-Dee pushed in beside me and peered into the hamper. 'It wasn't me. I never put anything in there!' I knew Dee-Dee well enough now to understand that that was exactly what she had done.

'So where did you put them?'

Dee-Dee's cache was in a shoebox under the cabinet beneath the back staircase. In it I found Lady Palin's penholder, several lipsticks and several pieces of costume jewellery . . . and a sticky melted toffee. But there were no papers.

'It's all here,' Dee-Dee said, looking at me out of the sides of her eyes. 'I swear, cross my heart and hope to die, stick a needle in my eye!' She squeezed them tightly shut in a gesture I had come to know all too well.

'Where did you put everything else you took from Lady Mary's room?'

Dee-Dee's Playroom

◆

Despite the shock of a second death, there was a definite air of relief in the house on Frangipani Hill. Sympathizers and well-wishers invaded the Residence on Thursday evenings and Saturday afternoons while official condolence notes flooded into Government House. I got the feeling that most people thought Sir Henry would be better off for having lost a second wife.

'Some men just don't marry well,' I heard a woman say to her female companion as they left. 'The more they need a good wife, the less they know about finding one.'

'Well, maybe he'll choose more wisely the next time,' the companion responded.

They were respectable-looking women of about Sir Henry's age, but as *ang moh* men tended to marry women much younger than themselves, I didn't think either of them stood much of a chance.

I had seen Le Froy on the fringe of the strangers who crowded into the Residence but had not spoken to him. He seemed to be studying the house, pacing corridors, looking out of windows – at the tree through which Charity had fallen to her death, at the bushes beneath Lady Palin's windows, now devoid of birds – and ignoring the people who eyed him and whispered.

Dee-Dee was highly excited by all the activity. She was not afraid of the strangers but wanted to talk to them and show off her reading skills to them. Sadly, most were not comfortable with her. If only she had been child-sized, they would have found her charming. Alternatively, without her childish mannerisms, they would have found her beautiful. But, given the unfamiliar juxta-position, they found her disconcerting.

Lunch that Saturday was mutton curry and a range of other dishes and cakes contributed by visitors. Overexcited, Dee-Dee would not try the unfamiliar food and, though she insisted she was not hungry, I made egg sandwiches for us. But there was the matter of where I could get Dee-Dee to sit and calm down enough to eat.

It was too hot outside, and too hot in her room, even if I could have persuaded my large charge to stay up there with so much excitement going on outside. Every time she heard footsteps in the corridor Dee-Dee dashed to the door to see who it was and tell them what she knew of events. And, with her room across the stairwell from the bedroom where her stepmother had been laid out, there were many pairs of footsteps. Not to mention inquisitive noses that rudely pushed through the door, their 'Beg pardon, I thought it was the Necessary' deceiving no one.

I decided that, despite the heat, it was important to get Dee-Dee out of the house before she worked herself into a full-blown tantrum.

'Shall we go out?'

'No! I want to go to Mary's room – everybody's in there. I want to go there too!'

'Let's explore outside the house today. Somewhere secret where nobody else is.'

Dee-Dee thought about it. 'Then I want to go to my playroom. Over in Papa's office.'

'But there are people working in there now.' I thought of the little play area I had created with standing screens in a corner of the drawing room. There were cushions and dolls and picture books to keep Dee-Dee quietly entertained. 'We can go downstairs and play colouring stories.'

'Not downstairs, silly Su! I want to go to my secret playroom in Papa's office. Come on, I'll show you!' I hesitated until she said, 'I'll show you my other secret things that I borrowed!'

It couldn't hurt, I thought. Sir Henry and his staff were in the Residence, accepting condolences. There wouldn't be any work going on in Government House.

We followed the path Sir Henry used daily and went into Government House through the back door, which was unlocked. The few people we met were occupied with their own business. They obviously recognized Dee-Dee and either nodded subdued greetings or ignored us. No one smiled. The governor's wife was dead, and they were all in mourning, though no one seemed to know what form the mourning should take. So, they nodded and let the pair of us through, but without the diplomatic smiles they would normally have been wearing.

I was unfamiliar with the official building but Dee-Dee clearly knew where she was going and pulled me along.

'Your papa's not in his office, sweetheart,' said an administrator, who had thrown a token black scarf around his neck despite the heat, as Dee-Dee confidently pushed open the door into the antechamber where his desk stood.

'I know. I'm going to my playroom.' Dee-Dee strode on without slowing.

'I'm sorry – is it all right?' I thought about state secrets but the young man just waved me on and turned back to his illustrated magazine.

Inside Sir Henry's private office, his polished-wood desk was bare, in sharp contrast to the piles of papers and stacks of folders on his clerk's desk outside. It was a large, comfortably furnished room with a round of upright chairs around the desk, an upholstered sofa and armchairs making up a conversation corner by the windows. It was also dark, because the heavy curtains were drawn. I guessed that was a sign of mourning, much as local people would have covered all the mirrors.

'Come *on*, slowcoach Su!' Dee-Dee pulled me impatiently towards a door set in the wall behind Sir Henry's desk.

Dee-Dee's playroom had probably been intended for storage. There were no windows and it smelt musty. A small mattress laid over a steamer trunk covered half of the bare concrete floor space. Dee-Dee's past presence there was obvious in a child's tea set and a pile of sweets that Dee-Dee fell on with cries of delight.

'Wait! Let me see them first.' Things could go bad so quickly in the damp heat, and Dee-Dee was less than discriminating. There was an open 3 Musketeers packet with only the strawberry and vanilla pieces left – Dee-Dee favoured chocolate – a Nestlé Baby Ruth bar, some Sugar Babies and violet creams. Apart from the leaking Musketeers, which I quietly secreted in my palm, the rest seemed safe enough and Dee-Dee was soon happily absorbed in arranging them on her tea set.

I heard voices in the outer office. Official visitors? Worried, I pushed the door open a crack and was relieved to see Sir Henry coming into the room with Miss Nessa.

'Didn't I tell you not to be so reckless? Didn't I warn you? You fool! You unutterable fool!' She slammed the door behind her even as she spoke. I was shocked. I had never seen Miss Nessa so uncontrolled. I had seen her angry before, but it had always been for good reason. Certainly I had never seen her angry with her brother, to whom she always spoke with respect even though he was her brother. I might have gasped because Miss Nessa's eyes whipped round and she saw me.

'You! What on earth are you doing in there?'

'Precious Papa!' Pushing past me, Dee-Dee bounded out of her playroom, answering the question. 'Look, precious Papa, look, Aunt Nessa, I found my sweeties! I'm having teatime with my sweeties! You must come for tea!'

'You had no right to bring Deborah here. This is a place of work, an office.' Miss Nessa spoke with her usual controlled dignity. Could I have imagined the wild accusing note in her voice a moment ago? Even if I had, I could not have imagined those harsh words!

'I'm sorry,' I said. 'I wanted to get her away from the house for a while. There were so many people and she was overexcited.'

'Good idea!' Sir Henry said heartily. He was clearly glad of the distraction. He put an arm around Dee-Dee's waist and meant to keep her with him. 'Right thing to do. Dee-Dee, if you'd like a bottle of pop, go and ask Malcolm to get you one from the pantry.'

'For goodness' sake, Henry, Malcolm is your secretary, not your houseboy!' Even that was out of character for Miss Nessa, I thought. I had never heard her telling off Sir Henry before. Either she was now comfortable enough with me to speak openly in front of me or Lady Palin's death had shocked her out of her usual composure. Either way, I made sure to keep very quiet.

'You should think about coming here to help me in the office,' Sir Henry said to me. 'You're one of those educated girls, they tell me. You can keep books and use a typewriting machine? That's more than that fool out there can do. He fusses over the thing like a baby and every letter takes half a dozen tries. This is where the real work gets done and there's never enough people to do it.'

It was as though Sir Henry had looked into my heart and seen my most secret dream. I could indeed use a typewriting machine, having taught myself using the Royal Portable typewriter in the Mission office. I had been doing most of Miss Johnson's typing by the time I left (how was poor Miss Johnson managing with her short-sighted two-finger typing now, I wondered). It was part of my Henrietta Stackpole lady-reporter dream.

'Su Lin has enough on her hands,' Miss Nessa answered for me. Perhaps to make up for her earlier harsh words she added, 'You are doing a very good job with teaching Deborah. We may find a way to make a teacher out of you yet! Unless, of course, you decide to stay with Deborah. Yes, that would work out very nicely for both of you.' Miss Nessa smiled at me in a way that I could see she intended to be encouraging.

Miss Johnson or possibly Miss Blackmore must have spoken to Miss Nessa about my getting a teaching certificate. I smiled and tried to look grateful. They meant to be kind. What right did I have to tell them, in the middle of their family bereavement, that I didn't want to spend my life as a school teacher or as Dee-Dee's paid companion? Reminding myself that reporters had to blend in to their environments quietly, I kept my mouth shut.

'If you really need help here in the office you should get young Harry in to do something useful.' Miss Nessa had not waited for a reply from me. 'He's on the payroll and he should be earning his keep.'

'You're the one who told me to put him on the payroll.'

'I told you to give him something to do! Wandering around with a camera isn't any kind of work!'

'Here we are . . .' Dee-Dee sang out, returning with two bottles of Fraser and Neave lemonade. They were cold and must have been stored in the refrigerator for just such occasions. Sir Henry produced glasses.

'To Mary,' Sir Henry toasted.

Dee-Dee echoed in a shriek of delight, 'To Mary! Dead Mary!'

A Memorial Service

◆

That Sunday, a memorial service was held for Lady Palin. Or, rather, the pastor mentioned the unpredictability of life in general and Lady Palin's brief stay on earth and in Singapore as part of the regular service. I was glad I'd found an old dark-blue, almost black frock for Dee-Dee and managed to let it down in time for her to wear it to church. Lady Palin's body was still with the police and Sir Henry had said there would be no public funeral service.

As I waited for the family outside the church, some of the town's tradespeople came to speak to me. They had not attended the service but had hung about to catch the Palins afterwards. It was not just from sentiment: several asked me to mention that they had not yet received payment for goods Lady Palin had bought in her last days. Some she had already collected but most were being packed for her to take back to England. They did not want to trouble the bereaved family but this was Singapore and money was money.

I agreed to bring it to Miss Nessa's attention but decided not to speak to her immediately. It was Sunday, after all. Not a day to worry about debts and bills.

'Please let's go to the sea front!' Dee-Dee had behaved very well, sitting quietly through the service.

'I don't see why not,' Sir Henry said, to Dee-Dee's delight. 'We're going for a little walk,' he called to Miss Nessa, who was still caught up in a group of what Harry called her good-works ladies. Harry, also on his best behaviour, tucked his sister's hand into his arm as we walked.

I loved the waterfront but had not been there for some time and the place was always changing. Now with the almost-new Ocean Building standing on Collyer Quay the whole look of the area had changed. Steamships had done for sea travel what trains had done for overland journeys, and the place was bustling with energy and people. Human beings could now cross the seas at will, without having to wait for favourable winds. It was all modern and efficient, but sometimes I found myself wondering whether the improvements were all for the good. My grandmother told me that in the old days, when certain winds were needed to bring ships from certain ports, the different seasons brought different cargos as surely as the rains brought different crops. In those days, a rhythm and an order bound people to the earth and water they depended on, but with modern steam engines we had lost that connection.

We paused in front of the Ocean Building. The enormous five-storey building was a tribute to modern Singapore: a combination of European and native investors running more than fifty ships. I encouraged Dee-Dee to try to spot ships' flags and identify the different countries they came from, but she quickly

grew bored and ran off to chase birds. I started to limp after her
but– 'I'll go!' Harry ran after his sister.

'Singapore is worth a lot more than people back home give
it credit for,' Sir Henry observed, his attention on the sea front.
'Back in England, in Europe, people are going crazy, I tell you.
Everything new is the magic pill to solve all problems. Out here
we've kept to the old ways, the old standards, things that matter.
That's why it's places like this that will anchor us when Europe
starts cracking at the seams.'

'Do you think there's going to be another war, sir?'

'Don't worry your pretty little head about that. There's a good
deal in the new Germany that's fine and great. Your prim and
proper missionary misses have got you thinking Germans are all
barbaric anti-Semites but, really, Hitler and his Nazi troops are
all that stand between Communism and the rest of us. The sooner
we accept that the better.'

Dee-Dee returned to us, cutting short Sir Henry's political
statement, and together we watched as Harry made his way down
the slippery iron steps to examine the stones and fish more
closely. From where we stood on Johnstones' Pier, I longed to
follow him down to the water's edge, my limp be damned.
I remembered sliding down those large smooth stones on my
bottom as a child – and suddenly I missed the girl I had once
been who hadn't yet known enough to see herself as Chinese or
crippled. I had to steady myself by telling Dee-Dee the stones
were dangerous and she might slip and wet her dress in the water,
though she had given no sign of wanting to follow her brother.
It was a beautiful day. The Brahminy kites were soaring and
calling high in the blue sky above, and the water below was so

clear that the sunlight glinting off seabed stones and dark darting fish shone and gleamed with every nuance of colour. The deep, warm, clear sea sustained Singapore. Standing before it that morning I felt capable of tackling anything, even hopping onto one of those ships and heading off into the whole mysterious 'rest of the world'. But would anything be really different there? For a moment all the beauty was no more than a shell for the trade and exploitation all those ships represented. Money and power: those were what everyone was after, whether they were aware of it or not. Even the selfless ladies at the Mission, in teaching young girls to read and write English rather than themselves learning Chinese, Tamil or Malay, were strengthening their hold over us.

But I stayed. I had put my arm around Dee-Dee's waist and Dee-Dee, uncharacteristically quiet, was holding my hand at her side. Dee-Dee's father and brother strolled away along the sea front and lit cigarettes. I could do good here: I could spend a little more time with this lonely not-so-little girl. After all, I knew only too well what it was like to be a motherless child in a house full of adults preoccupied with everything except you.

'Do you like it out here?'

Dee-Dee nodded so vigorously that I suspected today's excursion had come with the promise of good behaviour.

'Why do you like it?'

Dee-Dee looked around for an answer then, leaning closer, whispered, 'Aunt Mary didn't like the sea. That's why we couldn't come here when she was alive. And that's why I love the sea!'

I had to laugh. Her large trusting fingers grasping mine as she leaned against me made me feel old and wise simply for having lived longer and loved the sea longer. There is no place in Singapore more than a few miles from the nearest coast and true Singaporeans, whether born or adopted, feel most at ease within sight and smell of seawater. Perhaps Dee-Dee Palin was meant to stay on this island, after all.

But even then there were signs that our gentle sea could no longer ameliorate all ills. Although mass-transport steamships and mass-production factories made the island look prosperous, the number of men who had to resort to fishing to feed their families had increased. Even here around the main port there were a few dark men trying to look invisible over their lines and nets. If they were noticed they would be made to move, but they would return. Europeans who fished only for sport did not approve of men who fished for food, but hunger overruled colonial authority.

'I want an ice ball!' Dee-Dee demanded, pointing at a group of youngsters crowded around a hawker with an ice grater.

I started to say no, 'Foreigners don't eat ice balls,' but she had already dragged Sir Henry away for a closer look. I decided I wasn't responsible for what she ate when she was in her father's care, although I was the one who would have to wash her clothes and deal with any digestive upsets.

'I don't think you have any right to call us foreigners,' Harry said, in mock aggression. 'Look at me, for instance. I was born in Malaya. I've lived in Malaya for most of my life. If you think about where people come from, I'm as Malayan as you are. And if you say I'm not because of the colour of my skin then you are the one practising immigration restrictions!' Harry spoke in his usual light drawl, but I sensed there was more to it.

'Why would you want to be Malayan? Here you British are the ruling class.' I was careful to keep my tone light, too. I had no reason to pick a fight with him just when he was starting to be pleasant to me.

'I didn't say I wanted to be Malayan, just that if you disregard race and skin colour, what is there to distinguish someone like me from someone like you? Granted, I live in a nice house and there are servants to do the cooking but I don't think your family lives in the slums either. So what's the real difference?'

'That your stomachs aren't used to street food.'

'That's just a matter of hygiene,' Harry said.

'I eat it and I'm alive.'

'That's different.'

'Different how? You mean as in a different species, something that doesn't harm dogs and natives might give you a stomach-ache?'

'There's something in that, as the monkey said when he put his paw in the *jamban*.' '*Jamban*' was the local word for lavatory and Harry threw it in casually. But his grin said, 'Truce?' and I smiled to say, 'Yes.'

Harry Palin was bright enough. But our teachers at the Mission would have said that, without commitment and motivation, he had nothing to harness his cleverness to.

'The British have nothing to be proud of here,' Harry said flatly, 'unless the God who put this island at this spot with its natural deep-water harbour was British, and I seriously doubt that.'

Sir Henry returned to join us. He had somehow distracted Dee-Dee from ice balls and she ran over to take my hand. 'I saw fire ants!' she said importantly. 'Walking in a row.' She grabbed Harry with her other hand and started swinging her arms, holding on to me and her brother so we were swinging along with her. I felt sure there was some impropriety to this but could not resist the sea air and the child-woman's sheer joy in the movement.

Even Miss Nessa, finally spotting and coming over to join us, laughed at the sight. It was as though Lady Palin's death had lifted a huge burden off the whole family.

Bills and Accountings

◆

T hat evening I told Miss Nessa about the bills that the trades-
people in town had said were unpaid. It seemed Lady Palin
had ordered dresses and bales of furnishing materials from India;
they had been neither collected nor paid for. I had searched
unsuccessfully for the bills, but I was sure the tradesmen were
not trying to defraud a dead woman.

Then, when Miss Nessa came into Dee-Dee's room after
dinner, I had the perfect opportunity to ask about Lady Palin's
missing papers. 'I couldn't find any receipts or order slips in Lady
Palin's account books – in fact, I couldn't even find the account
books for the past few months.'

'Just pay them,' Miss Nessa said, to my surprise. 'We can't have
labourers not paid for their hire. Mary was so irresponsible. But
I suppose she had no way of knowing what was coming to her.
None of us has any way of knowing, do we?'

If Lady Palin had killed herself, she would certainly have
known death was coming, I thought, but the family's official stand
on the matter was that her death had been an accident and Miss

Nessa clearly meant to stick to that. I was coming to admire her more and more. Although she and Lady Palin had not been close, I could see from the strain in her face, her knotted shoulders and trembling hands, that her sister-in-law's death had struck her hard. I was going to tell her the amounts owed but before I could begin she distracted me: 'Oh, Inspector Le Froy wants to see you at his office tomorrow.'

'Me? What about?'

'He didn't say. He was looking for you outside the church but you had already gone off with Dee-Dee. I told him I would let you know. I will give you some money and you can go into town tomorrow and pay these people before you see him. Make sure they give you receipts. Tell them they can do what they want with the clothes and materials and see whether you can get them to discount the prices to cost. You can go after Deborah's breakfast. Bring her to me and I'll keep an eye on her . . . just when I have so many things to see to . . .'

'I can leave her with Cookie, or Sir Henry can take her to his office in Government House. Dee-Dee says Charity used to take her there all the time.'

Miss Nessa clearly didn't like the suggestion. 'It's about time Deborah learned to occupy herself. Make sure you bring her to me before you leave.'

The next morning Miss Nessa gave me the money for the trades-people. I was impressed by how close the amount was to the sum owed. She misread my expression and smiled wryly. 'Yes, it's a lot of money. You have no idea what Mary could get up to when she set her mind on making trouble. Take it all just in case. You can bring the change back. Buy Deborah something in town, if you like.'

At least Miss Nessa hadn't been difficult about the money, I thought. I wished I could have taken Dee-Dee with me. She liked going out. Being kept at home all day every day was as frustrating for her as it would have been for any seven-year-old, no matter how large the house and garden of her captivity. But I would be dealing with strangers and, given her size, it was not easy for strangers to understand her. It could also be very awkward because, physically, Dee-Dee Palin was a beautiful seven-teen-year-old with no qualms about lifting her skirts on the main street to scratch her bottom, if she felt like it.

I could not help wondering how Miss Nessa had estimated the amount of money owed so accurately. Had she really been able to work it out just from looking at what Lady Palin had brought home? But Lady Palin had not collected most of her purchases. Perhaps Miss Nessa had taken her papers?

If I had known that Sir Henry was going to town that day to see Chief Inspector Le Froy, I might have asked Miss Nessa if he would offer me a lift into town. It was considered quite proper for us to travel together, as long as I sat in front with the driver. But then again, I wasn't sure he would approve of my appointment to see Le Froy before I paid Lady Palin's debts.

———◆———

In many ways, social customs and conventions in Singapore were still antiquated. If anything, the propriety of the British ruling class was more unassailably superior on our tiny island than it was back in Britain. And in no one was this more so than in Acting Governor Sir Henry Palin.

It came as a great surprise to Le Froy when one of the junior officers put his head round the door and said that Sir Henry Palin wanted to see him urgently. Indeed, there was no doubt of Sir Henry's urgency or impatience as he appeared, pushing past his herald with a smile fixed on his face and his eyes fixed on Le Froy. 'Thought it was time I dropped by, just to see how things are going, eh.'

'Sir, your appointment is here . . .' The junior officer reappeared hesitantly.

'Not now, man. Tell whomever it is they will have to wait. We're handling important government matters here,' Sir Henry said, without turning. 'Tell them to come back another day.'

Le Froy snapped, 'Wait!' with uncharacteristic abruptness. Sir Henry looked surprised. The chief inspector appeared both tense and resigned, like a man bracing himself for a fight he didn't want to take on. 'Please ask them to wait. In the side room. What you have to say will not take long, Sir Henry. Or should I tell my officers to add a meeting between us to the schedule?'

'Of course not. This is just a friendly chat, eh? You can go now, my man.'

Sir Henry noticed the junior officer waited until Le Froy's nod dismissed him before he left. It was nothing short of insubordination, and the man was lucky that Sir Henry was not petty enough to make an issue of it. Although he would certainly mention it to Nessa, who was much more rigorous on punishing such breaches of etiquette.

'My condolences for your loss,' Le Froy said formally. 'Won't you have a seat?' He remained standing, a reminder that he had an appointment waiting.

'What? Oh, yes, certainly. Thank you. This is an unfortunate situation, very unfortunate. However, we must thank Providence that things turned out as they did. What measures have you taken to control the information?'

This appeared to be Sir Henry's standard response to tragedy.

'There is little information to control,' Le Froy answered as he had done previously, 'and there will be speculation and gossip.'

'It is my responsibility,' Sir Henry said again, 'to see this does not reflect badly on the Colonial office here. The best thing would be to treat it as an accident. My wife was unwell. While distraught by her inability to sleep, she accidentally took an overdose of her sleeping powders. In the opinion of the governor's office that is all that it is necessary to say.'

'And the first death at your house? The Irish nanny?'

'Precisely. Don't you see? There is no point in pursuing justice when justice has already been served in the most basic sense. An eye for an eye, a life for a life.'

'Are you saying you believe your late wife pushed Charity Byrne to her death, then killed herself out of guilt?' Inspector Le Froy's face wore a mask of exaggerated reasonable calm. His men knew this look well and the junior officers positioned just outside the not-quite-closed door were torn between the thrill of watching an impending storm build and heading for cover.

'I'm saying, what good will any further investigation do? If anything could help that unfortunate girl or my unhappy wife, I would be the first to encourage it. But now it is the living we must be concerned with.'

'All of your family, your servants and the doctor were witnesses. All their statements are on record.'

'Don't worry about my family and the doctor. They'll stand up all right. And as for the servants, those natives don't know what's going on. They'll say whatever they're paid to say. In fact, you should have a word with them before those damned reporters and Communists do. What we have to do now is keep everyone calm. There's no point in spreading panic and alarm around people who can't do anything about it.'

Chief Inspector Le Froy walked to the door and held it open for his uninvited guest without a word. Sir Henry left, but not without an envious glance at the three police officers standing at strict attention on either side of Le Froy's door. How did the wretched little man command such absolute obedience? He did not see his daughter's local nanny watching from the slightly open door of the small side room, partly blocked by the policeman who had snapped to attention in front of it.

Le Froy's Questions

———◆———

'I want to ask you some questions.'

'You don't think I killed Lady Palin, do you?' I was quite certain he didn't, but as with adding salt to soup, it is always better to stick your tongue out to taste the mix sooner rather than later.

Le Froy seemed amused by my response. 'No. But I would like to know what you think of this.' He took a letter out of a folder on his desk and handed it to me. It was neatly typed on plain bond paper: *Immoral slut, I have evidence of your shameful adultery. Terrible things will happen to you if you do not leave the island immediately.*

'Where did you get this? Who sent it to you?'

'It was sent to Charity Byrne.'

Charity, who was now dead.

'But who sent it to her?'

'We don't know. That's why it's called an anonymous letter. She thought it was quite a joke. She showed it to Sir Henry, who laughed at it. But, as Miss Palin quite rightly pointed out, all threats to the governor's household should be reported to the police, so she brought it to the station and it was recorded and filed away.'

'The police didn't take it seriously either?'

'The only person who seemed to take the letter seriously was Lady Palin.' He took back the letter. 'She pressed her husband to replace Charity to avoid any further trouble.'

I thought about Poor Mary. 'You really have no idea who wrote this?'

'The letter was typed, not written. No doubt an attempt to disguise handwriting. However, typewriters have their idiosyncrasies. See how the lower-case *e* here is slightly out of line? And the capital T is slightly tilted? Sir Henry made it possible for us to examine the typewriting machines in Government House and the governor's Residence and we discovered this letter was most likely typed on the machine on the work desk in Miss Vanessa Palin's bedroom.'

'Miss Nessa would never do such a thing!' I saw Le Froy's eyebrows rise at my quick response.

'We discussed it with Miss Palin. She made it clear that anyone in the household could have gone into her room and used the typewriter. She spends most of the day in town or in Government House and her door is never locked.'

'Harry might have done it as a joke. But he would have confessed if he'd known Charity had shown it to the police.'

'Miss Nessa and Miss Charity Byrne seemed to think it might have been written by Lady Palin.'

I thought about this. She had been concerned principally with ladylike behaviour and etiquette, and nothing could have been further from either than sending spiteful anonymous letters. But she had hated Charity . . .

'You're not leaping to Lady Palin's defence?'

'She might have written it. I don't think she meant it. She probably just wanted to spite Charity. I think she believed Charity was turning people against her.'

'Was she?'

'I doubt it. At least, not in the way Lady Palin thought. I don't think Charity would have bothered to make up slanderous stories about her. Why would she? Lady Palin did enough to upset people herself.' Le Froy's single raised eyebrow invited me to elaborate. 'She would boss everyone around, give impossible orders and shout at us . . . "Do you know who I am? I am Lady Palin, wife of Sir Henry Palin . . ." In a funny way, though, I think she was lonely and just wanted to be liked. But the more she tried to impress people with how important she was, the less they liked her. By contrast, Charity didn't care about such things. So what if her parents were poor and she was a nobody? She could still have a good life. I think Lady Palin thought it was unfair, that Charity didn't deserve to be happy if she wasn't. But why are you asking about this now? So what if Mary Palin sent the letter to Charity? Mary's dead, Charity's dead.'

'Say Mary Palin did write that letter. It implicates more than one person.'

It only took me a blink to see what he meant. 'Whoever Charity was carrying on with, you mean? But there's no way of telling who Lady Palin was referring to, and that's supposing she didn't just make it up— Oh, you think Charity's man friend found out she knew and killed her? But why now? With Charity already dead.'

'Perhaps she knew he had his eye on Charity's replacement.'

I had become so used to being Dee-Dee's invisible nanny that it took me a moment to realize he was referring to me. 'You think I'm having an affair with whoever killed Lady Palin so you brought me here to be questioned?' My first thought was of Ah Ma. Someone was sure to tell her I was being interrogated at the police station. All my uncles and their wives would be sure to say it was a direct result of sending me to school. I remembered Miss Nessa's manner the previous day. If she had asked me whether I was having an affair, I could have told her 'no' in private.

'I brought you here because I recently had a gas cooking stove installed at my quarters and I needed someone to demonstrate how to prepare a simple meal on it. I've been told you produce civilized meals out of local ingredients, that you won't pinch the silver, and the last meal you created for me from nothing went down very well. How about it?'

'Does Miss Nessa know you're investigating that?' I pointed at the letter now on his desk. He slid it into a folder, which he put into a drawer.

'I have no idea what your Miss Nessa knows. But we can talk over lunch,' Le Froy said, getting to his feet. 'Setting up the stove as an alibi took some doing and we might as well use it.'

———◆———

'Don't women know how much things cost?' Le Froy asked. He was talking not about his new gas stove or the headless, footless chicken ('Thought it would save you some work') with which he had presented me, but about the late Lady Palin's bills, which I would be paying with Miss Nessa's money later that afternoon. I could have said something about men not knowing the value of things – chicken necks and claws made good stock and 'phoenix claws', stewed with ginger, cloves and star anise, were a delicacy.

'Rich people don't have to worry about money.'

'*Au contraire*. Rich people worry more about money than poor people. That's how they get rich.'

I thought he was trying to annoy me and concentrated on adding more of the finely pounded red chillies to the sauce I was stirring. I had already made clear that the shopkeepers in town (including Uncle Chen and Shen-Shen) ran an account, paid monthly, for families like the Palins. The only things not put on it were alcohol and tobacco, and I doubted Lady Palin had bought either.

'I don't mean women like you, of course. Or any of your good Mission ladies,' Le Froy continued, apparently oblivious. 'But society women like Lady Palin, buying hats and dresses, stuff for dresses, ribbons . . . and with her never going to church or attending the socials, when did she wear all those things? That's like you buying half a pig and twenty gallons of coconut milk to feed four people.

'This chicken, for instance . . .' he prodded the curried chicken in rich yellow-gold sauce that I placed in front of him '. . . you can probably tell me exactly how old it is, how much it cost and probably who I bought it from, can't you?'

'That's different,' I said sullenly, only adding, 'sir,' when he was about to continue. 'And the woman probably charged you too much for an old bird.' But curry was good for flavouring and tenderizing old birds.

'No, it's the same thing. This is where your attention is focused. And you've chosen a far more valuable focus, I would say. Miss Nessa has probably been paying Lady Palin's bills since she married Sir Henry. That was how she knew how much money to give you. Su Lin, tell me about tapioca powder.'

Surprised, I obeyed. 'It's not used for milk puddings here. Tapioca costs about two cents per *kati* but most people grow their own or cut down wild plants so it's a cheap food. Here it's commonly cut into slices, wedges or strips, fried, and served as a snack, similar to potato crisps. Another method is to boil large blocks until they are soft and serve them with grated coconut as a dessert, either slightly salted or sweetened, usually with palm sugar syrup.'

That was clearly more information than the man wanted.

'Records show Nessa Palin went into town to buy tapioca powder and baking powder several times. Have you any idea why?'

Miss Nessa ordered the meals and kept an eye on the kitchen but she never did any cooking. 'Probably Cookie asked her to pick it up.'

'So, no purpose other than cooking?'

'Maybe it was for making dough for Dee-Dee to play with. Was this before I went to work there?'

'Before and after.'

'Tapioca powder is useful but harmless. Maybe it was for some project. I used some in the sauce to thicken it.'

Le Froy merely nodded. I was starting to recognize the signs: he had something on his mind he was not ready to discuss yet. I wondered if this was how men handled difficulties. Instead of sharing the problem, whether a missing cat or cash-flow difficulty, for community discussion and input as a woman would, men worried at it in their heads. It was as though they believed all the information they needed was already inside them, and that asking for help of any kind was a weakness.

He changed the subject, though he had not explained his interest in tapioca powder.

'Other than the shock over Lady Palin's death, is everything all right over there? They're treating you well? That boy Harry hasn't tried anything funny with you?'

'Harry not only hasn't tried anything "funny", he barely talks to me. I don't think he likes me at all.' I stopped, remembering the day on the sea front when Harry had seemed to forget his dislike.

'Probably you're better off that way. Has Sir Henry said anything about when they're bringing a new white nanny in?'

I sensed that Le Froy was watching me more keenly than usual, despite his apparent focus on his chicken. 'I don't think they've done anything about it yet.'

'Do you know the story of why Sir Henry came down here from Pahang?' He avoided my eyes while helping himself to some pickled vegetables. Le Froy was uncomfortable, I suddenly realized. He usually focused on whomever he was questioning, probably counting on his stare to make them reveal things they might otherwise not mention.

'I know the family were up north for a while after coming over from India. Sir Henry still owns some plantations, I believe.'

'Sir Henry was close to the sultan up there. He's very good at playing the white colonial master, if you know what I mean. Rubs in his friendliness and his superiority at the same time. Anyway,

219

they went out hunting together. There was a noise and Sir Henry took a shot at what he thought was a wild boar but it turned out to be one of the beaters. He got the man through the shoulder.'

'Oh dear.' I winced.

'That's not the worst. They were making arrangements to get the man back when Sir Henry thought he saw a tiger in the bushes. He wanted to set off after it at once, but the others were tending the injured man and not paying attention. Sir Henry took his rifle and shot the man through the head, killing him. "Put him out of his misery," he said. "Poor blighter was probably going to die anyway." And with that out of the way they could get on with the hunt.'

Now he looked at me but I had nothing to say.

'Sir Henry has great respect for the natives. Same way he has great respect for horses. He treats them well, he expects much from them and is proud of them when they do well, but he doesn't see them as people.'

I understood what he was trying to tell me. 'I'm not expecting to keep this post. I wouldn't want to. I like Dee-Dee and I hope she will always be well looked after, but I don't want to be a nanny.' Hearing myself, I wanted to apologize for sounding ungrateful but his look of relief stopped me.

'That's that, then,' he said cheerfully. He lifted the dish with the curry in it and emptied the rest of the cooling sauce onto the remains of his rice. 'Almost better than the chicken,' he said. 'Anything else?'

All men were like children when it came to food, I thought. I felt touched that Le Froy had wanted to warn me against disappointment. I also felt a little miffed that he had thought working as a nanny for the rest of my life might be a dream come true for me. If that was the best working life could offer me, I might as well have got married to whatever safe, boring old employee or distant relation Uncle Chen had picked out for me.

I was still far from my dreams of being an independent lady reporter. If anything, I was even further from becoming a secretarial assistant with my own typewriter: I was minding a child (not my own) and supervising a household (also not my own). Instead of a husband or sons who would be properly grateful for clean, mended clothes, with buttons reattached, the Palins seemed to think the miserable sum they paid me gave them rights over every one of my waking hours. I did not feel that when I was with them, but I was tired.

Cooking tired me in a way that trying to do accounts tired Uncle Chen, and I had eaten enough to feel comfortably sleepy and unwilling to go out into the noonday heat. I looked at Le Froy and saw he had a yellow curry stain on the front of his shirt. I prepared myself for an explosion when he noticed.

Unlike Sir Henry, Le Froy looked down and laughed at himself. 'Evidence that it was worth every mouthful . . . You haven't been in touch with your family recently?' he said. 'Have you written to your grandmother?'

It hadn't occurred to me to do so. It wasn't as though I had gone overseas. 'I see Uncle Chen's wife at the shop when I'm in town. If anything was wrong with Ah Ma, Shen-Shen would tell me.'

'Because your grandmother invited us to call on her.' There was a note of enquiry in his tone. 'Or, rather, Chen Tai sent a message asking me to bring you with me to drink tea with her after lunch. She seemed to know you were coming to see me today.'

'I didn't tell her.'

'I didn't think you had.' Le Froy looked amused. 'Let me put on a clean shirt first.'

Of course I had been expecting to hear from my grandmother ever since Lady Palin's death. Ah Ma had agreed I could work for the Palins despite the bad luck that came with one accidental death. After two, with the second tagged as either suicide or murder? But I had not expected the summons to come via Le Froy. Very little escaped my grandmother. I had sensed he felt responsible for my safety – did Ah Ma think so? Or could she have said something to Le Froy along the lines of 'If anything happens to my granddaughter, I'll have your private parts cut off'? Ah Ma loved the old martial arts and sword-fighting tales, especially the ones full of gore and vengeance.

'I don't want to go.'

'Why not?'

'Did she say why she wants you to bring me home?' If Ah Ma was worried, why couldn't she have sent a message via Shen-Shen? Why demand that the chief inspector escort me? Imagine being a schoolgirl summoned to the principal's office. No matter how fond you are of the woman, being hauled in to see her is seldom pleasant.

'To drink tea with her,' Le Froy said. 'Maybe she's concerned about you taking a bus or a tram alone all the way to Katong and she knows I have a car.'

I had been taking the bus to school alone for most of the seven years I had attended the Mission School.

'What's wrong?'

'I know my grandmother is worried about me, but the Palins need me more than ever now. I don't want to let them down. I don't want to leave Dee-Dee without saying goodbye.'

'You think that if I take you home, you won't be allowed to leave again? Is that why you haven't been back to visit your grandmother?'

That was rich, coming from him. Hadn't I spent my little time off cleaning his house and cooking for him? It was also true, but I wasn't going to admit it. 'My grandmother worries about me.'

'She has seen enough in her life to know there are reasons to worry.'

He might not be as old as Ah Ma but I could see he thought he had reason to worry too.

'Don't worry,' I said, on sudden impulse. 'I'm quite safe at Frangipani Hill. They are treating me very well. I know the post is only temporary and I'm not going to fall in love with Harry Palin, if that's what you're worried about. He's silly and selfish and immature, and I don't even like him. I just don't want to let Sir Henry and Miss Nessa down because they're counting on me and because I think it helps them and Dee-Dee to have me there.'

Le Froy nodded. 'Will you allow me to take you to drink tea with your grandmother? Let her see for herself that you are all right and not held prisoner or under threat. I promise I will take you back to the Palins afterwards.'

'Yes.'

He laughed. 'I know you can look after yourself. I have enough faith in the education your terrifying Mission School ladies gave you. But, Su Lin, you must remember, the Miss Blackmores and

Miss Johnsons and Miss Nessas of the world have their blind spots. Even I do. There are things we don't see because we can't. Like your Japanese neighbours, we can forget that not everyone sees us as the supreme race. It is when we forget to be aware of that that we are the most dangerous.'

Chen Tai Tea

———◆———

'**Y**ou know your uncle Chen controls most of the black market around here, don't you?'

I had been enjoying this ride across Singapore in Le Froy's Plymouth more than I had enjoyed the first. Back in those days Grove Road was the most direct route to Katong even if not the most scenic. After branching off Geylang Road, we drove through the vast mangrove swamps that stretched for miles all the way to the Kallang coast. In some places the road was like an uneven raised path, sloping down on both sides into mud and black roots. Beyond the swamp, I could see coconut plantations where the earth was more solid. Through the open windows came the sounds of birds and insects (fortunately mosquitoes stayed away from the moving car) and the sweet stench of swamp sweat. It reminded me of my long trips to and from school on the rattling benches of the open-sided old bus. In those days, I had never dreamed of seeing the inside of the governor's bungalow, even less the inside of a white man's motor-car! The car rattled a little too, but it smelt pleasantly of

Le Froy's tobacco and he did not spit betel juice out of the window as the bus driver had done.

'Did you know that most of the coconut plantations over there are owned by the family of Thomas Dunman, the island's first police commissioner? The man's a legend in the force. In his heyday he was the only white man welcomed at the tables of the heads of the secret societies in Chinatown.'

I was not distracted. 'Uncle Chen is not the head of a secret society.'

'It's not a secret society. It's a smuggling and gambling monopoly. Didn't you ever wonder why people call him Small Boss Chen?'

'It's a joke,' I told him. After all, Uncle Chen was huge, and not all of it was fat. No one could seriously describe him as 'little'. But I knew the answer in the instant before Le Froy spoke.

'Your late father was Big Boss Chen, but even he was working for your grandmother. Did you know that?'

'Of course. Everybody knows that. After my grandfather died, Ah Ma had to take over the family business so everybody was working for her. She always meant her sons to take over but my father and his brothers were so young then. Then two of her sons died so there's just her and Uncle Chen in the business now.' I had other uncles: they were my late mother's brothers or married to my aunts. Ah Ma made sure they had jobs and food but did not trust them. As far back as I could remember, my grandmother had distrusted her many relatives as much as she had 'outsiders' and 'foreign devils' and kept a strict eye on what everybody was doing all the time.

'You know about her side business? The loan sharks – *ah longs*

– who work for her?' Le Froy spoke conversationally, keeping his eyes on the road.

I didn't know where to start contradicting him. My grandmother was not a loan shark or even a moneylender. She was just better off than some, and people who knew this came to her when they needed something to carry them over until the next pay day or they found work. At least, that was what she had told me years ago when one of my schoolmates claimed Chen Tai ran an illegal loan-shark business. Yes, I had heard whispers. But I preferred my grandmother's version: 'When I lend people money, don't I have the right to get it back? It is my money, after all!'

Le Froy was not the first to try to shock me with the loan-shark accusation. Of course, being a frail old woman, Ah Ma had always left it to her sons, first my father and now Uncle Chen and his men, to arrange collection on her loans. They might have been responsible for giving people the wrong impression.

My grandmother was a strange mix of practical business sense and superstition. When I was growing up, the last day of every month was pay day and my grandmother paid every employee, from her accountants and medicine men to the coolies. There would be hundreds of workers in the front compound of the family mansion. Occasionally scuffles broke out between workers trying to collect debts or payments from each other but most of the time they were subdued and respectful in the presence of the big boss behind her giant ledger of financial records. After they had collected their money they would be given a cup of hot tea and a rice dumpling. Chen Tai had grumbled that her eyes were growing feeble and her fingers stiff. I had thought she was grooming me to be an accountant because now and then she would ask me for a calculation to confirm the sum that the bailiff in charge of a team of coolies named as their due.

If my uncle was running underground gambling and smuggling rings, there was no way my grandmother could be unaware of that. Years of studying in the Mission School had opened my eyes to things I might otherwise have taken for granted. For instance, my grandmother's spirit predictions. Chen Tai would shake her hollow wooden spirit box, which rattled and jangled till it dislodged the precious piece of paper upon which the gods dispensed their advice. These usually had to do with auspicious dates for business deals or marriage contracts but occasionally there were warnings of possible dangers and risks associated with certain dates. When this occurred the papers were burned and their ashes stirred into hot tea. I remembered being made to drink the concoction as a child, I more than any of the other children because I had to be protected from the spirits of dead parents who might try to reclaim me. The Chinese side of me half believed this. And, after all, what could it hurt to remember and respect the dead? Of course, there were also the spirits to whom Ah Ma prayed for a good husband for me. The Mission School side of my brain told me they were just superstitions, but I still kept a sharp eye open just in case.

'Su Lin?'

'Sorry. What did you say?' I rubbed my eyes and sounded disoriented, as though I had drowsed off looking out of the window.

'We're almost there. Is this the turning? There doesn't seem to be a sign.'

The Chen family mansion was unmistakable even from a

distance. It was large, with several extensions to the main building. As each son married, an additional wing had been constructed for his family, connected to the main house by sheltered walkways. Their widows and children still sat down to dinner with Ah Ma. There were servants' quarters behind, a three-car garage and drivers' lodgings by the front gate.

I was surprised by the rush of fondness I felt on seeing the high stone walls, topped by shards of green and brown beer bottles, that surrounded the property. Inside I knew starched laundry would be drying on colourful bamboo poles in every available patch of sunlight, with chickens, dogs and the servants' children moving on the bare earth and cow grass beneath them. I was even happy thinking of the vegetable garden at the side of the house, although it was so much less elegant than the carpet grass lawns and flowerbeds on Frangipani Hill. Here there would be leafy vegetables, lemon grass, *pandan* leaves, baby limes and *limau purut* . . . and the blue flowers of the butterfly pea plant that would be soaked in warm water to colour cakes and jellies. I had hardly noticed all these things while I was growing up there, just as I had hardly noticed the people around me.

The amount of ash and offerings lining the road in front of the house showed that the Chen family had already made liberal offerings to all wandering ghosts. Our own ancestors had their altars inside the house with daily food offerings and private burning bins to make sure they were well provided-for in the afterworld. It was one of the rituals I had mocked while I was living there – 'When you get the servants to burn money for you, won't it go to their ancestors instead of our ancestors?' – but now, suddenly, I felt protective towards my family.

'Wait,' I said. 'Stop the car.'

He pulled onto the grass verge at the side of the road without pretending to be surprised. 'Yes?'

'What do you want from my grandmother?'

'It was your grandmother who asked us to make this visit.'

'Lady Palin was always asking you to drink tea with her. Miss Nessa is always trying to get you to come to dinner at the house or buy tickets for her social evenings, and you never accept. You wouldn't have agreed to come here unless you wanted something from my grandmother. Are you going to arrest her?'

Le Froy laughed.

I glared at him. 'Well? Are you?' As all nice girls know there is a time to play nice and a time to defend a black-marketeer grandmother.

'I didn't come to arrest your grandmother. There is information that the police can't get, certain things the townspeople won't tell us. We may be able to pay once or twice for information but people here have their long-term livelihoods to think of. And their long-term livelihoods depend on Chen Tai. What do I want from her? All I want is any gossip or hearsay she may have picked up. Has anyone from Frangipani Hill been in the market for drugs, for instance? So many ships come in from China with something extra that we don't know about. Was Lady Palin sending a servant to buy extra "medicines"? Did Charity try to arrange an abortion? Does she know anything about them that someone could have tried to blackmail them over?'

'You think my grandmother would know these things?'

'Only because she has people everywhere and they can't help seeing what's going on. She has far more eyes on the street than the police do. I suspect she knows more than even your Shen-Shen does.'

'Do you think she will tell you?'

'It was your grandmother who asked me to bring you here.'

I had always taken it for granted that my grandmother was an old, old woman. I had already thought of her as old when she first took charge of me though she must only have been in her early forties then, less than half the age I am as I write this now, and sometimes I still find it difficult to remember that I am old. That day in Le Froy's car I saw Ah Ma through Le Froy's eyes. Perhaps my grandmother was not so very old after all, possibly not much older than he was.

'She probably wants to know what you intend to do. About Lady Palin's death and about Charity's death. Ah Ma always says, if you want to know what's happening ask the person holding the chopsticks, don't ask the chopsticks.' I thought of Uncle Chen, Shen-Shen and their helpers at the shop. Uncle Chen had ways of keeping his eye on things.

'She might still want to see you for herself. Talk to you herself.'

My grandmother might have preferred me to be safe at home with her, but that was not what I wanted. I was happy to see her again, but I did not want to end up back at Chen Mansion after a failed attempt at a job. I wanted to go back to Frangipani Hill and stay long enough to get a good recommendation from Acting Governor Sir Henry (that ought to count for something on future job applications!) or Miss Nessa, as 'Patron of the Ladies Mission Society'. Before they got a new (respectably white) companion for Dee-Dee, I hoped to earn a substantial amount towards a secretarial course. My grandmother was hardly likely to finance something that would help me get away from the family business! Also, I had grown fond of Dee-Dee. With a little more time, I was sure I could teach her to look after herself. After all, many seven- and eight-year-olds were already working in fields and factories and keeping themselves clean. Dee-Dee was at least as bright as a normal seven-year-old and a good deal stronger.

'My grandmother didn't stay safe at home either. She married a man her parents didn't approve of, and after he died she took over his business instead of going home to her family.'

'Maybe she wants to save you from going through what she did.' Le Froy hummed softly as he put the car back into first gear, then eased us onto the road and up to the gates of Chen Mansion.

——◆——

People always said how like Ah Ma I was, but I couldn't see it. My grandmother was shorter than I was and, thanks to her almost fanatical avoidance of direct sunlight, her skin was much fairer. She had dressed up for our visit and was wearing the traditional *nonya kebaya* and gold jewellery of the wealthy Peranakan matriarch she was. She smiled at Le Froy with her head tilted sideways in what might have been interpreted as either a flirtatious invitation or an innocently childish look.

'Chen Tai.' Le Froy greeted Ah Ma with a respectful bow.

'Ah, you are here,' Ah Ma replied in jerky but understandable English. 'How are you?' The look she threw me was both triumphant and uncertain. I nodded, approving her English pronunciation, and her triumph was complete. Now she had made her point she switched back to the familiarity of Baba Malay.

'The weather is so hot that I've got headache. I'm not in a good mood so don't ask to borrow money! Hello, Boss. Good of you to come so far to visit a useless old woman like me. Are you coming to complain about my no-good granddaughter? What bad things has she been doing now?' Ah Ma grinned fondly at me. She took for granted Le Froy would understand her. Ah Ma had been doing her own research. I should have been surprised but I wasn't.

'It's good to see you looking so well, and the governor's family is very pleased with Su Lin.'

'Sit! Sit! Why do you stand there all stupid like that? You, girl! Go and fetch drinks!' The last was to the maid, who had stayed to stare at the brown-skinned white man who had come to the house with the bad-luck granddaughter. 'Come in, come in. Sit down. Have you eaten yet? You'd better sit down. You're so tall. If I have to look up at you my neck aches.'

Chief Inspector Le Froy sat. He had clearly learned long ago that it was no use trying to resist such a force of nature as my grandmother. That was probably one reason why he had survived as long and well as he had in his Far East post.

'First, I'm sorry Su Lin was in the house with a dead body,' Le Froy said. He must have noticed my startled look but showed no sign. 'Please don't be angry with your granddaughter for not coming home straight away. The family wanted her to stay. She was a great help to them. And now I hope that you can help me.'

'I am old but not superstitious.' Chen Tai swept over her untruth without flinching. She turned on me. 'So now you are working as a maid for *ang mob*s. I thought you were going to be a big-shot secretary?'

'I hope you can help me,' Le Froy pulled her back on track, 'by giving me some information.'

'I am only an old woman. I don't know anything. Why ask me?'

'Because servants will tell their friends and relatives things they would not tell to their bosses or to a foreign-devil policeman. And I hear you know everything that anybody knows.'

'You think I spend my time listening to servants?' Chen Tai gave a disdainful flick of a hand and did not look up when the maid came in with the tea. In fact, she was known to be strict but fair with her servants. Plus she was generous with red packets at New Year, which always helped.

'You are trying to find out who killed the young girl, right? At first you wanted to blame the fat white woman for killing her but now you've got to find out who killed the fat white woman.' Chen Tai cackled in mischievous glee. I couldn't help smiling – at her delight, not the deaths – but Le Froy looked grim. 'Local girls here dying all the time but you policemen never investigate. Why are you so interested now?'

'It is an official investigation,' Le Froy said, with a touch of the pomposity that suggested he was uncomfortable.

'I'm too busy worrying about my own family to have time to busybody about *ang mob*s.'

'You worry about things like your son's business in Sungei Road?' Le Froy asked casually. Sungei Road was called the thieves' market not just because things were so cheap but because of how the goods had come to be on sale there. Uncle Chen's was one of the smallest shops in it but he got his share of what everyone else bought and sold . . . Effectively he was both landlord and underground police force.

My grandmother's sharp eyes darted towards me. I suddenly remembered seeing that look after a visitor had said something about my late father's prowess with women or drink. If I showed curiosity or alarm, that person did not reappear. I thought I saw why Le Froy had taken the time to brief me in his car and tried to look as though discussing Uncle Chen's little shop was the most natural thing in the world.

'What do you want to know?'

'Were Sir Henry and his wife close? Do you know if they had any problems?'

'They were living in the same house. How much closer would you want to get?' Ah Ma took pity on him and shook her head. 'Lady Palin had been sick for a long time. She was taking medicine because she could not sleep, because she could not do her toilet big business, because of her monthly pains.'

I had lived in the same house as Lady Palin and hadn't seen any of these things. Or, rather, I had seen (now that I thought about it) without noticing.

'I think she likes medicine as some people like drinking and smoking.'

'Lady Palin used to drink too.' I tried to show that I, too, knew about such things. 'In her room. She used to take the bottles down the back staircase so that nobody would know.' It was because everyone had known who left the empty Plymouth Gin bottles behind the kitchen door that no one commented on them. I could tell it was no surprise to Le Froy and Ah Ma because neither of them paid any attention.

'Their treasure chest is empty!' Le Froy leaned forward with more interest at this. Ah Ma looked pleased. 'There are stories about them from Pahang. In Pahang Sir Henry used to go shooting with the Sultan so he thought he was such a big shot. Do you get my joke? Big shot! Because he was friends with the sultan nobody chased him to pay his bills. He could buy things without money, order people around, but one day the sultan was no longer his friend, ha-ha! Everybody was coming to his door to ask for their money back! That was when he came down to Singapore to be acting governor. He still hasn't paid all his bills. But the *ang mohs* here close their eyes because they are all their own people. But I did not ask you here just to talk about *ang mohs*.'

'What did you want to talk about?'

'I cannot watch over my granddaughter in Sir Henry's house. If you tell her to stay with me she will be safe.'

'No!' I was on my feet and speaking without putting on my demure Chinese face or respectful Mission School veneer. 'Ah Ma, I want to go back.'

'It would be better for you to come home.'

Le Froy grinned. He added a little fuel to the fire by saying mildly, 'Your grandmother is right. You're only a young girl, and even if that house isn't bad luck, two people have already died.'

I turned on Le Froy. 'You agreed I would work for the Palins until they found somebody else to take care of Dee-Dee. They're happy with how I'm teaching her to look after herself.' Then to Ah Ma, 'There's no reason for anybody to kill me. If I break my promise, who will trust me again? And if nobody trusts me, how can I ever do business in Malaya or anywhere else?'

I knew that would strike her where it counted. Ah Ma was proud of keeping her word. That was what made the Chen protectors stand out against all others: when they agreed to protect someone they kept their word. Her expression didn't change but I saw she was assessing the situation and me.

'Ah Ma, you always say that any man, whether British or local, has the right to any job, provided he can do the work, yes? Well, I think anyone, whether man or woman, has the right to any job he or she can do. And I'm doing this job well.'

'If you want to go and be a servant to *ang mohs*, I can't stop you.'

'I will do what I can to keep her safe,' Le Froy said. 'But I'm not there with her all the time inside that house.' Their eyes met and some communication passed between them that I didn't understand.

'What?'

'I am only afraid this stupid girl will go and look for trouble.' Ah Ma spoke over my question. 'And she is stubborn enough to look until she finds it. What else do you want to know?'

'I want to know whether Sir Henry or his son have gambling debts, whether they are addicted to opium or to alcohol, anything Lady Palin could have found out about and used to blackmail them.'

I was shocked: saying such things could have got him charged with slander. But I saw my grandmother looking at him with interest and respect. 'Why ask me? You are the police.'

'People in their official position have ways of hiding things from people in my official position.'

'I don't know anything about that. If I did, I would tell you.

You should go and find out more about the dead girl. Next thing you know they'll be saying that the father of her baby was a Chinese man or an Indian man and then they'll kill Chinese men and Indian men.' Ah Ma grinned at Le Froy's discomfort. I guessed Charity's pregnancy was a nugget of 'privileged' information.

'We're working on that. Whether the girl was involved with Harry Palin or one of the soldiers in town . . . and whether Mary Palin knew about it. Any other funny business?'

'The big boss lady went to buy tapioca flour,' Ah Ma said. Le Froy looked as though her rapid patois of Chinese dialect and Malay had confused him. 'That's funny, yes? She herself went to buy it. More, she went to the store near the settlements, not my son's shop, which is nearer her house.'

'Miss Nessa?' I asked. I remembered the traces of tapioca flour I had found in Lady Palin's laundry basket. My grandmother nodded.

'The people there were so surprised to see a white woman buying *singkang*.'

'They recognized her?'

'Of course!' That was not surprising. Even if most of the whites could not recognize their own servants once they had doffed their uniform and servile posture, most locals knew all of the *ang mohs* by sight, as well as who outranked whom and where they belonged on the social visiting hierarchy.

'And they rushed to report it to you?' Le Froy seemed to have forgotten that that was precisely the reason he had come to consult my grandmother.

'Only because it's so funny. Another funny thing is Mr Harry following Miss Charity around. He did not *pak tor* with her, like boyfriend-girlfriend, but he would go into shops after her and ask what things she bought.'

Dee-Dee's Secrets

———◆———

'If she's not in her bedroom, then where is she?'

As I entered the front door I heard Miss Nessa's voice coming from the drawing room. Harry had been standing silently just inside the hall but when he saw me he turned and vanished. Apparently Charity was not the only person he spied on. I wanted to disappear too, but the door opened and Sir Henry emerged, saying vaguely and grumpily, 'I'm sure the girl is fine. She's— Ah, here is Miss Chen,' He looked as though Miss Nessa had just woken him from a nap. He also looked as though he needed his afternoon dose of whisky but he never drank when his sister was in the room. His face lit up on seeing me, though it might have been from relief rather than pleasure. 'Dee-Dee's somewhere around but we don't know where. She'll turn up. Can't be expected to keep an eye on her twenty-four hours a day.'

'No,' Miss Nessa said icily. 'Nobody expects you to. That's why we pay servants.' I knew she was talking about me precisely because she refused to look at me.

Sir Henry had no such problem. 'She wanted me to take her

into town so that we could have tea at the Jupiter. She seemed
to think that was where you went. She wanted to go and join you
there.' He laughed. Since Dee-Dee had had tea at the Jupiter on
her birthday, she had demanded every day, at least once, to be
taken there again. I had never been to the café, which was for
Europeans and Eurasians only. I suspected Dee-Dee had stuffed
herself with cream cakes until she was almost sick, which was
why she remembered it so well. 'Then she wanted to go across
to my office, but I told her I'd finished for the day.'

'Why did Chief Inspector Le Froy come for you? Where did
he take you?' Miss Nessa demanded.

'He drove me home to visit my grandmother. She was worried
about me. But after that I went to all the shops and I have the
receipts for Lady Palin's things.'

Miss Nessa waved them away. 'Dee-Dee is missing.'

'I'll go and see if she's in the kitchen. What time did you last
see her?'

They made vague sounds, Miss Nessa seeming more interested in why I had been in Le Froy's car than in her niece's
whereabouts, 'Did he ask you questions? What did you tell him?'

'We can talk about it after we find Deborah,' I said. Something
Le Froy had said came back to me: *The Palins treat people well,
but they don't consider you and me 'people'.*

But there was no point going into that now. Where was Dee-
Dee? I remembered the day of Charity's death, when she had
wandered down the long driveway to the main road. I was sure I
would have noticed if the car had passed her. Had she followed
a monkey or a tree lizard into the rainforest around the house?
I pushed the thought away. I could shudder later. Now I had to

find her – that was far more important than answering Miss Nessa's questions.

I went out of the front door and across the lawn to the back entrance of Government House. If Dee-Dee had been told not to go to her father's office there was very good reason to expect to find her there.

And I was right. The front of the building was locked but I found Dee-Dee fast asleep curled up on the little mattress in the annex to Sir Henry's office, the space she had called her playroom.

'Wake up, Dee-Dee, it's time to go back to the house,'

A sleepy, grumpy voice said, 'I thought you were never coming. Charity never came back.'

'Come on. Your father and Aunt Nessa are worried about you. You should have let someone know where you were!' I could hear the sharpness in my voice. It had been a long day and I was tired.

'Can't. Shan't. This is my secret place where all my secret things are. I'll show you one of them.' Dee-Dee fumbled under a corner of the mattress and pulled out a small object. 'You mustn't tell Aunt Nessa about it. Promise?' She wiped it on her dress before handing it to me. I took it gingerly (it was still sticky), then saw what it was: a tiny oval pendant on a fragment of chain. Dee-Dee was looking at me expectantly and I managed to smile at her, my tiredness forgotten.

'Where did you get this?' The locket wasn't mine and it didn't look like something Miss Nessa would own. It looked like gilt silver and its enamel plaque showed a shepherdess with a young man on his knees beside her, surrounded by turquoise and seed pearls. There were delicate floral engravings on the back and two compartments, both empty, inside.

'Found it.' Dee-Dee looked both proud and guilty. I knew that look well. It might mean nothing more than that she had 'borrowed' it from Charity or her stepmother because it was a pretty, shiny thing. On the other hand . . . 'Where? Where did you find it?'

'Under the tree,' Dee-Dee said. The guilty relief in her voice told me this was the truth. 'Where Charity fell.' Though we were alone in the room she leaned and whispered into my ear, 'I took it first. But it wasn't my fault.'

'What wasn't your fault?' I didn't whisper. 'Oh, Dee-Dee, what did you do?'

'I threw it, that's all. First I took it and I threw it over the balcony. I didn't know it would get stuck in the tree. I thought it would land on the ground outside, and Charity would run downstairs with me. I ran downstairs but she didn't. She tried to lean over and grab it and she fell.'

So many thoughts were darting through my mind but I answered automatically, smoothing down Dee-Dee's hair, 'And you found it on the ground outside?'

'Under the tree. Next to Charity after she fell. Give it back. It's mine now. I have to put it with my other things.'

'Let me just clean it for you first – it's dirty. And we'd better get back to the house. Aunt Nessa will be looking for you.'

I had put Dee-Dee's shoes on and got her back onto her feet and into her father's office when I realized it was no longer empty. Sir Henry had come in and was standing by his desk with a tumbler of whisky in his hand. He must have followed me. I remember thinking that, whatever people might say about Sir Henry as a governor, he was a good father. He watched us coming out of Dee-Dee's playroom.

'So this is where you got to! I thought so. Couldn't stay away, eh?' His voice was slightly thick.

He had turned down the lamps in the room and closed the door to the corridor. I suddenly felt uncomfortable, without knowing why.

'We should be getting back. I have to let Miss Nessa know I've found Dee-Dee and she's all right.'

'Don't worry about Nessa,' Sir Henry said. 'She'll fuss about something else if she can't fuss about this. Dee-Dee, my girl, what happened to the chocolates I gave you?'

'Chocolates? You never gave me any chocolates!'

'Of course I did . . . Oh, wait, let me see . . .' Sir Henry did a stage fumble and produced a little box from a drawer on the desk, which he opened with the flourish of a stage magician to reveal two chocolates. Dee-Dee shrieked with delight and pounced on them.

'But it's almost her dinnertime!' I said automatically.

Of course, that made Dee-Dee snatch them out of my reach and dart, giggling, into her secret closet.

'You're wasted as a nanny,' Sir Henry said, in a joking tone that made me even more uncomfortable. 'You worked out where she was in a flash, didn't you? That's why I think you should reconsider working here for me. Why not? Nice place to live, good pay . . . Not many girls would turn that down, you know.'

'Then you won't have any trouble finding a more qualified girl to take over.' I knew I was being pert but, given the circumstances, I was sure Miss Nessa would understand and even approve, not that I could ever tell her about this.

'You don't understand. I'll show you what I mean.' Sir Henry reached over and cupped my face in his hands. I could smell the alcohol and tobacco on his breath as his mouth came down towards me. I think he was aiming for my lips but I twisted away in time and he got the side of my head instead. In the confusion, I may have elbowed him in the ribs and kicked him in the shin, but that would have been assault. So, I have no idea what I was doing until I found myself standing away from him, holding a heavy paperweight in one hand and a letter knife in the other, in what might have been interpreted as a threatening manner. 'Keep away from me!'

Sir Henry held up both his hands, like a western cowboy surrendering to a Red Indian. 'What's the matter?' he said, in mock horror. Or perhaps his horror wasn't entirely mock and he was genuinely taken aback. Perhaps no girl had ever fended him off before, certainly not with his own stationery supplies.

'So, you found her.' The office door opened behind him and Harry was there. 'Occurred to me she might be here. Obviously I don't think as fast as some people. Come on, Dee-Dee!'

I'd never been so glad to see anyone in my life.

Harry moved behind me and pulled Dee-Dee out of her playroom by the arm. Then he took the paperweight and paper knife from me and tossed them onto the floor. 'Let's leave those things here. You won't need them any more.' He took my arm with his other hand and ushered us both to the door.

Sensing something, Dee-Dee made no fuss as we left. Sir Henry muttered about important work he had to finish off before dinner, and as we went out of the room I saw him drain the glass in his hand, then spotted the bottle of whisky on his desk. Somehow I was not surprised.

'I can't believe you did that!' Harry crowed, once we were out on the lawn between the two buildings.

'What?'

'You turned down the pater!' Harry's look was gleeful. All his previous scorn was gone. 'I heard you. You weren't even scared of him.'

'I don't want to be a secretary.' That was not strictly true. 'I mean I don't want to be his secretary.'

'With everything that that entails.' Harry laughed again. Suddenly he was completely different. It was as though the cloak of suspicion he had been wearing had dissolved and I was seeing the real Harry for the first time. He was looking at me with admiration and an almost conspiratorial air.

'What are you talking about?'

'You don't have to play innocent. I saw you fight off the old man.' Harry laughed again, loudly, like a child who had been waiting for the punch line of a joke. 'I can't remember the last time someone turned him down. I bet he can't remember either. Oh, that was worth seeing! I only wish Charity could have seen it!'

As his meaning dawned on me, I shivered. 'You don't mean – Charity didn't . . .'

'Charity thought she knew what she was doing.' Harry looked grim. He turned towards the house. 'We should get this one back.' So, I hadn't imagined it. He had deliberately walked us out of Sir Henry's office to save me from his father.

'I thought Charity hated you.'

'Charity only pretended to hate me. We were friends. We understood each other. Charity was only nasty to me in public.

She didn't want people to know how clever she was because people don't expect pretty girls to be clever, but she couldn't hide it from me. She told me that often the best way to get on with people is by being what they expect.'

'But isn't that dishonest?' I asked.

'It was part of the role she was playing. She wasn't really being dishonest because that was what they wanted from her for the salary they paid her. She was honest in her own way. I know she told little lies now and then, but she was honest with herself. Everyone else here thinks the only thing that matters is not rocking the boat. Charity saw life as an adventure novel. And she was the heroine.'

Charity had not been the only girl to build herself a fantasy future on circumstances she could not control.

'I once told Charity about going down the line – you know what that means, don't you? Off-duty soldiers going down the line looking for someone to spend the evening with. I thought it would shock her a little, maybe make her laugh. But do you know what she said? She said, "I wonder if those women get paid more than I do." Can you believe that?'

'How did she deal with it?' I asked. The ladies at the Mission School warned us that men have sex on their minds all the time. It was something they couldn't help, like dogs and pigs. 'Going down the line' was a euphemism for visits to the brothels catering for Europeans. Most of these were in the semi-rural fringe of the business city, the 'line' along MacPherson Road and Balestier Road. There, driveways led to darkened compounds. The only sign that they were occupied came from the dim red lights that guided visitors in. The line was the only place left for such commerce. Malay Street, a legend before the Great War, with its French and Russian prostitutes, was now only a memory.

'It's obvious, isn't it?'

'If it's obvious, tell me, did Sir Henry make advances to her? Did you?'

Harry looked as exasperated as I felt. 'You don't make small-talk very often, do you?'

'I don't make small-talk at all.'

Harry took a deep breath. 'The pater . . . He doesn't mean any real harm. It's been a topsy-turvy time or he would never have lost his head and approached you. You won't understand but in his clumsy way he probably thought it would be a compliment, that he didn't just see you as a servant.'

I knew what Harry meant, perhaps better than he thought I did. I had seen enough of Western courtship rituals to know European families did little to identify, research and arrange suitable marriages. Instead, to catch the attention of potential partners, Western males had to resort to shows of strength, aggression and virility, rather like wild boars in the mating season, and Western females had to decorate themselves and their homes, like bower birds. It was not surprising that some of this behaviour carried over, especially as Sir Henry was now single again. I was not angry with him – servants have no right to be angry with their employers – but I would take care not to be alone with him again.

For now, I decided to trust Harry. 'Have you seen this before?' I pulled the pendant out of my pocket.

Harry took it and turned it over in his hands. 'I saw Charity wearing it,' he said cautiously. 'Where did you get it?'

'Dee-Dee had it in her secret place in there.'

'Dee-Dee?'

'I found it!' Dee-Dee said. Harry looked at his sister, who had been uncharacteristically quiet. She had been drooping against him and he pushed her upright. She was almost as tall as he was, and even now, groggy with sleep, she was beautiful . . . and far too trusting.

'She found it under the frangipani tree where Charity died. She said she threw it over the balcony.'

'Dee-Dee?' Harry looked at her. 'Did you?'

'I threw it over the balcony. I already said I'm sorry. I wanted to race Charity downstairs. Only she jumped over the balcony instead. I'm sleepy.'

'Papa gave you one of his special chocolates again, didn't he? I told you not to eat them. Remember? Every time you bring me one of Papa's chocolates I give you two Cadburys?'

But Dee-Dee's eyes had closed and she was leaning against him again, humming to herself.

'What's wrong with the chocolates?'

'An extract of valerian root. It's a mild sedative. Harmless, but sometimes she wets herself afterwards,' Harry told me matter-of-factly. 'You didn't know Charity, but she was the kind of girl who would try to climb over a balcony to retrieve a pendant hooked on a tree branch. This was my mother's, you know.' He turned the pendant over on his palm. 'I saw Charity wearing it. I didn't know whether my father gave it to her or whether she'd found it somewhere, liked it and taken it. Dee-Dee, I mean, not Charity. And once Dee-Dee had it . . . well, Charity pretty much helped herself to everything that was Dee-Dee's, didn't she, pet? I suppose, to her, that was part of the deal. Sharing things.'

'Charity borrowed it.' Dee-Dee agreed, without opening her eyes. 'But it's mine. I want it back.'

'But if Lady Palin saw Charity with your mother's pendant, she might have thought your father gave it to her,' I said to Harry. 'She would have seen it as proof that Charity was having an affair with Sir Henry. That was why she was searching through Charity's things. She was looking for evidence. And maybe that made her depressed enough to take sleeping powders. You don't know who Lady Palin's doctor was, do you?'

'I don't like doctors!'

'Let's go up to your room and on the way we'll ask Cookie to send up some dinner,' I said to Dee-Dee.

Dr Leask's Prescriptions

———◆———

Harry not only knew who Lady Palin's physician was – Dr Leask treated the whole family – but suggested an immediate visit to him in town.

'I don't think your father approves of the motor-car being used at night, or by anyone other than his driver. Anyway, it will be time for dinner soon.' I didn't want to ask Sir Henry for any favours and had planned to avoid dinner because of a headache, which was a genuine enough excuse.

'We're not taking the government car and we'll grab something for dinner in town. I'm offering my own noble steed – my motorcycle!'

I hesitated. 'Will the doctor see us without an appointment?'

'The clinic will be closed. But the doctor will still be messing around in the mortuary or laboratory. He lives just across from it and he's used to people banging on the door. At least it's not after midnight and we won't get blood on his carpets! I'll tell Aunt Nessa you need something for your nerves. Don't worry, she'll assume poor old Pa upset you and won't ask too many questions. And don't worry, the motorized bicycle is as safe as a motor-car.'

I had always loved bicycles and been fascinated by motorized bicycles for some time. But the main reason I agreed to go with him was the chance to get away from Frangipani Hill for a bit – at least until Sir Henry was himself again. Dee-Dee was asleep almost before we got her into bed so there was no question of dinner. I almost wished I knew where Sir Henry got his valerian-root chocolates!

———◆———

'It's a 1910 Pierce motorcycle, with a clutch and two-speed transmission.' Harry's machine did not come with the side-car I had expected.

'How are we both going to—'

'Just get up behind me and hold on to me. It's like riding a horse, but not as high and totally under control. Don't worry, this is strictly part of the ride. I won't publicize our engagement till you're ready! Here, put these on.' He passed me a pair of goggles. On his motorcycle, Harry was all business. 'Bit big for you but they'll keep the grit out of your eyes. Ready? All right, hold on!'

Harry focused on his motorcycle. Skilfully and almost joyously he accelerated once we moved off the driveway and down onto the main road.

I squeaked involuntarily, part fear and part excitement.

'It's really safer to go fast than slow,' Harry shouted over his shoulder.

The road was not asphalted, like those in town. As we skimmed down the laterite surface, little chips and grit spun up, occasionally stinging my calves, but even that was exciting. There was no other traffic until we reached the main tributary into town, where the rickshaw-pullers were running two and three abreast. Some, laughing, raced Harry's motorcycle for a few yards before giving up. We also passed the occasional car and a bullock cart, with its thatched roof and a Chinese coolie driver in a wide straw hat, who grumbled at us.

We had to detour at Cavanagh Bridge, which was reserved for rickshaws and pedestrians, then make our way down Orchard Road, Stamford Road, and turn right into St Andrew's Road. By then the thrill of riding on the back of a fast motorcycle had blown away my headache and I had left my frightening encounter with Sir Henry far behind. I understood how people who travelled could leave their memories and parts of themselves far behind. Given the chance, I wanted to travel too.

St Andrew's was a part of town I loved. It was lined with huge old banyan trees on the cathedral side that cooled the hot red laterite road during the day and now housed sleeping birds, which occasionally fluttered and called. On the other side was the grassy expanse of the *padang*, as the public playing-field was known, and beyond that, Connaught Drive with its avenue of flame-of-the forest trees – masses of deep red, scarlet and orange blossoms – with glimpses of the gleaming waters of the harbour beyond that. All this was part of the order the British had brought. They might have taken away the original wild forest and undergrowth but in exchange they had planned and planted an environment where plants and people might coexist in an orderly manner.

———

'I would describe Lady Palin more as unhappy than sick,' Dr Leask said.

Harry had been right: the man didn't seem to mind seeing us at that hour. And he had still been inside his clinic when Harry had slid his motorcycle smoothly to a stop in front of it and tilted it at an angle for me to climb off. Neither had the doctor seemed surprised when Harry had said he wanted a private word about his late stepmother's health. He may have given the impression he was there on his father's behalf and I did nothing to disillusion the doctor: Sir Henry owed me something, I thought.

'Europeans here are all constipated. Not myself, of course. I make sure of that. And I don't consider myself a European expatriate so much as a white Singaporean. But all the others . . .' Dr Leask sounded gleeful. He was a tall, thin man. What was left of his hair was fine and blond and, in the evening lamplight, looked almost white against the brown of his face. The Singapore sun that had browned his skin had also bleached his hair but somehow left him looking as though he belonged on the island as much as any of the local fishermen did.

'Europeans eat too much meat, old and overcooked meat. They don't drink anything other than spirits and sweetened liquids, and they don't move their bodies, except to walk from their beds to their dining tables and from their dining tables to their motor-cars. It is not surprising their bodies slow down and become sluggish. But look at me! I eat everything the locals eat. I'll eat a stick of satay right off the roadside charcoals and chew sugar cane right off the stick—'

'Mary may have been trying to lose weight,' Harry interrupted. 'She was always saying how much weight she had gained since arriving here and she had to get her dresses let out several times. There were weight-loss capsules in her room. Did she get them from you?'

'I told her she was getting fat because she did too little and ate too much. It was as simple as that. If she'd had a couple of children to run after she would have been all right.' Dr Leask looked at me. I suspected he was hoping for a reaction.

'Did you sell her those capsules?' Harry was not diverted. 'Slim, Redusols, Formula 17?' They were all familiar names. I had seen the advertisements myself. But I had not seen any capsules among Lady Palin's things.

'Ah, the miracle DNP drugs. She did ask for them, yes, but I had to tell her no. There have been reports of skin rashes, jaundice, eye problems and other toxic reactions in America, where these are most commonly used. A doctor experimenting with them in San Francisco is said to have cooked himself from the inside! I told Lady Palin all of this, not that it did much good. I suspect she simply ordered them sent over, along with her biscuits and jams.'

'But she did get sleeping powders from you?'

'Oh, yes. For all the good they did her.'

'Beg pardon, sir?' I asked.

'Lady Palin kept telling me that my powders weren't strong enough. I was already stretching the limits for her. I was giving her a barbiturate, a commercial preparation under the brand name Veronal. It is very effective as a sedative but there is only a small difference between the prescribed dose and an overdose so I could not increase her prescription.'

'She can't have liked that,' Harry said wryly. I could imagine the fuss she would have made.

'Indeed. *Do you know who my husband is?*' Dr Leask shook his head wryly, 'Normally I insist on seeing my patients, even for standing prescriptions. Unfortunately Lady Palin found our consultations too wearing, especially after I refused her requests twice. So, in her case, I would send her monthly prescriptions to Sir Henry at his office when she requested them.'

'There's something else,' I remembered. I pulled out the remaining chocolate I had taken from Dee-Dee earlier. 'I took these from Deborah Palin. She really likes them but there's white stuff on them and I think they may be mouldy. I've never seen any on sale in town, at least not in my uncle's shop. Do you have any idea who brings them in?'

Dr Leask examined the chocolate with a curiosity I suspected he applied to every novelty that crossed his path. 'Can't say . . . That doesn't look like mould. It's some kind of powder, not sugar. Doesn't look like there's anything wrong with the chocolates.' He looked more closely. 'Where did she get these, do you know?'

'From Sir Hen—' I started to say.

'She picked them up somewhere,' Harry said over me.

'I'll keep an eye open.' Leask touched a finger first to the chocolate and then to the tip of his tongue. He did not offer to return it. I regretted mentioning the sweets. I had thought he would say, 'Oh, yes, a common sleeping aid,' but instead he was turning it into a big operation. I could see why some government officials found him difficult to deal with.

'Has your father decided about the funeral – or funerals – yet?'

'Chief Inspector Le Froy is still being cagey about releasing the bodies. Don't know what he's hoping to find.'

'Did the good inspector clear up the business about the young lady's photographs? Dr Shankar was quite upset about them when we were working on her. Her body, I mean.'

'What photographs?'

'Charity Byrne had him develop some photographs in his shop. Absolutely ridiculous, a medical man of his standing operating a shop instead of a surgery. But he wouldn't say more than that and it won't be any use you asking him. Perhaps his family might know more—'

'Shankar had no right to discuss Charity's photographs. It was a professional contract.'

I was surprised by the antagonism in Harry's tone. For a moment, he had sounded like Sir Henry. And the fear I sensed beneath his anger was also in Sir Henry. Dr Leask looked blandly innocent but pleased. I suspected he had provoked Harry much as he might have run a medical test.

'If Dr Shankar mentioned anything to his family, I know his daughter, Parshanti, quite well. I could ask her,' I said, watching Dr Leask.

'Oh, I'm sure he wouldn't mention anything,' Dr Leask said, agreeably enough. He had provoked the reaction he'd wanted. I decided he was one of those *ang moh* men who 'fish for sport, not for food' and tear the jagged hook through the lip of a struggling fish before tossing it back to bleed into the river.

———◆———

'I don't know what you're talking about,' Harry said, when I asked him why he had been upset at the mention of Dr Shankar and Charity's photographs. 'Look, shall we pick up some dinner here or go back and see if we can find some leftovers?'

He didn't speak again on our way back.

———

The dining room was empty when we got in. Sir Henry had a headache and a tray had gone up to his room, we were told, and Miss Nessa was having a sandwich in hers but had asked to see us as soon as we got back.

Of course Miss Nessa wanted to know where we had been. She looked at me with a suspicion I had not seen directed at me before.

Harry took charge. Without quite saying so, he implied I had had an encounter with Sir Henry earlier and had been so upset I had decided to leave immediately. He had taken me to town for a glass of pop and persuaded me to change my mind. 'Pressure of work and all that, you know. Hits the old man hard sometimes. Doesn't know what he's doing.'

'So that's what he—' Miss Nessa bit off the rest of her words and looked at me, her suspicion replaced by alarm and concern. 'Are you all right, Su Lin? Are you hurt?'

'Yes, Miss Nessa. No, Miss Nessa.'

'Whatever you think happened, be assured you were mistaken. It is a difficult time for all of us. It will not happen again. There is no point in dwelling on such things. We will not speak of it again.'

'Dear Aunt Nessa, surely you haven't suppressed your feminine

side so completely as to defend the patriarchy,' Harry drawled.
'Shouldn't you be standing up for disadvantaged maidens?'

'You can go now.' Whether she was embarrassed or not, Miss
Nessa clearly did not intend to discuss the matter further.

Once we were outside, Harry winked. 'We'll just look in on
Dee-Dee, then I'll join you in the kitchen and see what Cookie
feels like feeding us.'

Chain of Discovery

———◆———

G iven all the excitement of the day, I was sure I would never get to sleep, but a delicious dinner of fried noodles with prawns and spring onions took the edge off my excitement and left me exhausted. Fortunately, Dee-Dee had not woken. I barely made it to my own bed before I fell asleep, though not without anchoring our door handles. This was second nature for me now. I was responsible for the child-woman's safety as well as my own.

The next morning, I woke before Dee-Dee and went downstairs to ask Cookie for her breakfast instead of rousing her. When I ushered her into the kitchen, she seemed to have forgotten the events of the previous day and chatted over her milky porridge about bugs and bananas. Cookie had laid out some bacon left from Sir Henry and Miss Nessa's breakfast and she seized it eagerly, along with the grilled tomatoes. Cookie had had ready for me my rice porridge with stewed peanuts and *kopi*, the strong, sweet local coffee he knew I preferred. I tried to eat even though I wasn't hungry: this was rice and the Chinese side of me screamed guilt at every grain wasted. To my surprise I felt much better after eating. I hadn't noticed how hungry I was, probably because of all the questions tangled in my head.

The pendant kept coming back into my mind. Had Dee-Dee really thrown it? If she had . . . Fortunately, she seemed to have forgotten about it. Cookie saw I was tense and added a small dish of fried *ikan bilis* to the table. The tiny anchovies, which Miss Nessa wouldn't allow in the dining room because heads, bones, guts and all were consumed, were a special treat for the servants. Dee-Dee was so thrilled by their crisp saltiness that another dish soon appeared. She barely noticed me leave after Cookie had agreed with a nod to keep an eye on her.

The gracefully branching frangipani trees reached their maximum height at the level of the second-floor balcony. It was strange looking into the mature crown of leaves and delicate yellow-hearted white blossoms at eye level. Their faint scent in the gentle morning sunshine made it difficult to imagine that they could have anything to do with bad luck.

Then my eye caught a metallic glint. I yanked on the ropes to roll up the black and white bamboo blinds to their maximum. It required some effort. They had been installed as protection against sudden squalls during the monsoon season, but the family had simply abandoned the balcony during the rains. As a result, the ropes were fraying from the weather and the metal pulley was rusty.

Was it a glint of metal or just a trick of sunlight?

'There's something there . . .' Harry was suddenly beside me, leaning over. 'I can just about reach it . . .'

Startled, I lost my grip on the anchoring ropes. The rattan roll unfurled, thumping him on the back of his head.

'Ow! Let me do that. Do you see it? It's only about a foot away.' He twisted and knotted the ropes in a careless tangle on the rusty hook, then heaved himself up with both hands. 'Less than that – look, I can just about reach it.' He leaned forward and his feet lifted off the floorboards.

'No! Stop! You'll fall and break your neck, just like Charity did. Same place fall, same way die!' My hand smacked my mouth too late to block my unintended curse. A local would have been upset but Harry merely slid backwards onto the safety of the balcony floorboards. 'No point breaking my neck. But you can see it, can't you?'

'If it's the chain the pendant was on, it must have caught on that branch when Dee-Dee threw it over. She didn't make it up.' I'd been hoping it was another of Dee-Dee's stories.

Harry looked at the chain again. 'Dee-Dee threw it?' He panto-mimed a tossing action, first underarm then over. 'Most likely she did. If Charity dropped it by accident it would have gone straight down to the drain and flower border . . . but to have caught on a branch so far out, yes, she must have. And Charity managed to grab the pendant but the chain wouldn't come loose and she fell.'

Without thinking, I reached over the balustrade, anchoring my feet against the waist-high vertical supports. Charity had not been much taller than I was so if she had managed to grab the pendant . . .

'No, you mustn't. Stop. It's too dangerous. It is too much of a risk. Damnation, girl!'

'You want to just leave it there? You know Sir Henry and Miss Nessa don't want to hear any more about Charity's fall. And the servants are too scared of ghosts to do anything.'

'If I had a long stick,' Harry said, 'or if we had two long sticks you could use them like chopsticks, couldn't you, and just pick it off? Do you know where we could get two bamboo laundry poles maybe? Or two fishing rods?'

'Sihat!'

'What?'

'Who,' I corrected. 'Sihat, the gardener. He must have something to trim the high branches of trees. And we can trust him.' I couldn't say exactly how I knew that but it had to do with how carefully the old man treated the plants, the tools and the daily boys who worked under his supervision. And how gentle and patient he was with Dee-Dee when she interrupted his work with questions about birds and insects or gleefully kicked over the piles of leaves he had patiently raked together.

'Or Cookie.' I trusted Cookie for the same reason. Even if he was an old Indian man cooking for colonials, he had kept his dignity. I had seen the food he sent up to Dee-Dee when she wasn't well. It was nothing like the stuff delivered to the adults in the dining room. Bad people could produce fancy meals, but only a truly good person would make the effort to crush rice and strain stock to make porridge for a sick girl who probably wouldn't even notice it. Between Cookie and the gardener, one of them was sure to suggest something to reach it.

'The gardener's Malay, isn't he? And Cookie isn't even from around here. I thought you Chinese don't trust Malays and Indians?'

'That's just what you *ang mohs* want to think. Here we do what we have to do to survive. And sometimes you have to trust people so that they trust you.'

Harry nodded. 'I'll go and ask. Promise not to kill yourself before I get back.'

———◆———

Sihat obligingly produced a long bamboo pole with a string-activated clipper at the end. It was for harvesting rambutan and came with a netting bag at the end of another long pole. With me giving directions from the balcony, Harry had soon cropped and retrieved the tiny branch with the metallic gleam. He held it up between two fingers. It was indeed a segment of a chain, very likely Charity's pendant chain. 'Jesus Christ.'

'He would tell her to "Go and sin no more,"' I pointed out, 'after writing in the sand. But I want to know if what Dee-Dee said is true.'

'Dee-Dee may take things sometimes but she doesn't lie,' Harry said vaguely. His eyes were on the chain but his mind was clearly far away. 'She didn't know what she was doing.' It was automatic. Clearly he had been apologizing for his sister for years. 'Dee-Dee is always taking things. It's not really stealing. She always means to return them. And Charity wouldn't have minded. They were always sharing things. They were very close.'

Harry *wasn't really lying* in the same way Dee-Dee *didn't really steal things*. I knew it wasn't Dee-Dee he was worried about, and he wasn't worried so much as trying to work something out from the facts. Like many people who seldom analyse anything beyond their last meal or plans for their next holiday, he didn't find thinking easy. It was like watching someone whose only regular exercise was a stroll after church suddenly being obliged to run a marathon or trek to the South Pole – in his best Sunday brogues. I knew what was worrying him: had his father given the pendant to Charity? And, if so, had Mary Palin found out and been driven to stab Charity as she leaned over the balcony, reaching for it?

Something about that version of events did not ring true. I was pretty certain that no matter how much one woman wanted another dead, she would not stab her in the side before pushing her off a balcony in broad daylight. I could imagine Lady Palin giving Charity a good slap that might have toppled her over, but for her to have a *keris* in hand she must have planned ahead, which didn't sound like her at all. No, from what I had seen of Lady Palin she would have enjoyed creating a big scene too much to want Charity killed off so fast.

But Harry's thoughts had moved onto a different track: 'I wonder, could Poor Mary have loved Father after all? I always thought she was here to take advantage of him, because he couldn't throw her out, being married and all. She did try, when she first moved in. I shut her out because I thought she was just a gold-digger. But she couldn't help being stupid. She was like Dee-Dee in a way, wasn't she?' There was pain in Harry's voice as well as on his face.

'You loved Charity,' I said, without thinking. Harry looked shocked. I couldn't read the sudden horrible tension in his face and, for a moment, I thought he was going to hit me.

Instead he shook his head and let out a shaky breath. 'You said you weren't a spy,'

'I said I wasn't a police spy,' I said smartly, to cover the thoughts whirling in my mind. 'I should go and fetch Dee-Dee from the kitchen.'

'I'll come with you. I want to see what else of Charity's Dee-Dee has hidden away.'

———◆———

'Dee-Dee, what else did you borrow from Charity?'

Dee-Dee looked from me to the whistle Harry was playing with. She licked her lips. 'You're not going to tell Aunt Nessa?'

'We're not going to tell Aunt Nessa,' Harry promised.

'Oh. But it's my secret.'

Harry toyed with the whistle, artfully blew at the wrong end and looked puzzled. Dee-Dee whimpered. 'Fair trade?' he suggested. Dee-Dee nodded so hard I was afraid she would wet her knickers.

———◆———

There wasn't much in Dee-Dee's secret place, which turned out to be a Mackintosh's Quality Street tin hidden under a flowerpot behind the chicken house. There were some trinkets, some hairpins and bright buttons. And the photograph.

I was so taken aback to see a naked body posed on its side – one leg crossed forward to conceal the private parts, hair pulled over one shoulder above a generous freckled breast – that it took me a moment to reach the face, with its invitingly pursed lips. Then I recognized the young woman I had last encountered as a broken body beneath a bloodied sheet.

Of course I had seen Charity Byrne in town when she was still alive, but I can honestly say I had never seen that much of her. The Charity in the photograph posed seductively, looking at the camera through lowered eyelids. There was more make-up on her face than clothing on her body and I wondered how the photographer had felt about that.

But who had taken the photograph? And where had it been developed?

I could not imagine someone taking the film into Shankar and Sons Pharmaceuticals and Photographic Prints in town. Of course, Government House might have its own facilities for developing film: could Charity have been seeing one of the government aides? Had he taken photographs of Charity for himself or had he sold the pictures? I remembered that Shen-Shen and Lady Palin had commented on Charity having far more spending money than might have been expected. But there had been no sign at all that she was involved with anyone at Government House.

I flipped the photograph, glancing up to check on Dee-Dee. She was engrossed with blowing the three notes her new whistle permitted. Then I saw the message scrawled on the back of the picture in Charity's large, childish handwriting: 'To My Handsome and Heavenly Harry'.

I don't know how long I stood there, staring at the words. I jumped when Harry's fingers took the photograph from me.

'I didn't borrow that from Charity,' Dee-Dee remarked. 'I borrowed it from Poor Mary's room.'

Had Mary Palin wanted to kill Charity Byrne for having an affair with *Harry*? She must have, because if she hadn't, why had she felt guilty enough to commit suicide?

That Evening

———◆———

In the instant I read his name on the back of that photograph I knew I had been completely taken in by Harry Palin. How could I have trusted him, even after seeing how easily he had lied to and manipulated his own family? I, who had thought I could read people, had been totally deceived. No matter what he said now, I had seen his name written in Charity's hand on the back of that photograph, and I knew how right Le Froy had been to warn me against him.

I would have liked to send the photograph to Le Froy immediately but Harry disappeared, taking it with him. 'I've got to think. I need some time to think.'

I did not try to stop him. To tell the truth, I was suddenly afraid of him. I saw clearly that Harry had a motive for killing Charity (had she tired of him, fallen for some other young man in town?) as well as Lady Palin (especially if she had found out what had been going on between him and Charity). Now I knew why my grandmother and Miss Blackmore had repeatedly warned me against being headstrong and too trusting. At least I had learned the truth before it was too late.

I scribbled a note to Le Froy, telling him about the photograph and Harry's disappearance, and went to ask Cookie whether he was sending any of the boys to town for supplies. He said no, but if I needed anything he could spare Tanis. I gave the boy my note for Le Froy and told him to hurry.

After lunch I kept Dee-Dee out of the house for the rest of the afternoon, expecting at any moment to see Le Froy's motor-car appear, possibly at the head of a convoy of officers, ready to take in Harry Palin for questioning. I would feel much safer once he was locked up. I just hoped he would confess quickly so Dee-Dee wouldn't be dragged into it. But the hours passed and there was no sign of Le Froy. I couldn't understand it. Why was he ignoring me just when I had discovered the clue that solved his case for him?

It was evening and almost dinnertime when I saw Tanis again. 'Did you see Inspector Le Froy? What did he say when you gave him the note?'

'I did not give to him myself,' the houseboy said. 'Just now on the road I see Mr Harry. He ask me where am I going. I tell him. He say he is going to town to see the policeman. He will give him your letter.'

I felt a giant fist clutching my chest so I couldn't breathe. Le Froy wasn't coming. All afternoon, while I had been confidently expecting him, he had had no idea of what had happened. I cursed myself for not going into town to see him myself. I could have left Dee-Dee in the kitchen with Cookie and walked there in daylight. Then again, that might not have been a good idea either. I had not seen Harry all day and thought he had run away, knowing the police would come for him once they had learned about the photograph. But now it seemed that Harry had been lurking outside, waiting for me to try to get word to Le Froy. He had lied and taken my note from the houseboy, but what might he have done to me? Now that it was getting dark, Harry might come back at any time. I did not want to pass another evening in this house afraid to eat or drink anything he might have doctored and straining all night to hear his footsteps in the corridor.

I had no choice. I had to tell Sir Henry and Miss Nessa what I knew about Harry.

———◆———

In the drawing room, Sir Henry was dozing in his chair with papers on his lap and his pipe smoking in the ashtray beside him. Next to him, Miss Nessa was going through a pile of papers, peering through her *pince-nez* and marking out passages with a black pencil. She looked up when I knocked lightly on the door, and smiled when she saw Dee-Dee.

'Come to say good night, Deborah?'

'Yes!' Dee-Dee said. She ran to her sleepy father and planted her ample self on his lap, squeezing the breath out of him.

'Miss Nessa, I have to talk to you and Sir Henry. I found a photograph that Dee-Dee had hidden. It's a photograph of Charity.'

I saw Miss Nessa glance at Sir Henry, as though wondering whether I had suddenly gone mad. 'She's undressed in the picture. Completely undressed,' I went on urgently, keeping my voice low to avoid catching Dee-Dee's attention. 'And on the back there's a message from her to Mr Harry. A love message. And she calls him "her" Harry.'

For a moment, neither of them reacted. Dee-Dee started to sing a little song to herself, "'Roses are red, Violets are blue, Sugar is sweet, And so are you,'" but her father hushed her by actually putting his hand across her mouth.

'Where is the photograph now?' Miss Nessa asked. I could tell she had instantly grasped the implications and felt a huge sense of relief. Miss Nessa would know what to do. She always knew what to do, even if she wasn't always right.

'Mr Harry took it.'

'Harry?' Sir Henry's voice was high and artificial, as though he were acting a part in a stage play. 'Where's Harry? What photographs are you talking about? Naughty photographs of Charity, eh? I don't know anything about naughty photographs.'

'Quiet, you fool! And where is Harry now?'

'I don't know. He said he was going into town. But that's not all. I tried to send Inspector Le Froy a note about the photograph. I asked one of the houseboys to take it down to town for me this afternoon. Later, when I didn't hear back from the inspector, I asked the houseboy what had happened and he said Mr Harry had taken my note from him. He's probably destroyed it and the photo by now. Then there will be no proof!'

'Why did you write to Le Froy?' Miss Nessa asked.

'I thought he ought to know. You see, Charity died by accident. I found a piece of the chain from her pendant tangled in the frangipani tree growing next to the upstairs balcony. Dee-Dee threw Charity's pendant into the frangipani tree and I think Charity was trying to get it back and had just managed to grab it when she fell. When she screamed Lady Palin's name, it wasn't because Lady Palin was attacking her. She was calling to her for

271

help because she knew Lady Palin was on the second floor with her when she fell.'

Miss Nessa was shaking her head, as though to dismiss my explanation, but I pressed on, desperate to make her see its importance and implications.

'Mary could have grabbed at the damned pendant before the girl fell,' Sir Henry said. 'Women do things like that. As far as I can see, she grabbed the pendant when she pushed the girl over the balcony wall. She was strong, that woman. Then she saw what she'd done, threw the pendant after Charity and part of it caught on the tree. I don't see what all this fuss is about. One woman is dead. The other killed her and killed herself. Sad, but what can you do about it? Case closed. Time we all moved on!' There was a singsong storytelling lilt to his voice but no other indication that he was drunk. I found I was no longer afraid of him and focused my attention on Miss Nessa.

'Can't you see? If Charity died by accident because of Dee-Dee and the pendant, there was no reason for Lady Palin to feel guilty, no reason for her to kill herself. Anyway, she wouldn't have killed herself. She'd told everybody she was going home and was all excited. She was shopping in town and buying all those things to take back to her friends in England. But if Mr Harry believed Lady Palin pushed Charity off the balcony he may have killed her in revenge. Or perhaps she had found out about him and Charity and was trying to blackmail him. Dee-Dee took the photograph from Lady Palin's room, not Charity's. Mr Harry must have found out she knew . . .' As I spoke the reason dawned on me. 'Lady Palin must have threatened to tell you about him and Charity, so he somehow

272

changed her sleeping powders so that she took too much and it killed her!'

They exchanged a strange look, as though I had just answered a question for them. I was starting to feel desperate. Harry had already had hours to get away. Earlier I had been afraid of meeting him before Le Froy came to take him away, but now I just wanted him to answer for what he had done. Mary Palin had been a most unpleasant woman but that did not give Harry the right to kill her . . . if he had. Admittedly, part of me was hoping they would somehow prove me wrong. I had liked Harry Palin. I didn't want him to be a murderer. But who else could it have been?

Still neither of them spoke. I understood it was difficult for them. They had probably thought they knew Harry Palin, too. And to them he was an innocent son and nephew, as incapable of having lovers as he was of killing them.

'You can't just ignore it. If he hasn't destroyed the photograph you would see for yourselves. Charity wrote a note to him on the back.' I forced myself to speak calmly. Why should they believe me rather than the absent Harry? I wished I had gone through Dee-Dee's tin earlier and found the photograph when Harry was not around. Even if they didn't want to believe me, they would have had to believe the evidence of Charity's handwritten note. Then a sickening thought came to me: even if they believed me, they might choose to protect Harry rather than expose him. Wasn't that what my uncles always said? That white men were no better than us but always covered up for each other?

'Mr Harry couldn't have killed Charity because he was outside the house when she fell. I'm not saying that he seduced her but they definitely had some kind of affair. He must have been the

273

father of her child. And he used her death as an excuse to make it look as though Lady Palin killed herself. Mr Harry must have killed Lady Palin. He's the only one with any reason to.'

'You can't prove anything,' Sir Henry said. 'The girl was a liar. She said whatever suited her. You won't get anyone to believe anything she said.' He looked at Miss Nessa, cold calculation on his face. The good-natured bleariness had been an act. No normal head could have cleared so swiftly. 'All girls are liars, and no one is going to believe anything you say either. It's our word against yours.'

'What makes you think Harry was having an affair with Charity?' Miss Nessa ignored her brother.

'In the note she wrote on the back of the photograph she called him her "Handsome Harry". I'll swear to it!'

'No,' Dee-Dee said. We all looked at Dee-Dee in surprise.

'I saw it with my own eyes,' I said firmly. 'Dee-Dee, you don't understand—'

'You're the one who doesn't understand,' Dee-Dee said import-antly. 'Charity never called our Harry "Harry".' She preened a little, pleased to have our attention on her. 'Charity always called our Harry "Freddy the Frog". That's because Charity called Papa her only Harry because she said Papa was "Harry" only to her.'

Sir Henry stared at Dee-Dee with his mouth slightly open, as though he were a clockwork toy that had suddenly run down. So many new thoughts dashed into my head that I felt dizzy. I had to get away somewhere alone to think but I couldn't tear my eyes off Sir Henry. He looked so old and silly and helpless. Charity couldn't have been in love with him. Besides, Sir Henry was the acting governor. Governors did not kill people. Why didn't he close his mouth? Why didn't he say something?

Miss Nessa's mouth was stretched in a tight, thin line. Her eyes darted between Sir Henry and me, making me think of a king cobra preparing to strike. Despite the snake's masculine species name, the females are aggressive, much more so than the males, especially when defending their eggs. Even Dee-Dee picked up the tension in the room. 'I want ice cream,' she said, then fell silent, looking confused, when nobody responded. Miss Nessa started towards the door to the passage that led to the rest of the house.

'Nessa,' Sir Henry said. 'Nessa, you mustn't think that – it's not true. You know very well that that girl was just a little gold-digger. You said so yourself. Anyway, she was stabbed. It wasn't an accident. You can't believe that—'

'Shut up.' Miss Nessa closed the door. I heard the lock turn and she put the key into her pocket.

'I am certain Lady Palin wouldn't have killed herself.' My voice was only a little shaky. 'Please, Miss Nessa, you can't ignore this.'

'Nobody is going to believe any of it. Give me the chain and the photograph at once.' Miss Nessa's voice was calm and unemotional. She might have been giving instructions for the seating arrangements at a fund-raising tea.

'But I told you – they're with Harry. He took them.'

'Don't lie to me.'

'They'll be in her room somewhere,' Sir Henry said loudly. It was the first time he had looked directly at me since our encounter in his office. The jovial, slightly lascivious old gentleman was gone. Now he looked like someone caught stealing offerings from a shrine, but he seemed more embarrassed than guilty. Now, too late, I saw Le Froy's story had been a warning. The man was willing to shoot any native who got in his way. And now I was the inconvenient native.

'Miss Nessa,' I pleaded.

'Keep an eye on her.' Miss Nessa left the room, closing the door behind her. Again, I heard the key turn in the lock.

Sir Henry did not meet my eyes. Dee-Dee looked at him, then came quietly to my side. 'Bedtime?' she suggested.

'Good idea.'

But we were locked in. We could leave the house through the French windows but how would we get back in? Where else could we go? I moved towards the French windows.

'No,' Sir Henry said. He opened a drawer and took out a pistol.

'Not in front of Dee-Dee.'

'No,' he agreed. 'Not in front of Dee-Dee.'

They needed me, I reminded myself wildly. They didn't think anyone would believe me and I didn't have any proof, so they needn't feel too threatened. All I had to do was stay calm until I saw a chance to slip out of the house. I would head straight to town and tell Le Froy. Or I would find Uncle Chen and tell him to take me home to my grandmother. I would be safe there and I could take my time in telling her everything. Ah Ma would listen to me. And even if she didn't believe me, she would keep me safe. Suddenly the most important thing to me was to find somewhere safe I could hide from these *ang mohs* and their complications. Education, a career and adventuring to see the world were nothing compared to surviving the night to see morning.

'I should put Dee-Dee to bed.' My voice sounded normal, but neither Sir Henry nor Dee-Dee seemed to hear me.

All the times my grandmother had warned me to mind my own business came back to me. Why hadn't I listened? But, then, my grandmother was one of the most inquisitive people alive and everyone told me how much I took after her. I suspected that in my place she would have done exactly the same thing. And what would she do now? Someone like my grandmother, who thought all young *ang moh*s were wild and lascivious, would not have been surprised to learn that Harry Palin and Charity Byrne were having a love affair. But Sir Henry Palin, the acting governor, and his daughter's nanny? Even my mind balked at the thought. It was too close to *lèse-majesté*. My Mission School education had drummed into us that the governor represented the King of the United Kingdom and the Dominions of the British Empire, and King Edward VIII represented the God of the Church of England. (Although, of course, he was rumoured to be at loggerheads with the Church because he wanted to marry an American divorcée.)

I looked at the man to whose high position I owed allegiance, as a lowly member of the British Empire, and wondered if I could push past him and get out through the French windows before he shot me with his pistol. Outside, I would run round to the back steps, then down the trail to the servants' quarters . . .

I heard the door being unlocked. Miss Nessa came in, carrying a tray with the coffee urn and two cups and saucers, which she placed on the table by the door while she re-locked it without speaking. Sir Henry looked at her with a mixture of dread and hope in his face but neither spoke. I saw her put the key into her pocket. Then she picked up the tray again.

'I want coffee,' Dee-Dee said. She did not like coffee but she liked asking for it because being told 'no' by adults gave her an excuse to protest.

'I sent the servants back to their quarters,' Miss Nessa said conversationally, as she unfolded a paper sachet. 'There's nothing more we need them for here tonight. I told them I didn't want to see any of them anywhere near the house before morning.'

'I'll take Dee-Dee upstairs and put her to bed,' I said. Dee-Dee automatically took a deep breath to protest and I added quickly, 'If we go up early we'll have more time to read stories. We can read two stories!' which pacified her temporarily.

'I want to stay downstairs until Harry gets home.' Dee-Dee pouted. Being allowed to stay up wasn't very interesting when Harry wasn't at home to entertain her, but she was not going to give up without token resistance. 'I want Harry to come up to read to me.'

'I'll tell him when he gets back,' I said automatically. A contradiction that had been at the back of my mind surfaced: 'If Charity didn't write that note to Mr Harry, why did he run off with the picture? And why did he stop the houseboy taking my note to Le Froy?'

'Perhaps he has a greater sense of responsibility and loyalty than you seem to,' Miss Nessa said, still in her conversation voice. It was pitched higher than usual and she spoke through the bright artificial smile that was on her face now. Sir Henry had slumped back into a chair when she returned. Now he was watching her like a dog waiting for instructions. Miss Nessa poured coffee into the cups on the tray, then stirred in cream and sugar. Now she held one out to me. 'Drink this. Now.'

My hands accepted the cup with care, even as I said, 'Thank

you, but I don't drink coffee. It keeps me awake.' I tried to set the cup and its saucer back on the tray but Miss Nessa blocked my arm.

'You are going to drink it,' she said. 'Don't worry, it won't keep you awake for long. Nothing will keep you awake tonight.'

Her voice was controlled and controlling, her smile so confident that I nodded, politely holding the cup. The first and main thing you learn at school in Singapore is to obey instructions without question. I had spent ten years at school and had mastered the art of looking obedient.

Much as I longed for adventure, I have never seen the point in taking risks, especially physical ones. With my polio limp I was less than agile and I stayed away from rivers with crocodiles and storm drains with rats, and avoided going into town on Saturday nights when it was full of drunken white men. I had always thought of myself as an obedient coward, especially when faced with someone as pleasant and authoritative as Miss Nessa Palin. Looking into her cold blue eyes, with their hints of grey ice, I was frightened. I was frightened of what was in the cup I was holding, and even more frightened of the woman who had handed it to me. And, yes, I would probably have drunk the coffee if she had not held out the other cup to Dee-Dee.

'Deborah? You wanted coffee? Here you are.'

'Nessa,' Sir Henry said. 'No, Nessa.' He sounded as though he were miles away, instead of just a few steps across the room.

'Be quiet,' Miss Nessa snapped. 'Deborah! Come here!' Dee-Dee took the cup from her aunt, looking uncertainly to me for guidance.

It was the horror on Sir Henry's face that made me understand what Miss Nessa meant to do as she put a hand on Dee-Dee's arm and guided the cup upwards towards her mouth. 'Come on, you great silly girl. You said you wanted coffee . . .' Dee-Dee's mouth opened automatically.

'No!' I said. I had meant to shout but the words came out in a nervous squeak. 'You'll never get away with this.'

'You're a nice girl, Su Lin,' Miss Nessa said. Her voice was gracious and friendly, the voice that had encouraged donations of time and money to countless good works and projects. 'You were so good with Deborah, but you saw how attached she was to you, and you knew there couldn't be much of a life for her, no matter what happened. So, out of the goodness of your heart, you decided to put her out of her misery. You found poor Mary's Veronal after she died and that was what gave you the idea. But you knew it was wrong, so you took the rest of the powder yourself.'

I could see that people would believe her. Even now, looking at Miss Vanessa Palin's perfectly smooth hair and perfectly starched and ironed dress, I almost believed her. Surely this perfectly composed woman was far closer to godliness than mere cleanliness could ever hope to be.

'You can't just kill her!' Sir Henry gasped.

'She can't be trusted, and that fool Le Froy seems to trust her.'

'But Dee-Dee! Not Dee-Dee! She doesn't understand. She won't say anything. We'll find someone else for her. There must be someone else.' Sir Henry looked at me. 'Just keep her in the house, make sure she doesn't speak to anybody. It will be all right.'

'We can't keep her from the servants and the servants can't be trusted. And that fool Le Froy is sure to ask to see her.'

'But you can't just go around killing people like that, Nessa.'

'Somebody's got to clear up after you.'

I curled my fingers around my cup and lowered it. The coffee was still hot. Drawn by the movement, Miss Nessa turned to look at me, and as she did so I swung the cup up and splashed its contents into her face. Startled, Miss Nessa screamed, reeled away from Dee-Dee and stumbled, falling heavily into the chair behind her.

'Run, Dee-Dee!' I shouted. 'Outside! Go and hide outside!'

For a moment Dee-Dee hesitated, swaying from one foot to the other. She was afraid of being alone in the dark and shook her head. I could have slapped her. But if only I had been close enough to slap Dee-Dee I could have grabbed and pulled her out of the room with me.

Miss Nessa was back on her feet, looking furious as she wiped the coffee off her face with the lace antimacassar from the back of the chair.

'The coffee will stain both the upholstery and your dress if you let it set. There's baking soda in the kitchen.' My only thought was of how I could get myself and Dee-Dee away from there, but my voice was going on as though it were a recording machine playing back the text of a domestic-science lesson.

'Baking soda will dissolve the coffee compounds in the fabric if you apply it quickly enough. Or you can use an egg yolk with a little alcohol and warm water.'

Miss Nessa froze, staring at me as though I were the one who had just gone mad. That gave me time to move to Dee-Dee's side. There was no hope of getting the main door key away from Miss Nessa but I was sure the French windows out to the veranda that ran around the house were not locked – but Sir Henry stood between that exit and us. I hesitated.

'You miserable bitch!' Nessa Palin snarled. Like her expensive leather books, she clearly did not react well to being wet.

Dee-Dee gave a little trill of horrified delight, then shrieked, 'You said "bitch"! You said, "bitch"!' drawing Miss Nessa's attention back to her and the coffee cup she still held.

'Give your cup to Su Lin. Here, hand it to me and I'll give it to—'

Miss Nessa reached out to take Dee-Dee's cup but, with another almighty crow of delight, the girl emptied the cup's contents over her aunt as I had done. She sent her cup and saucer after the coffee, and at the sound of shattering porcelain Sir Henry gave an involuntary bellow of laughter. I acted.

'Outside!' I shouted to Dee-Dee, as I pulled her past Sir Henry to the French windows. Thankfully, they opened. 'Run! We're playing catch! Run outside quick!'

Dee-Dee whooped and shrieked in excitement and started running. I limped after her as fast as I could.

'Stop them! Stop them, you old fool!' Miss Nessa shouted, but Sir Henry was laughing again. It was a high, hiccuping laugh. I could have sworn I heard him saying, 'Run! Run! Run!' He didn't try to stop us. But as I pushed Dee-Dee into the garden ahead of me I heard a crash from inside the room that suggested Sir Henry had stood up just in time to collide with Miss Nessa as she had dashed past in pursuit.

In the Dark

———◆———

It was dark outside. Coming out of the well-lit drawing room
my eyes could see nothing but dark shapes. Luckily I knew
the place by now. I pushed Dee-Dee round the side of the
house and down the patio steps, then pulled her along the
lawn behind me.

'I can't see!'

'Close your eyes and hold my hand. Pretend we're playing
blind man.'

I heard her giggling as she hung onto me.

My first thought was to make for the track to the servants'
quarters and ask for help. Would they help us? So many times I
had heard Miss Nessa tell visitors that all of the servants were
loyal to the death to Sir Henry. I suspected what she really meant
was they were scared to death of her. That was the real reason
why none of them had said anything to the police about the two
deaths, though they must have had their suspicions. I couldn't
count on them to help us now. They might even force us to return
to the house and Sir Henry.

We came to where Sihat the gardener had been cutting and clearing wild grass that afternoon. I was sure he would have helped us to hide – as long as the White Boss didn't know about it.

'We're going to the monkey trees,' I whispered to Dee-Dee. 'Quietly. Like in hide-and-seek.'

Several times we had seen monkeys in the huge wild rambutan and mango trees that grew on the slopes beyond the servants' quarters. The trees were outside Government House property, but when the fruit was in season, the servants would join monkeys, squirrels, birds and tree lizards in scavenging for a share. The wilderness surrounding the official grounds was not true rainforest but it was thick and wild enough to keep us hidden for a while at least. And then what? Would the coming of day bring Miss Nessa back to her senses?

I strained to hear footsteps. The night was full of strange noises – rustlings, insect calls, the distant howl of a wild dog – but the servants' quarters stood dark and silent, and there was no sign of Sir Henry or Miss Nessa yet. I pulled Dee-Dee on. I didn't even know who was housed in each dark shed, except that Sihat was right at the end: his gardening tools were neatly laid out on a wood bench by the entrance. He always cleaned them at the end of each day, so they would be ready for the next morning. I knocked lightly on his door and called softly but there was no answer. He was either fast asleep or pretending to be. Sihat hated anyone touching his precious tools, and would yell curses if something were missing. But I risked it this time. No matter how angry Sihat got, I only hoped I would be alive to hear him rant again.

'When will they come look for us?' Dee-Dee whispered, panting in excitement.

'Ssh – quiet.'

We couldn't struggle through the heavy undergrowth all the way to town in the dark: we would have to take the road. The Palins could come after us any time they wished in Sir Henry's motor-car. They could run us down and claim it was an accident. That was a point in favour of horse carriages over motor-cars, I thought. It must be harder to get horses to trample someone to death than a mindless motor.

We would stay hidden, I decided, until I saw – or heard – the Palins' car go past us on the winding road down the hill. Then we would go back up to the house and I would lock us safely inside Dee-Dee's room until morning. Surely Miss Nessa would have come to her senses by then. Or once I was certain the Palins were gone we would retrace our steps and bang on Cookie's door until he opened it, no matter how long it took. I could leave Dee-Dee with him and somehow make it down the hill to town to find Le Froy – he was the only person I could trust now. Even my grandmother and uncle could not protect me from important *ang mohs*, who could confiscate property and detain them without trial. But important people in authority trusted Le Froy, and Le Froy seemed to trust me.

Now, as my eyes grew accustomed to the darkness, I saw the dark tree trunks stretching upwards out of the massed tangle of bushes in which they crouched. My arms and ankles were itching and I pinched away a flying bug attracted by the sweat on my face.

'I want to go back inside,' Dee-Dee whined. 'A mosquito bit me. I hate mosquitoes!'

'Ssh, sweetheart.'

Why hadn't Sir Henry and Miss Nessa sent the car out after us yet?

'Are we going to die?'

'Not tonight, darling.' I wasn't certain of that.

'If we die, will we see Charity again? I don't want to see Poor Mary. I don't want to die.'

'You're not going to die,' I said, hoping I was right. 'Not now.'

———◆———

'You win!' Miss Nessa's voice called out of the darkness. Distracted by Dee-Dee, I had not heard her coming. It was still her light social voice. So many times I had been happy to hear that voice, to know that more activities were planned, that everything was safely under control . . . It was only Lady Palin who had never wanted to join in. And now I knew how the poor woman must have felt. But surely Nessa couldn't be certain we were there. She had to be guessing, calling into the darkness. I clutched Dee-Dee's arm tightly, keeping her by my side.

'The game's over, Dee-Dee. Let's go inside and collect your prize. I have sweeties!' Nessa sang. 'You win!'

'Yay! We won!' Dee-Dee jumped forward, shaking off my arm. I grabbed at her desperately, getting only a handful of damp slippery cotton before Dee-Dee kicked at me with a gleeful shriek and dashed in the direction of Miss Nessa's voice. 'I want my sweeties! I hate mosquitoes! Where's my sweeties?'

Suddenly there was light as Miss Nessa switched on a lantern-style torch. The flat-based device was designed to be set

down for extended use, and as Miss Nessa held it up, it illu-
minated her and the area around her, allowing me to see her far
more clearly than she could see me. She was holding the lamp
in her left hand and Sir Henry's tiger rifle on her right arm.

Dee-Dee stumbled up to Miss Nessa but stopped uncertainly
before reaching her. Miss Nessa put the lamp on the ground in
front of her and, with both hands, pointed the rifle in the direction from which Dee-Dee had come.

'You might as well come out now, Su Lin.'

'I want to go in the house! I want my sweeties!'

Miss Nessa pushed Dee-Dee aside with the barrel of the rifle.
For a moment it seemed she would shoot the girl and I stepped
forward with an involuntary cry, 'No! Don't!' and saw the rifle
move to fix on me.

In that frozen moment, I thought I heard the sound of a car
engine in the distance, winding up the long road towards the
front of the house – several car engines, in fact. Miss Nessa heard
them, too, because she tensed and turned. As the sounds died
away, the rifle followed her eyes back in my direction. I kept my
hands behind my back.

'No one is going to get here in time to help you. You must
have sneaked out in the night to meet a lover. Everybody knows
that's what girls like you always do. Of course we had no idea
what was going on. When we heard noises out here, we thought
you were an intruder and one of the guards shot you. So sad for
you. But perfectly justified.'

I thought the rustlings in the undergrowth downhill from us
were increasing, as though bodies were moving through it, trying
to remain silent, but there was no way anyone from the cars could

have made it round so quickly, even if they had known where we were. Wild pigs, I thought – I had seen a solitary young male foraging a couple of times, though it was unusual for pigs to come so close to buildings. Or hungry spirits, anticipating my death and coming to collect me.

Miss Nessa walked towards me, the rifle pointed at my middle. 'I'm not very good with guns, so I want to make sure I get a good shot,' she said almost conversationally. Her diplomatic control was back. 'But don't worry. Once you're down the second shot will go through your head to put you out of your misery. It will be over very quickly.'

'Stop!' A man's voice came from the darkness some distance downhill to our left. Though it had spoken English, the accent suggested its owner was Chinese. We both turned and looked but could see nothing.

'Police!' I recognized Le Froy's voice coming from the trail leading back up to the servants' quarters. But how was that possible? 'Show yourselves and remain where you are.'

There were muttered discussions, the crashing sound of several bodies trying to run through the tangle of undergrowth and the darting yellow beams of tubular hand-held flashlights. At the same time, shouts and footsteps came from the direction of the house. I think we both realized at the same time that although people were coming towards us from two directions they were all too far away to stop Miss Nessa if she fired now. She could tell whatever story she wanted to once I was dead. Miss Nessa looked at me and raised her rifle slightly to press its barrel against my chest.

'The local girl Su Lin has kidnapped Sir Henry Palin's

daughter!' Miss Nessa said loudly. 'After threatening Sir Henry and myself, his sister, in our own home. She kidnapped Sir Henry's daughter and took her out here. We are afraid for the girl's life!'

Miss Nessa was so close now I could hear every rasping, quivering breath she took. There was a delirious grin of exultation on her face. I recognized the thrill of the kill that Sir Henry had talked about, the do-or-die moment when the rest of the world seemed to fade away and nothing else mattered. Well, I knew nothing else would ever matter again if I didn't seize that moment. Miss Nessa closed her eyes but I did not.

That Night

———◆———

I kept my eyes on Miss Nessa and heard myself say, 'Please. Help me.' I didn't know if I was appealing to Miss Nessa's Mission God or to any ancestral spirits that might be in the vicinity. Dee-Dee must have thought I was talking to her. As I swung the gardener's *parang* from behind my back and slashed at Miss Nessa's rifle, Dee-Dee launched herself at her aunt, grabbing and sinking her teeth into her right arm. Vanessa Palin fell forward, twisting away from Dee-Dee so that instead of whacking aside the barrel of her rifle as I intended, the *parang's* wicked blade slashed across her throat. A fountain of blood sprayed us as she fell, knocking the lantern on its side so it shone full on her face. Her lips moved but the only sound that came out was a terrible bubbling. Sihat was right: a well-sharpened jungle machete is a versatile and deadly tool.

Suddenly we were surrounded by people. I had not imagined the sounds of bodies moving up the jungle-tangled slope after all. Trembling so hard I couldn't move, I watched Uncle Chen push out of the jungle with about ten men, some familiar from his shop or Chen Mansion. Another group, now hurrying (skidding, tripping and swearing) down the steps and slope from the house, were in police khakis and I saw Le Froy, taller than most, taking in the bloody scene as he half strode, half leaped towards us through the crowd of men. Most of the police officers were carrying guns, and Uncle Chen's men were armed with knives and machetes. They all stared at each other, at me still holding my deadly weapon, and at the dying woman on the ground.

Then old Sihat was standing in front of me in his sarong and singlet. 'My *parang*.' Gently his rough fingers prised mine off the bloody wooden handle I was clutching.

'Sorry. I took it. I had to—'

Then Harry was there too, pushing through the crowd. He stopped at the sight of his aunt's body, bloody in the lamplight. Then his eyes darted round to settle on me and Dee-Dee. 'Good God. Thank God.'

Dee-Dee had been standing behind me, but on seeing her brother she started wailing.

'Take them back up to the house,' Le Froy said to Harry. 'Su Lin, are you all right?'

I nodded. I kept nodding, feeling like a chicken looking for bugs, as I struggled to find words. 'I can't – the house – Sir Henry . . .'

'Don't worry about him. Come on.' Harry put an arm around Dee-Dee and took my hand. I hesitated, looking at Le Froy. I wanted to explain, tell him Miss Nessa had gone mad and attacked us. I had only been defending myself and Dee-Dee.

'Later,' Le Froy said. 'Go.'

As Harry led us away, I heard Le Froy demanding, 'What are all of you doing here?'

'Hunting tapir,' Uncle Chen answered. Tapirs were mainly active at night and the jungle covering the slopes of Frangipani Hill was linked to the central Bukit Timah forests. 'We heard shouting so we came to see.'

'What did you hear?'

'Don't know, *lah*. My English not so good.'

———◆———

It was easier climbing up the steep steps now there were policemen with torches lighting the way. All the lights were on in the house and Dee-Dee pulled away to run to her father past the policeman standing by the French windows. Sir Henry held out his arms to her and they collapsed together onto the sofa. He didn't look at me or Harry.

Harry led me to the upright chairs along the furthest wall, and I saw through the open door that there were policemen there too, their khaki shorts looking out of place in the hallway, where all men, even servants, wore long trousers. I saw there was blood all over the front of my dress. It was all over Dee-Dee too, but Sir Henry didn't seem to mind or even notice. Harry poured whisky into a glass and handed it to me, then helped himself and downed it in one swallow. I took a mouthful and the fiery shock helped me to stop shaking. But I needed answers more than alcohol.

'Harry, why didn't you say something earlier?'

'You wouldn't have believed me. I saw how you were looking at me. You thought I was carrying on with Charity – you

292

thought I killed her and Poor Mary, and that I was going to kill you too!'

'That was only because I saw Charity had written "Harry" on the photograph. Of course I thought it was you! And why did you disappear? You must have known about Charity and your father as soon as you saw her love note. Why didn't you tell me? Why didn't you warn me? You almost got me killed! Dee-Dee too!'

Suddenly I was furious rather than afraid. If he knew there had been secret goings-on between his father and Charity, why hadn't he said so instead of skulking around looking guilty?

I was exhausted but still taut and tense. My body had been on danger alert for so long that I couldn't relax without collapsing completely. But I couldn't collapse yet: I wanted answers – and I still had to get Dee-Dee to bed. I saw she was fast asleep on the sofa with her head in Sir Henry's lap, which Miss Nessa would never have permitted, as he spoke to Inspector Le Froy, who had followed us back. Dee-Dee would be all right until I got my answers from Harry.

'I needed time to think. I didn't expect you to rush to tell Dad and Aunt Nessa.'

'I thought you killed your stepmother – perhaps somehow killed Charity as well! I thought you'd run away because I'd found out!'

'Would you have believed me if I'd tried to tell you? If it had been my word against Aunt Nessa's? And if the pater had taken her side? Anyway, I knew you didn't trust me. I read the note you tried to send to Le Froy. You were as good as telling him to come with his handcuffs and take me away! And you worshipped Aunt Nessa.'

That made me wince. He was right. I had admired Miss Nessa for so long. I had wanted her approval as much as I wanted to be like her.

'I don't blame you. I liked her too. I thought she was the only one who really saw me as I was.'

She did, I thought. And she saw me for what I was too. And she had used us both.

'I know you thought I was having an affair with Charity but I wasn't.'

'I thought you were in love with her. You were seen following her around in town.'

'I was, a little. At first it was just a game, and she encouraged it, flirting with me if anyone was watching. I suppose I thought, Why not let people think that? It's as good a cover as any.'

'Cover for what?'

He ignored that. 'I didn't know about Charity and my father. I should have guessed. She was always taking Dee-Dee across to Government House to see him, and he was always giving her presents that he pretended were for Dee-Dee if Poor Mary or Aunt Nessa saw. But I didn't think anything of it because that was just how men were with Charity. They liked her. There aren't very many white women out here, you know, so things are different here from how they are in England. You may not believe it but not all white colonials are out here to make money and live the good life. Some of us really believe it's all about organizing a better life for local people. You know, socialism and no more slums – all that. Good government is about making life better for people, whether or not they appreciate it. What you think of them doesn't affect how you treat them. It's nothing personal.'

'So you don't like the local people you want to help?'

Harry looked startled, as though I had interrupted him in the middle of a speech. Then his face relaxed and he laughed. 'Oh, Su Lin, I like you more than I want to. All right, I admit I shouldn't have run off like that, but I never imagined you'd be in any danger. It still seems crazy – impossible. I mean, Aunt Nessa?' He shook his head, still laughing, but I couldn't laugh and he stopped almost immediately. What had been so frightening was not that Miss Nessa had acted out of character but that she had not.

Everything Vanessa Palin had done was to preserve her broth-er's reputation and protect colonial authority. Acting to silence someone who threatened those things was completely in char-acter for her. I could not claim I had been taken in by some Jekyll and Hyde transformation.

'I didn't like Poor Mary but I wouldn't have done her any harm. She didn't deserve to die just because she was such a pain in the neck. Once I'd thought it over I took your note and the photograph to Le Froy. He saw the implications at once and was dashing about, rounding up his men, even before I'd finished explaining. I've never seen anyone move so fast – and he was so furious when he heard I'd left you here that I thought he was going to punch me. But it took me some time to find him – they finally tracked him down talking to coolies on Boat Quay. That was why we were almost too late.'

I didn't point out that they would all have been far too late if I hadn't got myself and Dee-Dee out of the house. Would Miss Nessa really have killed Dee-Dee as well? Sir Henry had clearly believed she would.

I could see why Harry had needed time to reflect, but I was angry. 'You could have warned me! Couldn't you trust me enough?'

'He decided to trust me instead,' Le Froy said. He had left Sir Henry and come across the room to us.

'How much trouble is my father in?' Harry rose to his feet.

Sir Henry had not tried to poison us or come after us with a tiger rifle. But he had threatened me with a pistol. Sitting and stroking his daughter's dirty fair hair, he looked ten years older and fifty times more tired than he had that morning. I hoped he wouldn't be in too much trouble.

'Sir Henry put a telephone call through to the chief of police,' Le Froy said. 'He said his sister was having an emotional breakdown and was hysterical. He needed assistance to prevent her harming herself and others. Of course we were already on our way here with Mr Harry by then, but the officer on duty passed on the message.'

I hadn't thought of Miss Nessa as hysterical or emotional, but perhaps that was how white men said, 'Need help with crazy rifle-carrying woman.'

'And when we got here Sir Henry told us where to find Miss Palin. He said he didn't know where you and Miss Deborah were, but Miss Nessa had taken a lantern torch with her and he had kept an eye on the light.'

'I told them they had to find her,' Sir Henry spoke up from across the room, 'before she found Dee-Dee. I couldn't let her hurt Dee-Dee.' There was a note of apology in his voice now as he looked at me for the first time since we had returned to the house. 'Or you. You aren't just another native servant, not when you've been so good with Dee-Dee. After all, you've been living with us, sitting at the table with us and drinking tea. You aren't just . . .' Sir Henry's voice trailed off.

I think he meant me to feel honoured and grateful because I was not 'just' a servant. Unlike Miss Nessa, who had preferred poison, Sir Henry had no qualms about putting bullets into those who were 'just' servants.

'I should take Dee-Dee upstairs to bed,' I said, half expecting to be told to leave the house immediately. After all, I was the reason policemen were now carrying the body of Sir Henry's sister, wrapped in a curtain, past the French windows to the front porch. We fell silent, watching the procession. The police were much more efficient this time, despite the hour. I realized that the delay over moving Charity's body had been due to Le Froy's desire to examine the acting governor's house and household. This time he needed no excuse.

Le Froy drew the curtains and had a quick word with the policemen by the door. Soon we were alone in the room. Sir Henry filled his tumbler from the whisky decanter by his side but Le Froy and Harry shook their heads when he tilted it towards them.

'Harry told me how you two found the chain,' Le Froy said, 'and the pendant.' When I nodded, he looked at Sir Henry as though expecting him to say something. But Sir Henry studied his whisky in silence and Le Froy turned back to me. I wished I knew how much Harry had told Le Froy to get him to rush his men over to the Residence. Now Miss Nessa was no longer a threat, I didn't want to get Dee-Dee into trouble. I didn't want her ever to realize that her throwing Charity's pendant over the balcony had triggered Charity's death – and those of Lady Palin and Miss Nessa.

'I should take Dee-Dee upstairs and put her to bed,' I said

again. If I could get the child-woman out of the way, it might be easier to gloss over her part in the story.

'No matter how the pendant got into the tree, it was Charity who decided to go after it. You can't call it anything other than an accident. There's no need to drag Dee-Dee into it.' In the yellow light, Harry looked pale and sickly and his voice shook a little as he spoke.

'I'm not trying to drag anyone into anything,' Le Froy said quietly. 'I just need to understand all the connections, to satisfy myself. Charity wasn't just a friend to you, was she?'

'Ah. Well. That. It has nothing to do with all this, but if it gets out, the repercussions would be bloody. Charity knew about . . . my visits to town. She was very friendly and supportive at first. I was stupid enough to confide in her and later she used it to blackmail me.'

'Times are changing,' Le Froy said. 'This friend of yours you slip into town to see, I suppose she is a native?'

'Yes,' Harry Palin said quietly. 'He is.'

'Some things may take a bit longer to change,' Le Froy said. 'But all things change in time. Even here in Singapore.'

'You should let Su Lin put my sister to bed.'

We all turned to look at Dee-Dee on the couch. She was already asleep, exhausted by the night's events. Le Froy turned down the oil lamp on the table beside her. His face was impassive as always, but the gesture was gentle, even protective, and I allowed myself to hope.

'I take full responsibility!' Sir Henry said, in his most pompous tone, but he looked far from confident. 'I'll say anything you want, but leave my daughter out of it. Harry—'

'Father?'

'Your sister. You will look after Deborah? You will make sure she . . .'

In that moment I understood that the man had betrayed the sister he depended on only because she had threatened his daughter. If Miss Nessa had wanted to kill only me, Sir Henry might have accepted it as something he had to close his eyes to for the sake of England. Somehow I still felt sorry for him.

But Le Froy was not after Dee-Dee. 'You stabbed Charity Byrne with the *keris* from your collection,' he remarked to Sir Henry. 'Why?'

'She was already dead.'

'Indeed.'

Sir Henry was known as a good man in an emergency, one of the fastest to assess a situation and take action. Of course, it might not always be the right action, but it was better than doing nothing while an enemy or a tiger attacked.

'I believe that, standing over Charity's body, you saw how her death could be used to drive your wife out of Singapore. You sent Harry for the doctor and Sihat for the police and, under the excuse of covering her body with a blanket, took one of the ornamental daggers from the display at the foot of the stairs and stabbed the body. Why?'

Sir Henry didn't seem to register the question. It might have been due to the whisky but he was certainly not responding quickly now.

'My second wife could not get used to life in the tropics. I offered to send her home, tried to persuade her to return home, but she would not return alone.'

'Poor Mary came out to marry someone else,' Harry supplied, 'but the poor bugger died of typhoid before she arrived and Aunt Nessa arranged for her to marry Father instead. I think Aunt Nessa thought it would be good for Father to have a wife to sit on ladies' committees and organize fund-raising, all the things she herself was doing. But Mary refused. She wanted to go back to England and live on a country estate with a London house and English servants.'

'Mary didn't understand money,' Sir Henry said. 'She didn't believe me when I said we couldn't afford to live in England in the way she wanted. I thought . . . if suspicion for Charity's death fell on her, if they found the *keris* among her possessions and she had to answer questions from the police, she would find it insufferable and agree to leave without me. I would have paid her passage home and got her a little house somewhere, of course. Lancashire, Nessa suggested. People are always disappearing into Lancashire. But then . . .'

'But then she found out you had been having a little romance with Charity.' Harry seemed to have forgotten that a police officer was present. 'She tried to blackmail you into taking her back to England, didn't she? Did you poison her?'

'No, no.' Sir Henry looked genuinely shocked. 'That was an accident. All I wanted was for her to get a little more rest so I suggested she take her powders. I thought if she could get some decent sleep she might be more inclined to be reasonable but she found it too hot, so . . .'

'So Miss Nessa gave her something.' I remembered Miss Nessa forcing coffee, with the promise of sleep, on me and winced. She would have found it much easier to persuade poor sleepless Lady Palin.

I remembered the paper with traces of powder I had found in the laundry basket in Mary Palin's room, and Miss Nessa's strange purchases of tapioca flour. 'Lady Palin said even Veronal couldn't put her to sleep here, but I don't think she was taking Veronal. Miss Nessa must have substituted cooking powders for the sleeping powders. That was why they didn't do Lady Palin any good. Miss Nessa would have held the Veronal back until she had a big enough dose. Then she put it into Lady Palin's hot chocolate.'

I remembered Lady Palin's sweet tooth and her fondness for over-sweetened drinks, desserts and medicinal whisky. She would not have noticed anything added.

Le Froy looked at Sir Henry. 'You ordered your wife's sleeping powders?' I knew his tone of mild enquiry meant that he had checked and rechecked this fact until he was satisfied it would stand. I don't know if it came from his readings of Sun Tzu or Socrates but he only sounded uncertain when he wanted to lure someone into challenging his facts.

Wisely, Sir Henry did not try. 'Yes. I ordered Mary's sleeping powders through the office. They came faster that way, packed and sent over in official boxes.'

'And you gave them directly to your wife?'

'Naturally!' Sir Henry was starting to look affronted. He had been happy enough to confess to sticking a knife into his dead lover's side in an attempt to frame his wife, but was offended by the suggestion that he might have opened his dead wife's medicinal powders. These nuances of British character are harder to understand than the intricacies of English grammar.

'You handed them to her yourself? Did you bring them back to the house as soon as they arrived? Did your wife come over to collect them? Or did you bring them back at the end of your working day?'

'Well, naturally–' Sir Henry cut himself off to think. 'Mary didn't like coming over to Government House. Said they didn't show her proper respect there. Got it into her head that Charity had turned them all against her. Women . . . Once they get that kind of fancy into their heads it's no use trying to reason with them. You can't talk sense into them. She wouldn't even come to meet the wives of sultans and such. Used to call them stupid for not speaking English and not wanting to shake hands. Nessa had to stand in for her. Didn't matter to the old boys that she wasn't my wife – doubt most of them realized it! As far as they were concerned, they were doing us an honour by bringing their women-folk in to meet us and I had to return the favour by producing a filly of my own. Nessa took on all Mary's duties. She did all the little things. Don't know how we're going to manage without her . . .'

'Perhaps Miss Palin brought your wife's medicine back to the house for her?' Le Froy persisted patiently.

'What? Oh, yes. Very likely. Nessa always tried to help poor Mary.' His face twisted and he fell silent.

I rose quietly and moved in Dee-Dee's direction.

'Your uncle Chen said to tell you that your grandmother sends her regards,' Le Froy told me.

'Did he say anything else?'

'Just that he and his men all agree it was too dark for them to see what happened,'

It was decided that I would stay on at Frangipani Hill until other arrangements could be made for Dee-Dee, certainly until after her aunt's inquest.

Less than two months later, Vanessa Palin's death was explained (with the help of medical specialists called in by Sir Henry) as being caused by her impulsively going outside alone in the dark after hearing something. 'A wild pig or a pack of wandering wild dogs,' the judge guessed. 'A most rash act on the part of a strong-willed woman, I must say.' It was clear what he thought of strong-willed women. He further surmised that the late Miss Palin must have tripped on the uneven ground and fallen onto a *parang* machete left out by the gardener. The heavy blade had caught her across the throat and she had died almost instantly. It was a tragic and unfortunate accident. He cautioned ladies in general against wandering around unescorted in the dark. Singapore might be a relatively safe island but that did not mean there were no wild animals around.

The judge also officially reprimanded Sihat bin Ismail, the head gardener of the Frangipani Hill property, for carelessness in leaving tools around. Sihat had been called to confirm the *parang* was one that he and his boys used. The Crown agreed and Miss Nessa's demise was ruled accidental death by misadventure.

I had thought the police would object. Inspector Le Froy, in particular, had been on the spot. He and all the men who had come to Frangipani Hill with him that night had seen Dee-Dee and me with our clothes covered in blood, yet there was no mention of us in the official report. Singapore, though, is a practical and pragmatic island and everyone was happy to go along with it.

OVIDIA YU

Of course, as we were to realize soon after, the colonial pow-
ers had their own problems in Europe. Spain was at war and the
British monarchy was threatened from within by rumours of its
first abdication for centuries – the last was Richard II's. In retro-
spect, the deaths of two women in faraway Singapore must have
counted for very little.

Although Le Froy told me not to worry, I had felt sure I would
be imprisoned for killing Miss Nessa. When we left the court
after the ruling, I drew my first deep breath since that terrible
night. Perhaps things would return to normal, after all. But I no
longer knew what 'normal' was for me. I would be leaving
Frangipani Hill soon, but I couldn't imagine returning to a life of
beading slippers and making *achar* in my grandmother's home.

Back at the house, I went out to Sihat's shack to apologize to
him before collecting Dee-Dee from Cookie in the kitchen. Given
how particular the old gardener was about safety and keeping
his tools in order, it was unfair that he had been reprimanded
for causing a fatal accident by leaving tools out.

He brushed off my explanation without allowing me to finish.
'It is not my *parang*, what. It belongs to Government House. Why
should I feel bad because the boss missy goes walking at night
and falls on it? Maybe the boss missy own self take! It is not my
business!'

Of course, I knew by then that Uncle Chen and his men had
turned up on Frangipani Hill for their nocturnal pig hunt only
because Sihat had ridden all the way to Chen Mansion on his
bicycle to tell my grandmother I was in danger.

'But how did you know I was in trouble?' I hadn't thought to
ask Sihat till now. It was the first time since that terrible night that

I had gone down the steep steps to the dirt track with its zinc-roofed servants' shacks.

After they had received Miss Nessa's orders to return to their quarters and lock themselves in until morning under threat of being shot for treason, I had expected all the servants to obey without question. After all, the *ang mohs* had the right to conduct their top-secret matters (and drunken parties) in private. But Sihat had not been asked to light the torches set along the winding driveway for visitors. He had come quietly up to the house to see if his lights were needed and had heard enough to make him haul his bicycle down the track and hurry to my grandmother's house.

'I didn't know you even knew my grandmother.'

Sihat looked uncomfortable and my suspicions were immediately confirmed.

'How much money do you owe her?'

'Chen Tai say I don't owe her anything any more. She already return back to me all the guarantee notes. In fact, she want to give me more money but I tell her no need. I tell her I never go to her to get money, only because I don't want more bad things to happen here.'

'Why didn't you take the money? My grandmother was giving you a present – you wouldn't have to pay it back.'

Sihat shook his head. 'I don't need it.'

My grandmother would have said a man who took only what he needed would stay poor. I thought he would stay happy.

I knew there would be other benefits, though. The men who had come to my rescue that night had all seen Uncle Chen shake the old gardener's hand with both of his and tearfully put an arm around his shoulders, and soon all would know that Sihat had

OVIDIA YU

Chen Tai's gratitude. Outside the courthouse, packets of Lucky Strike cigarettes and coveted box matches had been pressed on him, and now I saw generous bundles of cooking charcoal, dried squid and salted eggs stacked outside his shack. Anonymous gifts, I guessed. Even if he lost his job in the Government House gardens, Sihat would not go hungry.

Epilogue

———◆———

There was some talk of holding further hearings on the supposedly accidental death of Lady Palin and the apparent murder of Charity Byrne but they came to nothing. I knew I was not the only one to wonder how much Sir Henry had known about his second wife's 'accidental' overdose. However, given that he was alive and well connected and his sister was dead, all the blame landed squarely on Miss Nessa.

'So Charity's fall really was an accident?' Parshanti pressed. 'And they're sending him up to Terengganu and letting him get away scot-free? How can they?'

'They have no evidence. And he is not very likely to repeat the crime.'

'He might marry again!'

I knew enough from Uncle Chen's trading contacts to view Sir Henry's posting more as penal servitude than freedom. Siam had ceded Terengganu to the British, along with Kedah, Perlis and Kelantan, without consulting the rulers of those states and the sultans were understandably unhappy.

OVIDIA YU

I was visiting Parshanti in her parents' shop because I had taken Dee-Dee to the Mission's kindergarten. She fitted in perfectly, the children young enough to accept her without question. When I left, promising to return in an hour's time, she barely looked up from the cross-stitch alphabet she was working with a large round-tipped needle. Harry, who had driven us into town, accompanied me to Shankar and Sons but stayed outside with a cheroot. Dr Shankar subscribed to modern German theories linking lung cancer and tobacco use. He closed an eye to Mrs Shankar's thriving business in tobacco products (Parshanti's mother melded all the thriftiness of her Scots ancestry with the pragmatism of her adopted island) but did not permit pipes and cigarettes in his store.

In truth, I was not sorry to be away from Harry's gloom for a bit. I sympathized with his family situation and suddenly uncertain future, but he was healthy, educated and better off than most people. And I had missed my gossipy chats with Parshanti dreadfully. Nobody chatted at Frangipani Hill.

'I can't believe she just fell. Charity was so sporty and good at jumping! Do you remember them challenging her to jump over the water barrels?' Parshanti kept her eyes on the French seam she was back-stitching as we chatted. Her mother had more orders than she could handle and there was always hand sewing or lace edging to be done. I could have offered to help but, unlike Parshanti, I could not sew and talk at the same time and I preferred to talk.

'It's the sporty ones who take the risk and risk the falls,' Mrs Shankar said firmly. 'When will you be moving back to Chen Mansion, Su Lin? Your grandmother must be missing you.'

I could not tell Parshanti's mother that I was desperately looking for ways to avoid returning home. I dreaded the pushy matchmakers with their eligible bachelors who would be waiting. As the effects of the Western depression stretched on in Singapore, people were paying less attention to my 'bad luck' and more to my grandmother's money. My time at Frangipani Hill had let me glimpse a world of twentieth-century possibilities and I did not want to let it go.

Parshanti was so used to her mother's words that she no longer heard them. 'Prakesh said that Sir Henry was outside when he saw Charity fall. When he got to her she was already dead and he looked up and saw Lady Palin at the upstairs balcony. Prakesh says she must surely have—'

'Prakesh Pillai should not be talking so freely,' Le Froy said. He was standing behind me, having entered in his usual soundless manner. I had grown used to his ways but Parshanti squeaked – he had startled her into stabbing a finger with the needle, and Mrs Shankar dropped the bead she was threading.

As she bent for it she asked serenely, 'Chief Inspector Le Froy, what can I get you today?'

'Nothing for me, Mrs Shankar. But there is a young man who needs an outfit for the Royal Air Force that's being set up in Tengah.'

Harry, who had come in behind Le Froy, was smiling for the first time in weeks. 'I'm going to start training on gliders.'

'What do you know about flying planes?' I demanded.

'Nothing. That's why starting at RAF Tengah is perfect for me.' Harry looked at Le Froy and grinned. 'We're all new. Apart from the trainers, nobody knows anything. But I still don't know how you pulled it off!'

'I told them you're skilled with a gun and on a motor-bicycle, have a good head under pressure and can be trusted,' Le Froy said. 'Since the powers-that-be balked me on all major fronts, I thought it a good time to make a trivial request they could satisfy their consciences by granting.'

'How have they balked you?' I guessed Le Froy had come straight from a meeting with his superiors. He had a look of a dog recently released from its chain: glad to be free but its jaws aching from being clenched.

'I was lectured interminably on the honour of the Crown and the importance of maintaining the public image of the colonial authority. I was also reminded several times that it is my responsibility to keep the peace, not to interfere. In other words, the deaths of two colonial Englishwomen are none of my business. And there was no threat to the lives of the governor's child and her nanny.'

Yet Le Froy seemed far from frustrated. I sensed excitement – even delight – in him that he could barely contain. And, though he was talking more than usual, I could tell there was still more he had left unsaid. Mrs Shankar sensed something too: I saw her looking from Le Froy to me as though she were trying to work out what it was.

'Did you come here to look for Miss Chen?' she asked pointedly.

Le Froy bowed acknowledgement. He turned to me, 'Yes, as a matter of fact. I called in at the Mission Centre and they said—'

'Dee-Dee! Is something wrong? What has she done? Did they send you to get me? Why didn't you say so at once?'

'Not at all, Su Lin. Please sit and calm down. In fact, when I asked where I might find you, Miss Tey asked me to let you know that Miss Deborah has joined the other children in a nap and there is no need for you to hurry back. Schooling her with six- and seven-year-olds was a very good idea. How did you come up with it?'

'If you disregard appearances, Dee-Dee *is* a seven-year-old.'

'You mean the Palins are just going to get away with everything?' Parshanti had returned to what she was most interested in, her sewing pushed aside. 'Su Lin could have been killed! That's what's important. Don't you care?'

'Sir Henry Palin's image is more important than Sir Henry the man, because the acting governor is the figurehead, the upstanding symbol of just and generous colonial rule. And of course I care. Miss Chen is my responsibility as long as my name and signature are on her Mission employment form.'

'Not for long, I hope,' Mrs Shankar said. 'If Deborah Palin settles in with the children at the Mission Centre, Su Lin won't be needed any more.' Mrs Shankar had championed education for women and encouraged Parshanti and me in our studies, but the recent events had frightened her back into conventionality. If she could have shut us away in purdah from all white people, I believe she would have.

I knew it was no use asking Le Froy if I could train to fly planes like Harry. I couldn't ride a bicycle or shoot a gun. But surely . . . 'Now things are going back to how they were, I can be your housekeeper and cook as—' *As Miss Nessa had arranged*, I was going to say, but could not. Becoming Le Froy's housekeeper would be taking several steps backwards, but I knew that if I returned to Chen Mansion it would be as though I had never stepped out at all.

'Things are not going to be the same. I'm being transferred,' Le Froy said.

A promotion with which his superiors had bought his silence?

'You know I was hoping to train for a profession – I could be a teacher, perhaps, or a nurse. Before you go, if you have any contacts who could men–' I broke off as he shook his head. 'Well, that's really too bad of you!' Feeling betrayed – how could I ever have thought that selfish, self-centred *ang moh* would help me? – I prepared to storm out before he saw the tears in my eyes.

'Wait!' Le Froy caught my arm.

'Let me go!'

'I'll be transferring to the new detective headquarters at Robinson Road once the building is completed.'

'Congratulations. Now let go of me.'

'I am recruiting officers and specialized agents familiar with various Chinese and Malay dialects to monitor Chinese secret societies, commercial crimes, prostitution and gambling. And, of course, to monitor political threats.'

He had dropped my arm but I stared at him and did not leave. I tasted the salt of my forgotten tears as I asked, 'You mean like a Singapore Scotland Yard?'

'Not just Singapore. We'll also have to keep an eye on China, after last year's revolution. There's no telling how long Dr Sun Yat Sen will last as president. And, of course, there's all the activity in Japan . . . You don't speak Japanese, do you? At least it will be easier for you to pick up the script characters . . .'

Le Froy could have gone on, but I interrupted him: 'Inspector Le Froy, are you asking me to come and work for you?'

'You already work for me, Chen Su Lin. And I have the papers to prove it.'

Acknowledgements

———◆———

So many people helped me in the writing of this book, which came from an idea I had years ago, when Singapore's National Arts Council (thank you, NAC!) sponsored me on a writing retreat at the amazing Toji Cultural Centre in South Korea. Being away from Singapore made me think more about early Singapore (thank you to the wonderful organizers, all the other writers and the gardener-cooks for the wonderful food at Toji!).

I want to thank my agent Priya Doraswamy, who made this book possible; my adventurous editor Krystyna Green, who took a risk on a manuscript before it had an ending; the amazing team at Little, Brown/Constable, including desk editor Amanda Keats and super copy-editor, Hazel Orme, who did all the real work of putting this book together.

And, finally, thank you to you for picking up this book. I hope that you enjoyed reading *The Frangipani Tree Mystery*. And if you enjoyed reading about Su Lin in early twentieth-century Singapore, please visit my Facebook page and say hello – I would love to hear your feedback and any suggestions for future books!